WIRED REVENGE

TOBY NEAL

***

WIRED REVENGE

A Paradise Crime Thriller

By Toby Neal

✤✤✤

"If you prick us, do we not bleed? If you tickle us, do we not laugh? If you poison us, do we not die? And if you wrong us, shall we not revenge?"
-William Shakespeare

Chapter One

Six months after Wired Strong

Fashion week in Paris could be deadly.

Pim Wat retrieved a name card in gold lettering spelling out *Vivian Moran* from the brocade seat. She settled herself carefully on the tiny gold Louis Quatorze imitation chair. The long black runway that she faced was trimmed in rippling lights and set off by draped tulle in luxe purple, this year's favored color.

"Pleased to be in a front row seat," she told her business partner in French, tweaking the folds of her flowing white silk pantsuit so that it draped gracefully over her legs. Her heart fluttered with an excitement that echoed the thumping bass of the heavy techno music.

"Of course, *ma petite*," Enrique Mendoza said, as he settled in his place beside her. "They wouldn't dare do otherwise."

Pim Wat didn't contradict her new partner, though the reason for her favored status was quite different than it had been in the past. Still, a front row seat for the Dior show was always a big deal.

She'd come up with the Vivian identity years before but had not actually used it since her complete facial overhaul and departure from Thailand six months ago. Fortunately, she'd had all the photos in each of her go-bag identification documents updated before she'd had to flee so abruptly.

Pim Wat had landed on her feet, as she always did. "More lives than a cat, my Beautiful One," her dead lover's voice whispered in her mind.

Thank the gods her old compatriot Mendoza had responded positively to her contact when she'd arrived in Paris. He'd helped her build her new identity into the fully fleshed woman who sat beside him now, and he was the only one who knew who she really was.

Mendoza's loyalty was a weathervane that swung to the highest bidder, but she'd been able to secure that with her hidden source of funds.

Besides, Mendoza knew her history, and was thus aware that betraying her would have deadly consequences.

She was playing a long game now that she was on her own. In due time it would culminate in revenge upon those who'd killed her lover, given her to the CIA for torture, taken her grandchild—and expelled her from her former life into this one.

Pim Wat adjusted square framed tortoiseshell glasses on her nose, scanning the room for threats.

The glasses, embedded with a facial recognition program, circled each face briefly, then flashed identities and employers in the upper left corner of the clear lenses. She'd learned, through many hours of practice, to be able to monitor that input as she glanced about in a normal way. "A good crowd so far."

"And an even more exciting collection." Mendoza scrolled through his social media feed on a diamond-encrusted phone. Dressed in a lavender silk suit, he played the part of gay man about town flawlessly, hiding a sharklike constitution that Pim Wat found comforting—she always knew where she stood with her old friend.

The huge room dimmed. The runway lit up with lines of embedded lighting zipping back and forth. Strobes circled the ceiling; a pulse-pounding song filled the air.

Spontaneous applause broke out as the first model strode out in that ground-eating way they affected. Pim Wat checked the rapt faces turned up to watch the progression of the model down the runway, the spin-turn, spin-turn at the end, a hand on a protruding hipbone, the outfit shimmering under the lights.

No one she needed to worry about was watching the show, at least so far. She'd do another scan before it ended.

Pim Wat took off the glasses and stowed them in her golden clutch purse.

She sat back to enjoy the spectacle, her phone at the ready to photograph the outfits she might want to buy.

So far, she was loving her new life—and the delicious irony that her main source of income was still as a very expensive assassin. "Stay with what you're good at," her lover had told her more than once, and as always, his wisdom was sound.

Connor sat upright on a tilted ergonomic stool he used in lieu of a work chair, facing three large monitors in the large stone tower room of the fortress of the Yām Khûmkạn in Thailand. The screens absorbed his full attention as he surfed through reams of data sifted by his Ghost software, as well as his beloved Sophie's DAVID software.

The computers were all at work scanning for keywords and photographic traces of Pim Wat, Sophie's deadly mother. Pim Wat had been the longtime lover of the espionage organization's enigmatic former leader known only as the Master, and one of the premier assassins in their stable.

Newsfeeds flashed by faster than Connor's eyes could interpret, but that was fine; the programs were his eyes, ears, and touch anywhere in the world that technology could reach.

He'd been searching for Pim Wat ever since she escaped through a hidden tunnel leading from somewhere in the bedroom of the original Master's suite on the day Connor had killed him—and assumed the man's position.

"You'd think, with the best facial recognition software and hunter/seeker programs in the world, we'd have found her by now."

His loyal compatriot Nine's voice jarred Connor out of his 'wired in' hypnotic trance. Connor blinked; his eyes were gritty. He lifted his hands from the keyboard; they were cold and stiff from lost circulation.

He'd been sitting for too many hours and hadn't noticed his body's depletion.

"The plastic surgery Pim Wat had was evidently extensive enough to wipe her out of the facial recognition system. Her new identity must have been carefully created, and she's been lying low— not in any of her usual haunts." Connor yawned, his jaw cracking, and stretched arms corded with muscle high over his head. "I didn't expect it to be easy to find her."

"The former Master didn't keep anything on her?" Nine cocked his head. "A record of her identities and accounts?"

"Not that I've been able to find. In some ways, he was old-school. Kept his most important information up here." Connor tapped his temple. They'd been over these same questions several times, but Nine kept bringing them up. Connor squelched a stab of annoyance; problem-solving was not one of Nine's strengths.

"You work too hard." Nine squeezed his shoulder. "I brought your lunch."

Connor's physical needs, immersed in the mental energy of the online hunt, had been suspended. Now they came back in a rush. A steaming clay pot of meat-laden curry and vegetables on the tray Nine held smelled rich and aromatic, looked delicious, and elicited a rumble from his empty stomach.

Connor turned away from the workstation, reminded of why he appreciated his somewhat pedantic friend. "Thanks, Nine. I'd forget to eat if you didn't bring me something."

"I know, Master."

"Dine with me."

"I have partaken, but I will have tea with you." Nine moved the tray of food over to a small round table in the corner of the large, airy stone room.

Situated in the highest tower of the Yām Khûmkạn's jungle

fortress, this room's elevation was where its satellite communications system experienced the least interference. The view from a bullet-proof glass window faced out over the rest of the ancient compound, and the courtyard where men training to be ninjas drilled each day.

Connor stood up from the stool, interlacing his fingers and stretching them high above his head, then bending forward to place his hands flat on the floor. He shut his eyes; he could see and feel energy flowing in his veins, pumping through his muscles and organs, coursing in a river along the bones of his spine. The veil between the physical and metaphysical worlds was thin, now that he wore the robe of the Master of the Yām Khûmkạn.

After a few more stretches and side twists, he walked over to sit opposite Nine at the table.

Nine was a compact and muscular man with the wide cheek-bones, jet hair and golden skin of the Thai people. When Connor had joined the clandestine agency that some called a cult, he and Nine had become close as he trained under the ruthless and exacting hand of the former Master. Through the rigors of testing, the drama of the previous Master's surprise choice of Connor as successor, and even the battle for supremacy that had ended in the earlier Master's death, Nine had unquestioningly had his back. The Thai man occupied the functions of bodyguard, personal attendant, second-in-command, and friend.

Nine had Connor's food tested for poison at every meal; there had been enemies within the compound who had not appreciated the former Master's choice of a white man to succeed him. Thankfully, those malcontents had been weeded out one by one.

Connor opened the lidded pot of curry and dug in with a pair of bamboo chopsticks. "Good stuff."

"The new cook is dedicated." Nine poured tea for both of them into small, handleless ceramic cups. "Everyone is pleased so far."

"Appreciate your help with that."

"Turns out one of the new trainees was a culinary student. He has been happy to leave drilling on the yard for creating nourishing meals."

Connor slurped at the tea. "Excellent." He raised his eyes to meet Nine's. "I have issued a bounty on Pim Wat's life on the darknet. Five million dollars, dead or alive. I provided a sketch of her as I last saw her, a DNA sample, and fingerprints. Someone will find her for us since I have not yet been able to."

"A wise move, Master. Your reach is long, and your pockets deep."

Connor grinned. "You sound like a fortune cookie."

The reference was clearly missed by his friend, who raised his brows in question.

Connor sighed. "Never mind."

He should not have felt so alone, surrounded as he was by acolytes, but Sophie was lost to him in the United States—and so was anyone who would get his American humor. He was the Master of the Yām Khûmkạn now, whether he'd sought that position or not.

Connor stood up and shrugged out of his gi, enjoying the sensation of his muscles as they rippled with life force. "Let's go down to the courtyard and run some drills with the men."

⚜

Sophie Smithson, CEO of Honolulu-based Security Solutions, gestured to the small round conference table in the corner of her office. "Let's all have a seat."

Sophie's colleague and friend, former detective of French police Pierre Raveaux, took a chair. Raveaux, an elegant blade of a man, had a silky accented voice. "I appreciate your invitation to this strategy meeting, given that I'm your newest employee."

"Not quite the newest." Kendall Bix, the buttoned-down President of Operations for the company, drew out a chair. "I don't believe you've met our most recent addition to the team, Lono Jones."

Raveaux shook hands with the former Maui Police Department detective. Sophie's friend Lei had originally introduced Lono to her on Maui; Sophie'd recruited the investigator to try to fill Jake Dunn's position.

"We're glad to have you both aboard in a full-time capacity, Pierre and Lono," Bix went on. "Sophie and I thought bringing you two on full-time to cover her maternity leave would give us the help we need. She'll be gone four months. Covering her position will give you a crash course in the company's operations."

Raveaux cocked an ankle on a knee and straightened the pleat of immaculate black trousers. "I appreciate the chance to move from contract work to permanent employee."

Jones nodded to Sophie. "Thanks for taking a chance on me. I won't let you down." The former detective had shaggy blond surfer hair and deep-set greenish eyes set off by a neatly trimmed beard. Full sleeve tattoos on both arms were visible in his aloha shirt.

"I'm glad to have you both aboard." Sophie hefted herself out from behind her desk to join them, carrying her tech tablet. Nine months pregnant and due any day, she wore a simple A-line shift that minimized her girth—but just maneuvering from one side of the room to another was a challenge at this stage. "Let's get down to business. What have you brought to discuss, Kendall?"

Bix took out unfamiliar reading glasses and slid them onto his nose. He caught Sophie's eye and grimaced. "Yes, I'm wearing these things now. That time has come." He woke up the tablet he'd set on the table and consulted it. "My proposal is that Raveaux and Jones occupy this office during Sophie's maternity leave and basically take on her administrative duties, plus any active investigations she would have participated in." Bix peered over the tortoiseshell glasses at the seated men. "As you're likely aware, Sophie has a dual responsibility with Security Solutions—first as its administrative head, and also as senior tech investigator."

Raveaux shook his head. "I do not pretend to have Sophie's skills with computers. In fact, I'm a bit of a Luddite by choice." He patted the pocket of his jacket, distorted by the fat outline of a paperback book. "As you've both had occasion to notice."

"I can pick up whatever Pierre doesn't feel up to tech-wise," Jones stated confidently. "I spent ten years in Hawaii as a detective, first on the Big Island, then on Maui, before leaving the force. Tech investigation was one of my specialties."

"A good part of why Bix and I hired you," Sophie said. "Why don't you tell us why you left Maui Police Department? My friend Lei Texeira introduced us some years ago and you seemed embedded over there."

Jones shifted uncomfortably. "Just needed a change of pace, career-wise."

Sophie decided not to press. "We don't expect you to clone hard drives and do forensic tech investigation unless you're comfortable with that. But one of you will have to peruse expense spreadsheets, overtime logs, and handle other personnel matters. If an investigation requires basic background checks and data searches, I expect you to take care of those."

"None of that is a problem." Raveaux said. He inclined his immaculately barbered head toward Jones. "Glad I'll have a partner in the CEO's office."

"Sophie, when do you want to begin your leave?" Bix took off his glasses and tucked them in a pocket.

"Let's talk through our existing caseload and figure out a date," Sophie said, just as a sharp stab of pain wrenched her lower back. She bit her lip, stifling a gasp.

Probably just a bit of gas.

She stood carefully, avoiding the men's concerned gazes, and headed for the tea service on the credenza. She forced herself to breathe evenly through a knifelike sensation. "Ooh. Got a little back spasm." She pressed a fist into the affected area. "Bix, familiarize Jones and Raveaux with our current cases, would you?"

She kept her back to the room, breathing shallowly and holding onto the edge of the credenza, as Bix showed his tablet to Raveaux and Jones and began the review.

This didn't feel at all like the Braxton-Hicks contractions she'd been enduring for the last month.

This didn't feel like a normal contraction of any kind.

Something was wrong.

As she reached for the hot water pot, a sudden gush of fluid broke loose between her legs.

Sophie dropped the pot with a clatter, holding herself steady against the sideboard as she waited for the pain to ease.

At last she turned to face the men.

All three of them stared at her, open-mouthed in alarm. "I'm afraid you'll have to carry on without me. It seems I'm having this baby sooner than I expected."

Chapter Two

Three months later . . .

Connor arrived in the Yām Khûmkạn's fortress tower room after a day spent in meetings and drilling with the ninja trainees; the Master's work was never done.

An alert blinked on the computer he used to run Sophie's DAVID software, notable for its ability to sift keywords and images on the Internet.

One of his latest approaches had been to take the sketch of Pim Wat's new face that he had worked up with an artist and have the crude image made into a photorealistic avatar. He'd recently uploaded and inserted it into the facial recognition programs he'd hacked at airports around the world.

This latest image was yielding more results, though so far, he'd ruled out the pings that had landed in DAVID's cache.

He logged into the cache.

All it contained today was a small news item retrieved from a Paris periodical dated three months prior: "Kaleidoscope Tastemakers Ltd. welcomes their newest member. President of the well-known lifestyle design company, Enrique Mendoza, is pleased to welcome socialite Vivian Moran to his exclusive group of consultants. Ms. Moran is pictured with Mendoza at the Dior fashion show this spring."

The pixelated photo showed a well-dressed man and woman, heads tilted back as they watched a Paris runway. The ping had come from the face of the woman, and as Connor narrowed his eyes—even with the woman's large fashionista tortoiseshell glasses—the main recognition points of her face matched that of his digitally manipulated avatar photo.

The woman's height and build were not mentioned in the article, but now that he had a name and a possible employer, it was only a matter of time until he found out more.

He squinted at the photo, then sat back. "Is it you, Pim Wat?"

In the months that he'd been intensively looking for Sophie's mother, this face was the closest match that he had found. Still, he felt no sense of recognition gazing at the petite platinum blonde in a white pantsuit at the Dior show.

That Vivian Moran had managed to evade any other photographs besides this one was remarkable, and a little bit of a confirmation in itself.

How long had Vivian Moran existed?

Why weren't there more images of her if she was a "socialite"?

Connor stretched high, cracked his interlaced fingers, and then leaned forward to apply them to the keyboard.

He dug for every bit of information the Internet could provide on Enrique Mendoza, Vivian Moran, and a company called Kaleidoscope Tastemakers Ltd., based in Paris.

Soon there would be little about any of the three elements of this current puzzle that he did not know.

As often happened, Nine was the one to break Connor's trance before the computer. "Master. It's three in the morning. You must rest."

Connor had not heard the man come in, and when he turned his head, a lance of pain shot up the stiff muscles of his neck. "I think I've found her."

Nine's dark eyes narrowed. He peered over Connor's shoulder at the monitor, but what he saw—lines of code and segmented windows filled with clips—must not have made sense, because the man shook his head. "I never doubted you would."

Connor rolled off the ergonomic stool and onto the floor of the tower room, which was covered with luxurious carpets. He stretched his stiff, aching muscles. "I need the Healer tonight, or I will not be able to sleep."

"I will summon him." Nine stepped over to an old-fashioned bell pull that snaked down the stone wall through a hole to somewhere in the depths of the fortress. "Let's get you back to the massage room."

Connor allowed Nine to help him up, but he was filled with urgency about the information he'd uncovered. "Wait."

He turned back to the computer and hit a few keys, quickly composing an e-mail to a man named McDonald at the CIA. Once that was sent, he could rest.

Pim Wat had been found. This was his chance to trade her for his freedom to return to the United States and be with the woman he loved.

He felt dizzy with hope at the possibility.

The international multiagency task force that had been hunting him for years due to his online vigilante justice activities had offered him a deal: amnesty and restoration of his assets in the USA in return for the lives of Pim Wat and the Master.

The Master he'd delivered. That alone hadn't been enough for the State Department and killing the Master had put him in even deeper bondage. He shut his eyes, trying to suppress the horror of the memory, and stumbled.

He accepted Nine's strong shoulder to lean on as his friend helped him away from the computer and down hand-hewn stone steps to his luxurious apartment chambers.

Connor hadn't wanted to occupy the space he so associated with the former Master, but the men had insisted. He'd redecorated with all new carpets and hangings in natural fibers and a modern minimalist aesthetic that suited him more than the previous Master's love of rich color and luxe decor; still, he seldom spent time in the place where their final showdown had occurred.

A vibration of that dark night still haunted the stones of the walls.

Nine helped Connor all the way to the bathing and massage chamber that was part of the suite. He removed Connor's robe and assisted him onto the table, then poured herb-laced oil into a small pot and lit the mini brazier that warmed it. "The Healer is on his way."

Connor tried to relax, but his mind was still churning as he lay waiting. Would McDonald take his offer and provide a written contract as he had asked?

Truth was, he hoped to kill Pim Wat regardless—but he wanted clemency, too.

There was no way to know what would happen now. He had to wait and see.

The Healer arrived. "Master. You have been working late again."

"Yes."

The older man, his shoulders thick with muscle, approached respectfully, and lay a warm, gnarled hand on Connor's shoulder. "Let go of your tensions and worries. See the energy of them and allow it to pass through and away. Carrying them only blocks your power."

Connor shut his eyes.

The color of his own energy field, normally a strong, bright blue, had darkened almost to indigo.

The Healer passed his hands, pulsing with yellow light, back and forth above Connor's body, drawing the darkness up out of him and casting it away with flicking gestures. The technique was only one of the many the Healer was well versed in.

Connor felt the heaviness and internal conflict he'd been struggling with softening. Gradually true relaxation came; his muscles slackened.

Finally, when the energy cleansing was done, the Healer dug his strong fingers into the rock-hard muscles along Connor's neck and spine, loosening them with deep, intense kneading.

Connor wept silently, tears pouring from his eyes as the pain stored in him released.

He grieved for the Master.

But more, he grieved the loss of his beloved Sophie.

They'd been friends, then lovers, then he'd lost her through his stupid choice to run from the law and hide in Thailand. She'd made it clear when last they saw each other, that she wouldn't take him back.

He was a murderer—and soon he could be her mother's killer, too—if he was lucky enough to catch that evil witch. How could they ever make it past a barrier like that?

"Let it all go," the former Master's resonant voice spoke in his mind. "Life is full of surprises. Let it surprise you."

The man's presence and wisdom lasted even beyond the grave.

Chapter Three

Sophie held Momi's slightly sticky hand while pushing the jogging stroller with baby Sean in it. The infant was covered against a breeze flowing up from the beach park they were headed for on their usual evening walk.

Momi pointed excitedly to a hot dog stand nestled in the shade under one of the spreading trees that shaded the sidewalk. "Mama! Hot dogs?"

"On the way back, honey. That's when we pick up something to eat."

Armita, the kids' nanny, snorted from behind Sophie. "Not a nutritious dinner."

"That's why we only do it once a week." Sophie smiled over her shoulder at the slender, stern-faced woman dressed in her usual ninja black.

Raveaux, who had been wrestling Sophie's rambunctious Lab, Ginger, and well-behaved Doberman, Anubis, away from the hot dog cart, tipped his fedora in Sophie's direction. A bit of sparkle brightened his dark eyes. "I could be persuaded to cook everyone something that would be both nutritious and tasty upon our return."

"No! Hot dog!" Momi yelled, stamping her foot.

Sophie passed the handle of the stroller to Armita without a word, drawing her child off to the side. She gestured with her chin for Armita, Raveaux and the dogs to continue as she squatted down in front of the toddler, gaining Momi's full attention.

Momi had large, long-lashed eyes, a head of glossy black curls, and tawny brown skin; African American, Hawaiian, and Thai heritages had resulted in a beautiful blend. "Momi. If you keep up the fuss you will not be having a hot dog. You will have plain rice and vegetables. Then you will go straight to bed."

Momi's plump lower lip trembled. Her daughter was mercurial and strong-willed; Sophie already dreaded the teen years. The little girl threw her arms around her mother and rubbed her curly head into her chest. "Okay, Mama."

Yes, her daughter was a handful, but she was also affectionate, energetic, loving, and eager for new experiences.

Sophie kept hold of Momi's hand, quickly scanning the surrounding area as she caught up with the others.

The group perambulated without incident to their favorite part of Ala Moana Beach Park, an area where the dogs could be turned loose to frolic in a fenced pet zone.

Armita set out the picnic cloth. Pierre took Momi and the dogs to the loose pet area. Sophie settled herself with her back against one of the great spreading monkeypod trees that made the park such a treasure, to nurse baby Sean. She enjoyed the intimacy of breast-feeding her son, knowing it wouldn't last much longer since she returned to work in a month.

She peeked in at the baby's sweet face beneath the cloth she'd covered them with for privacy and stroked his plump cheek with a fingertip. Though Sean was lighter in coloring than Momi, both children shared dark curls. Sean's eyes had an interesting gray-green cast to their brown color. His cheerful, active nature and robust constitution were already apparent; Sean was his father Jake's son.

Sophie would never forget her fiancé's bold, energetic presence with Sean in her life to remind her of him.

Grief gave Sophie's heart a familiar squeeze. Jake had given his life to save hers on one of their cases. It was of little comfort to her that it was how he'd have wanted to die; he'd been taken far too soon.

Sophie felt a twinge of pain from her abdomen, leftover nerve damage from the emergency C-section necessary for Sean's birth; she'd had a sudden rupture that had led to his emergency delivery after her water broke dramatically in the Security Solutions office.

Sophie shut her eyes, trying not to revisit the traumatic memory.

She and Sean were both healthy, and she was healing. Though she would have no more children, her arms and her heart were full with these two.

Armita brought Sophie a bottled water. "You must hydrate to keep your milk supply up."

Sophie accepted the chilled liquid with her free hand, noticing that the screw top was thoughtfully removed. "Thank you, Armita."

She relaxed, sipping the water, and watching Pierre Raveaux play with Momi.

Pierre took his duties as a godfather seriously, as she'd known he would when she asked him to assume that role.

Once the dogs were loose in the enclosure, he brought Momi outside the fenced area and showed her a present. He had brought a new kite for her; it was an elaborate construction made of interlocking Asian-themed fish to celebrate Girls' Day.

Sophie smiled as she watched Pierre and Momi running with the kite as they launched it into the sky. She continued to enjoy the mix of diverse heritage and history in Hawaii, where so many races coexisted peacefully.

They stayed at the park until Momi grew tired and fussy after falling and skinning her knee.

Armita already had everything packed and stowed by the time Sophie got up from her spot against the tree and settled Sean in the stroller while Pierre wrangled the dogs and Momi.

Soon their little party was passing the hot dog stand; Momi got her promised treat, and so did Ginger and Anubis.

Pierre accompanied them all the way to the door of Sophie's apartment in the swanky Pendragon Arches building. She'd lived in a company apartment there for years now, but she was finally closing on a house with a fenced yard that would be more safe, secure and have more room for the kids and dogs.

Armita took Momi and Sean inside, and Sophie folded up the stroller. Once she had done so, Pierre handed Sophie the dogs' leashes.

"Thank you for another lovely evening," he said. "Sure you don't want me to come in and fix the family something to eat?"

"Not tonight. We still have leftovers from last time, chef Pierre." Sophie produced a wrapped hot dog from inside her purse; she had hidden its purchase from him. "A surprise for you from Momi. She insisted Uncle Perro get a hot dog too."

"That's my girl."

Jake used to say that phrase.

An arrow of grief slammed through her, and Sophie's eyes filled.

Raveaux saw it happen because the twinkle in his gaze died. He set his free hand on her shoulder and leaned in to kiss her cheek. She smelled his cinnamon aftershave. "Whatever I said, I'm sorry to take the smile from your face. You know that's the last thing I want to do."

"It's just that Jake used to say that." Sophie blinked the moisture from her eyes.

"I will strike it from my vocabulary forever."

"No. I welcome reminders of Jake—of what we shared. See you tomorrow, then?"

"Yes. Meantime, I have an adventure scheduled with Jack Reacher." Raveaux patted the bulge of a paperback in his jacket pocket. "I thought I'd have time to read it at the park."

"Momi never gave you a moment's rest. You probably can't wait to get home for some peace and quiet."

"Oh no. Never that."

Sophie glanced away from the longing in Raveaux's gaze. "*Bonsoir*, Pierre."

Shutting the door on him was becoming more difficult by the day.

Chapter Four

Pim Wat smoothed a sleek cap of platinum blonde hair as she stared down at her phone through reading glasses she'd begun using in the last year. Other than the glasses, she defied aging: her skin was as smooth as money could buy, her makeup perfect, her outfit a flattering creation by a famous designer.

She had an image to maintain that was part of her new persona, and she loved it.

The scene on her phone was nothing extraordinary: a tall, bronze-skinned woman, holding a toddler by the hand, pushed a stroller containing an infant.

A petite, wiry woman in black walked beside her, carrying a diaper bag.

A well-dressed man wearing a straw fedora brought up the rear, holding the leashes of a rambunctious yellow Labrador and a dignified Doberman.

The scene went grainy as the small cavalcade passed out of the eye of the traffic camera across from her daughter's building.

Pim Wat had paid for a surveillance hack to watch her daughter's comings and goings in Honolulu—an easy thing to contract. She tuned in daily to watch them come and go, noting any changes in their patterns. She wasn't yet ready to take them, for several reasons

—the first being that there was a hit out on Pim Wat's own life for her to deal with.

She'd been informed of it by Mendoza at their last business meeting. "Don't make it worth my while to take the job to kill you." He'd smiled with false humor. "You owe me, so I don't get tempted to collect on that five million."

Mendoza wasn't joking.

She'd taken care of a Turkish businessman he'd sent her just the other day and hadn't billed. Hopefully her partner was satisfied with that quid pro quo, but she doubted it.

Pim Wat's hand tightened on the phone as she waited for Sophie and her children to reappear in the next camera's coverage.

She should have expected that the new Master would try to take her out; Connor had a long reach and plenty of money. Eliminating her had to be one of his priorities. Still, it was damned inconvenient that he'd put out a hit order. She'd have to be on guard even more now, and Mendoza was a tricky ally who could easily turn against her.

Pim Wat logged out of the surveillance app when Sophie and her family took too long to reappear; Momi probably needed her shoe tied or something—the girl was a spoiled little brat.

Pim Wat frowned, noticing the well-defined tendons and spots on her hand that held the phone. The skin was wrinkled and thin, her knuckles bony. Those hands told a tale that countered Vivian Moran's stated age of thirty-eight.

She had to find a solution to that—fat injections and lasering, perhaps. It wouldn't be a quick process.

For now, she'd wear gloves. Something nice in kid leather or silk; maybe even lace fingerless. Gloves could be her new signature look; maybe she'd start a trend.

Meanwhile, fantasies of revenge were the cold broth she fed on.

She wanted revenge on many: first, on Connor, for the murder of her lover, the former Master. Pim Wat preferred to do her own wet work, and killing Connor was going to be a special pleasure—if she could get to him, with all those damned ninjas around every corner at the compound.

Sophie and her nanny Armita were next on her list. Taking them was going to be almost too easy; the two were exposed many times throughout the day. Penetrating Sophie's busy apartment building would be a piece of cake, as the Americans said.

Cutting Armita's throat was one of Pim Wat's favorite daydreams.

Armita had been her handmaid for close to twenty years before she'd betrayed her mistress by helping Sophie capture Pim Wat and turn her over to the CIA. Pim Wat still missed Armita's skillful service daily, and that stoked her sense of outrage and loss.

She'd play with Armita for a while when she captured her. Make sure her former minion had plenty of time to see what was coming. Then, she'd make Armita choke on her own blood.

Pim Wat took no pleasure in the necessity of killing Sophie; it would have to be quick, and from behind. Sophie was her only daughter, after all.

But easy as it would be to take out Sophie and Armita, she wouldn't survive long if she did so with her archenemy, the deadly new Master, searching for her.

"I must deal with the usurper first," Pim Wat growled. "Damn it." How she hated her lover's former protégé, that bastard upstart murderer . . .

A chime brought her gaze up to meet that of her perky young assistant, who had cocked the door ajar and stuck her head in. "Can I get you anything before I go out to fetch the mail, Vivian?"

For a moment Pim Wat was nonplussed. *Vivian?*

Oh, right. Her new name. And this was her new place of work; a lovely office done in shades of ivory and touches of gold. She'd been so deep in her ruminations she'd lost track.

So annoying; the girl needed training. But the little slip was a reminder that she, herself, needed to truly own her new identity. From now on, she was Vivian—even in the privacy of her thoughts. "Do not open my door without permission. Ever."

The assistant's eyes widened. "I'm sorry. I meant no disrespect. Of course, madame." She shut the door gently.

Pim Wat would be Vivian from here on out. A lifetime of deception had taught that immersion in a character was essential.

Vivian leaned back in her chair and closed her eyes. "So tedious to have to reinvent myself at my age. How I miss you, my Master, my love," she murmured aloud. Her occasional use of male escorts for a night of pleasure had scarcely blunted the edge of longing she still felt for her lover and his skillful hands. "There will never be another like you."

Done with the moment of emotional indulgence, Vivian sat up and set her phone aside. She turned her attention to the sleek monitor on her desk, logging on.

Technically, her new job was as a lifestyle consultant who assisted wealthy clients with taste decisions—from wardrobe to the type of pet they kept, to the decor and staffing of their many homes. But lifestyle guidance wasn't all Mendoza's agency provided for their well-heeled clientele; fixes of various illegal kinds were their bread and butter, and that included murder for hire.

Vivian reviewed the specifics of her latest target: a man in his sixties, Korean, living aboard a yacht in Thailand.

The location made a habitual wrinkle form between Vivian's brows, a wrinkle that couldn't take shape due to a recent Botox treatment. She smoothed the spot with a fingertip, instead.

"I don't want to go anywhere near Thailand. I told Enrique that," she muttered. Was her colleague and erstwhile boss testing her?

Vivian's eye was caught by the small, silver-framed photo on her desk of the pristine crescent-shaped beach of her favorite retreat, Pali Island in the Philippines. She used the photo to keep her motivation high; she was a believer in the use of mental rehearsal. She swiveled gently back and forth in her chair, visualizing playing with her grandchildren Momi and Sean on the sand of her special hideaway.

When her enemies were gone, she'd be able to relax and enjoy the fruits of her many trials and tribulations. "I deserve to be there. And I will be a good mother to them." The children would never know the difference; kids were simple clay, easily molded, and she'd hire help.

But taking out Connor?

That would require all her skills and contacts and calling in every favor she could.

Vivian had been hesitant to bring up her real agenda to Mendoza initially when she arrived; but now that she was more established and had proved her usefulness, she could offer to do several jobs for free in return for help in taking out her greatest enemy.

Vivian stroked her nonexistent forehead wrinkle thoughtfully, then picked up the phone on the desk.

Chapter Five

Pierre Raveaux slid his key into the door of his ground floor apartment in a quiet corner of downtown Honolulu. He'd given up immediate access to the ocean from his original apartment in Waikiki in favor of a larger place that allowed pets, only a ten-minute walk to the beach for his daily swim. Lisette met him at the door, winding herself around his legs.

"*Bonsoir, ma petite.* Did you miss me?" he crooned in French, stroking the striped arch of the cat's back. A smoke gray tabby with a white bib and socks, Lisette filled the emptiness of his home with her playful presence. Still a kitten, she was lanky with adolescence and yowled a loud complaint about how long he'd been gone.

"I know, my darling. Let's get you fed." It had been many hours since he'd been home, and mindful of that, he'd put up an electronic fence in his minuscule yard and asked a neighbor boy to come play with Lisette when he got home from school. Now, he glanced out through the glass sliding door where a cat door led to a basket of toys on the patio; they were scattered about, evidence that Timmy had come by at some point. "I see you had company. You are not neglected, *ma jeune fille.*"

He opened a can of top-quality food and put it down for Lisette, then headed to the bathroom for his swim gear.

Raveaux treasured the evening walks with Sophie's family, but it was Sophie's company he craved most. He would welcome a chance to be alone with her even if nothing personal passed between them, but that seldom happened. Sophie had given him no reason to hope his feelings were reciprocated, though she clearly liked and relied on him.

He didn't mind. He was in no hurry.

Raveaux slid a hand into his pocket to remove his late wife Gita's gold Ganesh charm, a gift he'd given her on a long-ago anniversary. He slid the precious reminder of Gita into a small safe with his ID, Security Solutions creds, and weapon.

Raveaux jogged the short distance to the beach and did his swim workout in the cool, calm night water, enjoying the silken dark ocean, the moon and stars overhead, the lighted palms silhouetted along the beach. Getting out, he showered at the park and walked back to his apartment with his towel around his neck, letting the tropical breeze dry his hair and skin.

He mulled over the cases he and Lono Jones were covering at Security Solutions, and the coming day's assignments.

Jones was turning out to be a hard worker with a quick mind, good tech skills, and an edge of competent violence that was useful in their world. He was also a quiet man, which Raveaux appreciated. He'd come to like his new partner very much.

Back at the apartment, Raveaux checked his phone and frowned —someone had phoned while he was out: a blocked number. The caller had left a message. Often those turned out to be European contacts from his law enforcement days.

Raveaux dressed in sleep attire of a lightweight cotton tee and boxers, then fixed himself a cup of herbal tea. When the beverage was ready, he seated himself in an armchair with a lamp he favored for reading. Lisette promptly jumped into his lap and circled a few times, kneading the fabric of his clothing with her needle-sharp claws. She settled on his stomach, purring.

He stroked Lisette's silky fur as he listened to the blocked number's voicemail on his phone.

"Pierre, it's Connor. We only met the one time, on the Big Island of Hawaii, when we rescued Jake and Sophie." Raveaux's eyebrows rose in surprise that he was hearing from the mysterious man in Thailand. An international, multiagency law enforcement team had caused Raveaux untold stress as they tried to leverage him to help capture Connor the year before. "As you know, I am the founder of Security Solutions, though I deeded the company to Sophie." The man blew out a breath. "As the company's founder, I would like to send you on a special assignment to Paris. Call me back, ASAP." The man left a phone number. The voicemail ended, and auto erased.

Fortunately, Raveaux had years of practice memorizing numbers.

His gaze flicked to the wall clock above the sliding exterior door: the hour was well after 8:00 p.m., but this call deserved his immediate attention. Months of harassment and pressure on Raveaux from the task force bent on bringing Connor "the Ghost" cyber vigilante into custody had eventually subsided as the group failed to build a case.

What could Connor possibly want Raveaux to do in Paris? Excitement sang along his veins; it had been years since he'd been to his birthplace in France.

Maybe some new threat had come up.

Connor picked up right away when Raveaux called; the Ghost had an upbeat voice that Raveaux recognized. "I hoped that message would pique your interest."

"Indeed. What does the founder of Security Solutions want or need from this humble investigator on the company payroll?" Raveaux sipped his tea, trying to stay cool.

"I have a lead on a mutual enemy. I can't think of anyone better than you to follow up with a possible sighting of Pim Wat, Sophie's assassin mother."

Raveaux froze, the mug halfway to his lips. He set it down on the little table that held his book. "I'm familiar with the hunt for Pim Wat, and why Sophie wants her found. What is your interest?"

"Pim Wat wants to kill the woman I love and steal her children,"

Connor said flatly. "She is an ongoing danger to Sophie, and to me since I killed her lover, the Master of the Yām Khûmkạn."

Connor, that man of many identities, also loved Sophie?

It made sense, unpalatable as it was. Raveaux had already observed Connor's attachment to Sophie when the man rescued her and Jake from a lava eruption on the Big Island.

Raveaux no longer had time on his side; he had competition.

Connor went on. "I understand you've been harassed and threatened with deportation by the task force that's been trying to bring me—or I should say, my alter ego the Ghost—in. I'm in touch with them through an agent McDonald with the CIA, and we've brokered a deal. A pardon for me, in return for Pim Wat, dead or alive, and any of her associates we can nail along the way."

"Does Sophie know?" Raveaux frowned. Sophie would greatly resent any withholding of information.

"No, and I don't want her involved. Pim Wat's too dangerous."

"Sophie will see being kept uninformed as a betrayal," Raveaux said, his belly tightening.

"Let me worry about Sophie, and about dealing with Bix at Security Solutions and getting your trip okayed. Deal?" Connor sounded impatient, clearly eager to move on to details.

"I cannot keep this kind of secret from Sophie," Raveaux said. "I will not. Our relationship is founded on trust. I have given her my word I will never lie to her, even by omission."

A long pause.

Connor sighed. "You want her too, don't you?"

Raveaux continued to stroke the purring kitten in his lap and said nothing.

"All right. I will call Sophie and tell her about this likely sighting. I just don't want her to go after Pim Wat herself. You understand where I'm coming from, right?"

"Sophie is on maternity leave with a three-month-old infant. She will not be foolhardy with the safety of those dearest to her," Raveaux said stiffly. "But she deserves to know everything; it is a matter of respect that will also help her take precautions." He paused. "You of all people know how capable she is."

Connor's voice was measured and deliberate when he finally spoke. "You're right, Raveaux. Thanks for your perspective. I will discuss all of this with her."

"I agree to go wherever the case takes me, then," Raveaux said crisply. "Proceed."

"There's a company called Kaleidoscope with central offices in Paris. Ostensibly, it's a lifestyle consulting company for the rich and famous, but according to my sources, Kaleidoscope also fences high end art and collectibles and deals in murder for hire. I would like you to go to Paris and investigate them in person. A woman matching Pim Wat's sketch description is a consultant with them. Her name is Vivian Moran."

"A good lead. Pim Wat would return to what she knows, and that is murder, fashion, and style," Raveaux said. "How soon would you like me to depart?"

"I will send on a secure file with everything I've gathered on Kaleidoscope tonight. I'll also contact Sophie and Bix, and after I do so, we'll get back to you with a departure date and time. I will also be providing you manpower support in the form of . . . ninjas, for want of a better word. The Yām Khûmkạn has many resources, and they will all be available to you."

"Ninjas could be useful. I will wait for your go." Raveaux ended the call with a punch of his thumb. He reveled in the tiny triumph of having the last word in a conversation with Connor, aka the Ghost, aka the Master of the Yām Khûmkạn.

Pim Wat.

Ninjas.

An incoming file on a murder-for-hire company called Kaleido-scope, based in his hometown of Paris.

Unlikely he'd be getting much sleep tonight.

Raveaux didn't mind that a bit.

Chapter Six

Sophie was in the secret office on the other side of her apartment, boxing up the private records and computer equipment for the move to her new house, when Connor's burner phone rang.

She hadn't heard that unique Thai ringtone in so long that she jumped. She had to search for the source and finally found it: she'd put the seldom-used phone on a charger in the corner and it was buried under equipment.

BLOCKED NUMBER showed on the screen, but she'd taken too long to answer; the melody had stopped. Sophie stared at the device, frozen for a moment.

The caller had to be Connor, but she'd cut off all communication with him almost a year ago. She couldn't think of any positive reason he'd be calling.

The phone rang again.

She answered. "This must be Connor."

"Sophie." Her former lover's voice sounded nearby and cheerful, with a hint of the Australian accent he'd affected for one of his aliases. "You knew it was me? Even after all this time?"

"You're the only person with this number." Her tone was brusque. "This call had better be important. That damn task force on your tail has finally given up, and I'm not interested in getting them excited again."

"I'm calling at the insistence of a friend." Connor still sounded amused. "Pierre Raveaux."

Sophie's pulse picked up. "I'm listening."

"Raveaux said I had to loop you in on this." Connor cleared his throat. "I'm sending him to Paris to follow up on a lead on your mother."

"Son of a flatulent yak!" Sophie cursed in Thai. "Of course, I must be fully informed of anything to do with my mother!"

"It's just a lead. We don't know if it's her, for sure. I didn't want to tell you because of that."

"And because you didn't want me to try to go after her myself," Sophie snapped.

Connor's silence confirmed it.

"Well, I'm on maternity leave and about to move my family into our new house. I'm a little occupied right now. I have no intention of going after my mother. *At this time.*"

"Thanks for that." He paused. "A new house? I hope it's more secure than the Pendragon Arches apartment."

"It is, and that's one of the main reasons I'm doing it. Now tell me what you know."

Connor described intel he had gathered; he was the only one who knew what Pim Wat's made-over face had looked like--he'd seen her before she fled, hidden behind a new face. "I've been looking for her ever since she got away from the fortress; this is the first time I've had enough of a visual match to put boots on the ground to look closer at a suspect. I chose Raveaux because of his French connections." Connor paused; Sophie mentally watched him run a hand through his short blond hair in a habitual gesture. "I've cut a deal with the task force through the CIA—Pim Wat in exchange for amnesty. I'd like to come home to the United States, Sophie."

Sophie's thoughts whirled. She sat down abruptly in an office chair nearby and spun Jake's heirloom diamond ring on her finger.

The last time she'd seen Connor, he'd been struggling with accepting his new role, but he'd seemed to step into it.

Now he wanted to leave.

Could any leader of that shadowy Thai organization just walk away from his position?

She had to focus on what they knew right now, not on future repercussions. "Raveaux is a good choice. Trustworthy. Competent. An investigator who knows the culture and speaks the language. He will verify what we need to find out about your lead."

"I'm glad you approve." Connor's tone was dry. "But I don't need your permission to deal with Pim Wat however I see fit. And until recent discussions with the CIA, I saw fit to have her taken out for a price. That's still our best option in dealing with her."

"I don't disagree, and expected as much," Sophie said with equal asperity. "And while I also agree that the current Master of the Yām Khûmkạn need not check with me about anything in the whole wide world he cares to do, we're still talking about *my mother*." Her voice rose. "And I have a right to know anything and everything about whatever is going on with that she-devil!" She panted with fury. "Pim Wat has sworn to kill me, and Armita, and take my children! My babies, raised by that *daughter of a fork-tongued viper*! I'd sooner die than see that happen." Sophie's eyes stung, though all she was conscious of was blinding rage. "Don't ever try to cut me out of anything to do with her."

"I hear you. Loud and clear." Connor sounded chastened. "You got it, babe."

"And don't call me babe." Sophie unclenched her fists and regulated her breathing. "Jake used to call me *babe*."

Connor cursed softly. "I put my foot in my mouth, didn't I?"

"So it seems," she growled. *"Hind end of a flea-bitten dog."*

"You just called me a mangy dog's ass, Sophie." His voice smiled. "And I still love you. The last time we saw each other didn't end well. But I want you to know . . . I'm ready to give up my vigilantism if it would give us a chance to be together. I've had a lot of time to think."

Sophie made a fist again. "It's too soon to discuss this."

He still loved her. Why did that make her heart do a backflip? Wasn't she over him yet, damn it? She'd tried so hard to forget what they'd once had . . .

Pim Wat might have been found. That took precedence over anything else.

"I am glad you told me the news, and I'm glad you let me know Raveaux insisted on it," she said at last. "This company in Paris, and Vivian Moran's function in it, fits perfectly with my mother's modus operandi. She has always loved being a tastemaker as well as a killer; she enjoys the irony of it."

"Good. I'm talking to Bix next and setting up Raveaux's departure. Everything will be lined up in a day or so. I will have him check in with you directly prior to his flight."

"That's fine," Sophie said woodenly. Pim Wat might have been found! She needed time to digest the intel.

"How are you, Sophie?" Connor's voice softened. "Feeling okay after the baby?"

"Childbirth is rigorous on a woman's body, but I am recovering as best as can be expected. I'm glad to be on leave and able to spend Sean's neonatal period with him, and have more time with Momi as she adjusts to being a sibling." Sophie softened her stiff tone. "Momi still asks for her Uncle Connor. Those days on Phi Ni were special."

Sophie and Connor had vacationed with Momi on Connor's private island in Thailand before its seizure by authorities, and that sweet time had made a big impression on her daughter.

"Happy to tell you that part of my deal is going forward already. The Phi Ni property has been released from the asset freeze. Nam and Kupa aren't happy here at the compound, so I plan to let them go back soon. I hope we can all reunite on the island when Pim Wat is in custody."

"I miss Phi Ni." Sophie shut her eyes to better recall the tiny island off the Thai coast with its cliff-straddling house, pure white beach, private airstrip, and boating bay. She missed their retreat more than she cared to admit. "I hope this woman is who we're looking for."

"I do too." Connor cleared his throat again. "How is Anubis?"

Sophie glanced over at the Doberman, curled up with Ginger. The two were so intertwined they looked like a jelly roll, curled up in a dog bed sized for only one large canine. "You're not getting Anubis back. He's a part of the family now; Ginger adores him and he's happy with us."

"Well then, I'll just have to move in with all of you, too," Connor said, and ended the call abruptly.

Sophie stared at the buzzing phone in her hand. Her heart was thumping. Her cheeks were hot.

She felt more alive than she had since Jake had died.

Was it because her mother had been found?

Or because Connor had told her he loved her and there was a possibility of his return?

She didn't have to know right now.

Sophie got on the Bowflex machine and did chest flies and arm reps, then sit-ups on the slant board. She was still trying to rebuild her core after the ordeal of carrying and birthing Sean.

She felt a twinge from her breasts, filled with milk for Sean's midmorning feeding, and another twinge from the surgery area on her lower abdomen.

Time to stop exercising.

Done were the days when she'd ignore her body and its needs and press through. She was a mother now and had to go easier on herself to keep her recovery steady.

Sophie exited through the secret doorway in the apartment's master bedroom closet and entered her apartment. The sound-proofing between the two units was so good that she hadn't heard baby Sean's hungry crying.

She took the infant from Armita and sat with him in the comfortable padded rocker installed in the living room. She fed him as Armita prepared an early lunch in the kitchen with Momi.

"There's a lead on my mother," Sophie said, once she had the baby settled.

A stillness fell over the nanny as Armita chopped vegetables; her knife paused midair. "Where?"

"Paris."

"That is indeed where Pim Wat would start a new life." Armita brought the knife down with a whack. "We told them to look for her in all of the major fashion and art centers."

"Yes. But there has been nothing until now. Connor found the lead with art generated by his memory of her new face." Sophie gazed down at the baby and stroked her hand along his silky hair. The infant's jaws worked vigorously as he took his nourishment, his eyelids fluttering. "Raveaux is going to investigate. I told Connor that I needed ongoing updates."

"As well you should," Armita said darkly. "We have to get into the new house as soon as possible. It's more defensible."

"We already have the highest degree of security that's available here, but I agree," Sophie said. "Nothing has changed with this news. We've always known that she would come for us at some point. This is a good thing. Connor and Raveaux might be able to head her off. And Connor is making a deal based on bringing her in."

Sophie filled Armita in on the plan so far.

Momi, seated on the counter with a cucumber and a butter knife to "help," piped up. "What is a deal?"

Armita rolled her eyes and tickled the little girl. "Nothing, Little Bean. Just deal with me putting you down for rest time."

That distracted Momi into a fit of "no!" while giggling as Armita teased her.

Sophie smiled at their antics. Armita had the toddler well managed, but they had to watch their words now that she was older.

Once Sophie had fed, burped, and diapered Sean and put him down for his nap, she, Momi and Armita ate a delicious lunch of stir-fried vegetables, tofu, and rice. Armita then carried Momi off for rest time.

Sophie headed back to her office and, once inside her quiet sanctuary, got on the phone with the movers.

Armita was right.

It was time for them to get into the new house, with its security upgrades, as soon as possible.

Chapter Seven

Vivian folded her hands serenely in her silk clad lap as she faced Enrique Mendoza. Her boss sat across from her at his desk. His choice of meeting place was no accident; it put her in the regrettable position of a penitent asking favors.

In fairness, he'd offered to take her to coffee, but she was still limiting possible camera exposure, and never went anywhere outside the office without the screen of a hat, wig, sunglasses, or all three.

"So, that's my situation, Enrique. I hope you understand why I took my time bringing this to you. I was showing my value to your organization before I asked for your assistance."

Mendoza stroked the mustache on his top lip. Today he wore a fall suit in lightweight oatmeal tweed with a cream silk tie. Gold cuff links winked at his wrists, and he smelled of clove and lemon, an oddly delicious combination. "I never took you for a fool, Vivian. I knew you weren't telling me everything when you called me that first night, distraught."

Vivian narrowed her eyes in annoyance; she hadn't been distraught. A tad desperate perhaps, but who wouldn't be, when she'd had to flee for her life with an army of ninjas on her trail, not to mention an international crime task force? "However you need to frame it, *mon cher*."

He gave a little bark of laughter. "You continue to amuse. Part of your charm." He leaned forward. "So. You need help with an assassination list, and you're willing to trade hits. Or did I miss something?"

"That's a bit crude, but yes."

"Meanwhile, there's still a bounty on your own pretty head that you're working off, so I don't cash in on it." Mendoza leaned back with a smug smile. "It seems you'll be in my debt for the foreseeable future."

Vivian cast her eyes down modestly; he mustn't see the scorn she hid.

Enrique Mendoza would die when his usefulness was over.

She pictured slitting his throat: the stab, the wrench across all those tough cords and tendons. The satisfying spray of hot blood all over the desk, the wall, the floor, her own skin. The razor-edged knife she carried was, even now, warm against her thigh. "Since I'll be working off debt, it's a good thing I love what I do."

"Indeed." With an air of getting down to business, Mendoza turned to his computer. "Your first personal target, the Master of the Yām Khûmkạn in Thailand, is a formidable one. I have just the asset to help you with that." He typed rapidly, then turned the monitor for Vivian to see. "The Chameleon. He specializes in deep cover, long-term penetration jobs."

The man in the photo had lightly tanned skin, dark eyes, black hair. His physical stats showed a medium height, trim build. No outstanding traits at all.

Mendoza flicked through a series of photos, and Vivian drew in a sharp breath: the Chameleon was able to change his appearance as easily as his namesake.

He was a young woman, an old man, an Asian, an Arab, a Turk, Chinese complete with coolie hat, a hipster youth with a skateboard.

"Chameleon will be able to penetrate the fortress of the Yām Khûmkạn with no trouble," Mendoza said. "He's quick and quiet. Likes to use poisons on his weapons, as do you."

Vivian let go of her pique for the moment and smiled. "Oh,

Enrique, you are truly the best! How did I not know about this man?"

"If you did, he wouldn't be much of a chameleon, would he?" A tiny diamond winked from one of Mendoza's incisors. "I'll set up a meet between the two of you. You can do the latest assignment together, orient him on what he needs to know, then monitor the job he does from outside the compound."

"But I don't want to go anywhere near that compound," Vivian protested. "Too much exposure. They're all looking for me."

Mendoza's eyes were steely and opaque. "We aren't running a charity here, *ma petite*. You must earn your keep." He reached across the desk and touched the lace of her fingerless glove. "Nice touch. No one can guess your age from your hands, now."

Yes, Enrique Mendoza was going to die—but now it was going to be slow.

"Vivian Moran." She extended her gloved hand to the man called the Chameleon.

The Chameleon merely nodded; his limp handshake was of the barely civil variety. "I find names meaningless in our line of work. For this assignment, my designation is Tik Panh."

Vivian inclined her head; the name was a common one in Thailand.

The mid-height, wiry built assassin was dressed to blend in Paris: black slacks, good shoes, a designer sweater. She would never have noticed him in a crowd except that he, too, wore a hat—a black wool cap with a brim and the ornate antique badge of some unknown brotherhood pinned to one side.

The detail elevated his appearance to stylish, but not loudly so.

She seated herself at the small outdoor table across from him at the street café, one of so many in Paris. Dressed for the brisk weather in a wool fedora with a little net veil that drew attention to her eyes and a blonde wig that hung in curls down her back, Vivian felt secure from prying eyes—and facial recognition cameras. "I assume Enrique briefed you. We will be traveling to Thailand together on the company jet and working in Bangkok on our assignments."

Panh leaned forward slightly. "I need to know everything you can tell me about the target's habits, the routines of the trainees, and a floor schematic of the fortress."

Vivian's pulse picked up. This was really happening! That upstart Connor was going down. "What do you know of the Yām Khûmkạn?"

"I know enough. The Master is a hard target." Panh's mirthless smile showed slightly pointed teeth, like those of a ferret. "A worthy target."

"That man is not the real Master," Vivian said sharply. "He is a Trojan horse for the CIA. A usurper, who took advantage of the true Master's trust to get close enough to murder him. He does not have the skills that the true Master was legendary for."

"He had enough skill to kill your lover in hand-to-hand combat," Panh said. "That can't have been easy."

Mendoza must have told the Chameleon of her relationship to the former Master—another thing he would answer for at the right time. "It's true that Connor is not unskilled in close fighting and weapons. My advice is to use a quick-acting poison in conjunction with whatever you bring to bear on him. Catching him alone and unawares is essential."

The Chameleon's stare was cold. "I told you what I needed from you, and advice is not a part of it."

Vivian regrouped with difficulty, fiddling with her napkin. "I will work on a map of the secret tunnels and layout of the building for you, and the daily schedule of the trainees as best I knew when I left. They may have changed everything with the advent of the new Master."

"I will be entering the fortress as a new trainee, or possibly a service or food provider, whichever position is more expedient,"

Panh said. "The layout and access tunnels that will take me to the target's private areas are the most critical."

Vivian shut her eyes, remembering the hidden passageway that she'd escaped through. Unless they'd discovered and blocked it, that route would lead directly to Connor's bedchamber.

"Not a problem." She accepted the espresso a waiter deposited in front of her; Panh had ordered the same.

They sipped in silence for a moment.

Vivian relished the strong flavor and wonderful smell of the black coffee. She gazed around the cobblestoned street; bike and foot traffic were encouraged on this route lined with tiny jewel box shops. Only the smallest cars could fit through, but they did occasionally roll by, as tiny as toys. All part of the ambiance of Paris, her new home. She was safe, hidden behind her new face and little net veil.

Yes, she'd landed on her feet. "Of course you did, my deadly viper, my Beautiful One," her lover said in her mind.

"When?" she asked at last.

"As soon as Mendoza provides us our covers and paperwork. He told me two or three days." The Chameleon leaned back in his chair and tipped his face to the weak sunshine. "Might as well enjoy the City of Love while I'm here."

Vivian reached into her small designer handbag and extracted currency. "You do that. I'll get started on the schematic."

She rose and left, feeling the man's focus between her shoulder blades like the red dot of a laser sight on a distance rifle.

Chapter Eight

Connor pressed his faithful servant Nam close, holding the smaller, older man in a hug. "I will miss you, my friend."

"Thank you for letting us go home." Kupa spoke from beside her husband.

He embraced the pretty Thai woman next, once again marveling at the transformation Pim Wat's surgeons had wrought on Kupa's face and body, a makeover that had been a form of torture for the modest woman. "I have McDonald's assurance that the island has been released from the asset seizure department of the U.S. Department of Justice. If you have any problems, contact me immediately."

Nam nodded. "I wish you could come with us, Master."

"It is not the time. We are moving on Pim Wat," Connor said.

Nine, beside Connor, straightened his gi as the breeze on the ramparts lifted it. "Travel safe, my friends."

"Look after our Master for us," Kupa told him.

"I always do," Nine replied. "I am interviewing a new personal attendant, though. The Master needs someone to care for him."

Nam frowned. "Maybe we shouldn't . . ."

Connor rolled his eyes. "Get on the damn chopper, Nam, Kupa. I need you to get my house in order so I can come visit, and hopefully bring Sophie and her children too."

The couple both broke into smiles at this prospect; they adored Sophie's toddler Momi and couldn't wait to meet baby Sean. "We will work hard at it, then. I'm sure the grounds and house are a mess after all this neglect," Nam said. "Who knows what that typhoon has done to the island?"

"Exactly." A typhoon had ripped through the area only a month ago; Connor had seen the destruction via one of his satellite hacks and it looked significant. "Send me pictures of the damage and what is needed. I will order more materials and send a team over when you are ready for them to help with repairs."

"Of course, Master."

Connor suppressed another eye roll—it didn't matter how often he told them not to call him that, they continued. "I hope to see you both soon."

The two turned away at last and got aboard the Yām Khûmkạn's chopper. Already loaded with materials and food supplies, the craft rose gently, swaying in the wind, and arced out from the compound's raised helipad.

The pilot was new; authorities in Bangkok had discovered the body of the previous one, his throat cut, near the abandoned craft in Bangkok six months ago when Pim Wat had used it to escape. She'd wanted no further witness to her new appearance; he'd be a fool to ever let that slip his mind.

The weight of that sat uneasily on Connor as he and Nine watched the craft fly toward the coast, moving out over the dense jungle that surrounded the fortress. The clear blue sky promised a smooth flight for his beloved servants.

Nine turned to him. "I would like you to choose the men we will be sending to Paris to assist the Frenchman. And of course, your new body servant."

"I don't need one," Connor barked, turning on his heel to head toward the opening in the stone wall that led back through tunnels to his chambers. "I can take care of myself with your help."

"I have other duties, Master. I cannot be everywhere at all

times," Nine argued. "You need me to keep an eye on the squad leaders too."

Connor clenched his jaw without replying.

As he always did when he came this way, he scanned the stone walls for any sign of the passageway Pim Wat had used for her escape.

The ninjas had searched and tested every stone in his chamber and every rock of this wall for any egress; they'd found nothing. The walls were carefully fitted together with a system of notches rather than mortar; wherever the opening had been, it was well disguised.

A sudden intuition stopped Connor as he stepped over the lintel into the fortress; a sense of wrongness permeated the stones in that area. He knew better than to disregard such things.

Connor placed his hand on the wooden door frame.

Nothing.

He pressed his palm against the nearby stones.

A faint reverberation, almost too soft to perceive . . . *something evil this way came.*

Connor opened his eyes.

Nine had stopped beside him, dark gaze assessing.

"I am moving out of the former Master's chambers," Connor said. "I never liked it there. Too many memories. The fact that we still haven't located Pim Wat's escape route from the Master's chamber concerns me."

Nine opened his mouth to argue; he'd been the most vociferous that Connor needed to slip seamlessly into the former Master's role to reassure the men. One more glance at Connor's face, and he ducked his head in agreement. "I will have your personal things moved to another set of appropriate rooms. But I insist on a new attendant for you. I cannot do all you require of me, as it is, and keep up your wardrobe, food, and personal space as well. The men will not understand if you don't have a body servant."

Connor turned away, fighting the sense of being hounded. He had no privacy, no personal life, no freedom. He was owned by the responsibility he'd inherited through no choice of his own.

He was trapped in this dank stone fortress, surrounded by hundreds of ninjas who looked to him for purpose and leadership.

And if he didn't provide that, they would turn on him and tear him apart.

He shivered in the chill that came off the stones as he headed down the hall, dimly lit by braziers and a series of high slits reflecting off brass mirrors set along the route.

In his former life, he'd lived alone with just his dog for company for many years. Why did this variation on that bother him so much now? But the culture of the Yām Khûmkạn, with its layers of hidden hierarchy and pride in servitude, was still foreign to him.

He'd had a taste of something better with Sophie, and it had ruined him for anything else.

Maybe he just needed a dog. With Anubis beside him in those days, he hadn't been lonely. Sophie'd told him he couldn't have the Doberman back, though. He smiled at the memory of their conversation. It had been so good to hear her voice . . .

"Perhaps a female attendant would be better for you," Nine said as he trailed behind. "She could meet . . . all of your needs."

Connor's spine stiffened. "I don't want a woman."

"Then . . . a man?"

"No!" Connor speeded up, his sandaled feet flying over the flagstoned hallway. "I just want to be alone!"

"You still long for Sophie, then," Nine said imperturbably.

"Yes." The response had been startled out of him. Connor whirled to face Nine. "I understand that you are trying to serve me to the best of your ability. Hear this: I do not want another person near me. Have someone clean and freshen my rooms daily when I'm out. Have the laundry staff take care of my clothing and the kitchen send up food which you can have tested. The Healer can attend me when I need it. But no personal attendant. That's final."

Nine's dark gaze was compassionate but unyielding. He ignored Connor's statement. "Perhaps, when Pim Wat is gone, Sophie will come to you on Phi Ni and bring her children. The dogs, too. You could visit them there."

Nine never contradicted Connor; he just ignored what he didn't want to hear, and the man could be stubborn as a rock.

Connor shut his eyes.

Calmed his breathing.

Loosened his fists.

Deliberately purged the darkness from his energy field.

He opened his eyes and smiled at his dear friend and loyal compatriot. "I hope so."

"I will hope with you, too, Master." Nine bowed in his respectful way.

Connor turned and walked on, heartened. "Sophie turned me down the last time I saw her, but it's not over until the fat lady sings."

"You wish a fat singer to be brought to the compound?" Nine asked.

Connor laughed this time; his spirits had lifted with the action he'd taken to manage his emotions. He might be trapped in this position, in this place, but within it he still had power, and some autonomy; he always had control over his own attitude and responses. "Never mind the fat lady for now. Let's review the men and choose some backup for Raveaux in Paris."

Six fully trained ninjas, survivors of the rigorous gauntlet ceremony of the Yām Khûmkạn and seasoned assassins all, stood at attention before Connor and Nine in one of the smaller courtyards.

Misting rain slicked the stones of the yard. Connor's new personal attendant, a young graduate chosen by Nine, held an umbrella high above his head.

Connor assessed the six men visually first, probing the colored energy mantle surrounding each man. He looked for pale colors, incongruities, dark spots. Each of them had several, which was to be expected.

He dismissed three of the men based on that alone.

The three remaining candidates faced him, elevated breathing and heart rates revealing tension and excitement.

"Tell me what your strengths are," Connor said.

The boldest of the three spoke first. "I am Four-Hundred-Eleven. I excel in target penetration, shock and awe. I prefer the sword as my weapon."

The shortest of the ninjas said, "I am Three-Twenty-Three. I am best at concealment and disguise. My weapons of choice are my hands." He held them up; long fingered and densely muscled, they radiated strength and deadly skill.

The last man said, "I am Seventy-Seven. As you can tell from my name, I have been here training for many years." Indeed, the ninja showed silver at his temples. "They call me Dove because I am deceptively gentle in approach to a target. My weapon is a wire." He held up a curled garrote.

Connor inclined his head. "Four-Eleven, you may go. This job requires a subtle approach. Thank you for your service."

When the boldest of the three had departed, disappointment evident in his posture and energy aspect, Connor turned to Nine for advice. "What next?"

"Have your men display their skills in a match, and we will see if they are right for the assignment, or if we need to choose others."

Connor felt the change in the room as the two warriors went on high alert, adrenaline pumping through their systems. He met each of their gazes with his own, giving them witness of his full attention. "Fight to first blood or surrender, whichever comes first."

Connor and Nine stepped back to give them room. The two faced each other. They bowed as was customary, then moved forward to meet.

Pad of careful, barefoot steps circling on wet stone.

Sibilant whisper of fabric against flesh.

Hiss of breath.

Smack of skin on bone.

Guttural grunt.

Thump of blows and kicks.

Muffled sounds of pain.

Cut off cry.

The thump of a hand on the stones.

"Dove, you are the winner," Connor said. "But you are both fast, quiet and skilled. That is what is needed for this assignment. You will be going to Paris, France, for this assignment. Nine will send you maps of the city and a primer on the language so you can study en route. You leave at first light."

The jubilation in the men's backslaps as they left was contagious.

Connor turned to Nine. "I want to go. I want to see if it's Pim Wat myself. I'm the only one who can tell for sure."

"You cannot," Nine said. "You are too valuable."

Connor growled and fisted his hands. "I need a sparring partner. Send some trainees to meet me in the square. Five or six ought to do."

He had to discharge his frustration somewhere—might as well take it out on the hides of men who'd signed up for it.

Chapter Nine

Sophie wore a loose dress and a floppy sun hat, baby Sean wrapped close against her chest in his sling. She walked around the perimeter of the grounds of her new house in Kahala, an upscale suburb just outside the city limits of Honolulu. The sun shone down brightly; fall on Oahu featured lovely weather, and she enjoyed a light breeze off the nearby ocean, tangy with the smell of waves.

The estate was enclosed with its original native lava stone wall, but the ground was torn up with new plantings and landscaping that was going in. Sophie picked her way around holes in the lush lawn, consulting a clipboard.

Sophie and Armita had been searching for the right home to buy ever since she'd found out she was pregnant with Sean. She hadn't wanted to live in a high rise with a second baby to manage. With her mother still on the loose, they'd decided a private home could be made more secure.

Sophie'd closed on the house two months ago and had been taking her time having the remodel work done and security upgrades put in, but now that Pim Wat had potentially been located, their move-in date had been accelerated.

Kahala, around the corner from Diamond Head and just outside of Honolulu, featured a lot of older homes as well as modern new mansions. Sophie's purchase was a vintage home—a large Mediterranean done in stucco with wide verandahs and deep terra-cotta roof overhangs built to capture ocean breezes for natural cooling. Built in the fifties, the house had belonged to a movie star who had retired there; it already contained many of the security features, including a "safe room", that Sophie had been looking for.

The biggest security upgrade Sophie had invested in was a high, bulletproof, clear Plexiglas ocean-facing wall with an electronic sensor system embedded in it. This part of the estate had been left open when Sophie bought the house; she couldn't move in with it that way.

Each massive, expensive clear panel had been shipped over from the mainland for the build. Sophie had worked closely with the engineers at the Security Solutions lab to have it installed and then hooked up with her firm's newest video AI monitoring system. All the "bells and whistles", as Jake would have called them, were routed through a self-contained portal and ended up on Sophie's phone for easy monitoring.

She passed the painting crew heading into the house and waved, then paused to examine nearby windows. Additional protection measures were added to them, which included metal shutters that could be let down in case of heavy storms or intruders. The shutters were painted to match the roof and looked like louvers; currently retracted, she was pleased with their integrated styling.

But Sophie had chosen the house more for its fireproof walls and impenetrable terra-cotta roof than for any aesthetic. She'd bought it to be her family's personal fortress.

The "safe room" deep inside the house was a basement that contained plenty of survival supplies and had been built originally as a bomb shelter. The safe room area also had its own independent power source and computer satellite setup in case lines of power and communication were ever breached.

They would be safe here. She'd sleep easier once they'd moved in. Pendragon Arches had been all right, but there were just too many ways a stranger could gain access.

Sophie reached the corner of the property and gazed through the clear security wall to admire the way the sun sparkled off the surf. A barrier reef just beyond the beach created a nice, sheltered swimming area in front of the house that the kids would love when they were a little older.

She'd stolen the idea of the clear security wall from a job she and Jake had worked on Maui for a rock star who was being stalked. "This house is my happy place," Shank Miller had said. "Hell if I'm going to let crazy people steal it from me." He'd insisted on security measures that didn't detract from his view and the lush tropical plantings at his home.

Sophie had gone one better with her Plexiglas panels, working with the manufacturer to have camera and motion sensor nodes embedded in the plastic. The wall was being tested by Sophie as an option to add to Security Solutions' offerings for upscale clients.

But Jake had been the one to come up with the clear security wall idea at the Miller estate.

Jake.

Sophie's heart squeezed painfully at the memory of her fiancé's face, animated with excitement that he'd solved the challenge to everyone's satisfaction at Miller's place.

He'd love what she'd done for their home.

Sophie kissed the top of Sean's soft, fuzzy head, resting peacefully on her chest. Sometimes she could almost feel Jake, as if he had an arm around her and their child. "I got you, babe," he said in her mind.

"If only," she sighed aloud. "You'd love this."

Sophie continued her leisurely inspection of the security wall and the edge of the property, ignoring the noise and voices coming from inside as the workmen finished up the painting.

Once she'd checked all the mounts and inserts and verified on her phone that the AI system was live and online, she deactivated the program with a push of her thumb.

No point in keeping it all going when the gates were wide open, and workers poured in and out.

Armita appeared on the verandah, Momi's chubby hand held tight in hers, as the toddler tugged and fought to run back inside and watch the painters. "Are you done? Please say you're done. This one is trying to escape."

"I am. We should be good to move in as soon as the paint's dry and the fumes are out of the house," Sophie said.

"Good. I'll meet you at the car; Momi stuck her hands in the paint, and I don't want her to get away again." Armita marched off with her reluctant, protesting charge in tow.

Sophie snuggled Sean's plump weight close as the baby napped. "Are you going to give us a hard time too, like Momi does? Don't answer that, little man. You'll be worse if you're anything like your papa."

Sophie's landscaper approached, carrying a plastic tray of new starts. "Hey, Sophie. You wanted to look at the native Hawaiian plants I suggested for around the property walls?"

"Yes, please," Sophie said, approaching the lanky older Japanese man. "I don't want anything to block the view, but as we discussed, I'd like to use indigenous Hawaiian plantings along the sides for more privacy. What have you got?"

They discussed a barrier outside the wall consisting of native *hala* trees, with their long, spiky leaves and umbrellalike shapes to cast shade. Around the *hala* they'd plant *naupaka*, a beach-loving bush that didn't mind the salt air and sandy soil.

Directly in front of the house on the beach they would plant low-growing *ipoema* vines to hold down the sometimes-blowing sand with their heart-shaped leaves and purple flowers that looked like morning glories.

Done consulting with the landscaper and remembering Armita's understandable annoyance, Sophie hurried around the side of the house, mentally visiting each of its high-ceilinged, airy rooms. They wouldn't need air conditioning out here with the oceanfront setting and a house built to make the most of the prevailing winds.

The sides and back of the dwelling that faced the street had been walled long ago with gorgeous native lava stone; Sophie'd had holes drilled in it and inset motion and video security nodes already, carefully camouflaging them.

A steel security gate on a motion sensor stood open to accommodate the traffic of the workers, and Sophie was reassured by the two burly Security Solutions personnel at the gate. They checked in everyone that came or went from a vetted list complete with ID photos that had been created for each worker.

Sophie was making her home both as safe and appealing as it could possibly be. The effort and expense would be worth every penny when she finally moved her precious family into it.

Armita had Sophie's Lexus SUV turned on as she waited. Momi, restrained in her car seat, had been appeased with a graham cracker and an apple juice box.

Sophie opened the side door and undid the straps of Sean's carrier. "Did you get into the paint, Little Bean?"

Momi popped the plastic straw of her drink out of her mouth and grinned, her smile a row of perfect pearly teeth, a dimple in her cheek. "Yah, Mama. It was pretty."

Armita rolled her eyes from the front seat. "That's why we put that color on your bedroom walls, sweetie, but it's not for touching."

"I like purple!" Momi declared loudly.

"And that's why you have purple walls in your room," Armita replied.

Sophie eased the sleeping infant away from her warm body and slid him into his car seat.

Sean Dunn Smithson slept on, his plump cheek pink and creased from where it had rested on Sophie's chest. She buckled the seat's straps over him and covered the whole thing with its sun hood, draped with a thin gauze cloth to keep air currents off his skin. Hopefully, that would help him sleep a bit longer. "Shh," she whispered to Momi, holding up a finger to her lips.

Momi nodded. "Baby Sean sleeping."

"You're a good big sister, you know that?" Sophie leaned across the baby's seat to kiss her daughter's forehead. "Love you, darling."

"Luv you, Mama."

Sophie withdrew, shut the door with a gentle click, and got into the passenger seat up front.

Armita maneuvered their vehicle around the circular driveway, past the workers' trucks, and out through the gate. The house had a separate garage, but that was currently the domain of the landscaper, his crew and supplies for the yard project.

"As soon as that paint's dry and the security's online, we're moving in," Sophie repeated in a low voice.

Armita nodded. "Pendragon Arches is okay, but there are too many points of entry."

"On that we agree." Sophie settled back and adjusted an overhead rearview mirror so she could watch the children: Momi was dropping off, and Sean was still sleeping soundly.

These two were everything. Pim Wat would not have them, not ever.

"Over my dead body," Sophie whispered.

It wouldn't come to that, though. Her children needed her too much.

Chapter Ten

Raveaux stood on the sidewalk at Charles de Gaulle International Airport, holding his small carryall and the leather satchel that was never far from his side. Fall nipped at his nose, and his heart thumped with excitement as he looked around his familiar birthplace.

Paris was beautiful in fall, with the plane trees flaunting their colors and attractive goods in the windows alluring shoppers. Well-dressed, stylish people hurried along; even the dogs were precisely groomed. He breathed in deeply, wincing a bit at the smell of exhaust fumes from the cars whizzing by—but then, a whiff of fresh bread from a bakery wafted across the street.

Paris was full of these contrasts. Just one of the reasons he loved her.

A silver-gray Mercedes limo pulled up at the curb in front of him. The driver hopped out, came around and opened the back door for him. "Welcome to Paris, Monsieur Raveaux."

"Music to my ears to hear those words spoken in my language, in the city where I was born." Raveaux surrendered his bag and slid into the buttery leather of the back seating area, carrying just his satchel.

"Pierre. It's been far too long." His wife's friend Delphine Arles, seated in the corner, leaned forward with a smile. "I was so happy to hear you'd be in town."

"You are as beautiful as ever, *ma cherie*." Raveaux kissed both of her cheeks, and she kissed his with a sparkle of appreciation in her eye. "Thank you for meeting me on such short notice."

"Gita would be glad to see you looking so well."

"She would have agreed with my choice to move to Hawaii for a fresh start." Raveaux clasped Delphine's hand in both of his. "She is never far from my thoughts."

"Nor mine, even after all these years." Delphine sat back, reaching for a tissue in the side pocket of the limo. "I am still lonely without my best friend. Seeing you really brings her back."

She dabbed her eyes as Raveaux settled himself and put on his seat belt. The limo moved out smoothly, cutting into the dense Paris traffic—a shark moving through a school of lesser fish.

Delphine's beautifully made-up eyes looked him over. "I recognize that old leather bag." Delphine Arles hadn't aged a day in the five years since he'd seen her last. A petite blonde dressed in her signature look of cream with jewel-toned accents, she had been a useful contact in his detective work in the field of art theft as a philanthropic widow and socialite. On the board of the Louvre and an art collector in her own right, she knew everyone who was anyone in the art scene of Paris. "Tell me what brings you here."

Raveaux cut his eyes to the uniformed chauffeur.

Delphine pressed a button. A soundproofed, darkened barrier rose to separate them from her driver.

Raveaux reached into his bag and took out a small device. He pressed it, and a buzz of white noise filled their space. "Forgive me. A signal jammer in case there are more than human ears listening."

Delphine's blue eyes widened with excitement. "This is all very cloak-and-dagger, Pierre."

"I can't be too careful with this particular case." He paused to gather his thoughts. "Are you familiar with a company called Kaleidoscope?"

"I am." Delphine wrinkled her pretty nose. "Tastemakers to the tasteless. Anyone who has to hire a company like that should not be living in Paris."

Raveaux smiled. "Obviously. Even so, I am investigating them for a private case. Do you know anyone personally who works for them?"

"Ooh!" Delphine rubbed her hands together with glee. "I hope you are planning an ignominious arrest of that awful poseur, Enrique Mendoza. I know him from events around town, unfortunately."

Raveaux's pulse quickened. "Good. I am also interested in his staff. Have you met any of them?"

"Mendoza is the main face of the company. He has several style consultants, apparently, but they do not run in our circles." Delphine sniffed.

"I need to get closer to him. To that business. Can you arrange a chance meeting, perhaps?"

Delphine narrowed her eyes. "What is this about?"

"I can't tell you, darling," Raveaux said firmly.

She pouted. "I want gossip. Just a little. Just a whiff. I'd love to let slip that they were involved in art forgery or some other skull-duggery."

If his friend only knew! "Nothing must leave this conversation," Raveaux said. "Not a whisper of any sort of rumor. This is an active investigation. We can't spook them."

Delphine lowered her eyes. "You know how arousing that is, don't you?" She touched his knee with a slim hand and lifted crystal-blue eyes to his.

His dead wife's best friend wanted him. Had wanted him for years, the longing in her gaze proclaimed.

"Delphine," he whispered, and covered her hand with his. "I am —not available."

"Oh, ha! I was only teasing!" Delphine's laugh was a brittle tinkle. That flash of bone-deep hunger must have been another of her ploys because she fluttered her lashes and flashed a dimple as she with-drew to her corner of the seat. "Silly man, you flatter yourself. But tell me what to do, and I'll do it. For Gita's memory, of course."

Raveaux sat back as well, keeping distance between them. "After we've got what we need for the investigation, you can throw them to the gossip wolves; I'll even give you the material you need to ruin Kaleidoscope's reputation. But for now, I must get a closer look at Mendoza, and his staff. Some sort of interaction, to begin with."

Delphine's smile was a humorless curve. "I know just the thing. Leave it to me."

Chapter Eleven

Raveaux checked the white bow tie of his tuxedo in the mirror on the back of the hotel room's door. He still remembered how to knot one, though it had been another lifetime since he'd done so. He assessed his appearance: not bad for a man who'd left any kind of formal socializing when his wife died almost six years previously.

Raveaux had taken the free day since he arrived in Paris to get into his character: a close, classic haircut, a professional shave, a facial, massage, and a manicure completed careful preparation for arriving at a major art charity fundraising event with socialite Delphine Arles on his arm.

He would be playing the part of freelance art evaluator for the evening. Delphine was known as a collector in her own right, not just for her function in attracting and securing art for the Louvre. Bringing an independent expert to evaluate the silent auction offerings was expected.

Raveaux brushed a bit of lint from his sleeve, enjoying the way the suit enhanced his lean, muscular frame. Only a few years ago, he'd been a scarecrow, his robust tan gone sallow, permanent bags under his eyes.

He looked ten years younger. Living in Hawaii and working for

Sophie at Security Solutions had given him a new lease on life, as the Americans said.

He checked the gold watch Gita had given him for an anniversary—he'd visited the safe deposit box downtown where he'd stored all valuables before he left for Hawaii. It had been hard to see his dead wife's jewelry and the little pearl necklace and bracelet set Lucie's grandparents had given his daughter—but it was evidence of how far he'd come that he was able to do so at all.

His phone buzzed. A text from Delphine's number.

"I'm here in the car."

Raveaux tugged his lapels, buttoned his jacket, and headed for the door: it was time for a high society party. At least he looked the part—and that was essential in Paris.

⚜

When they arrived at their destination, Raveaux opened the door of the limousine for Delphine and took her hand to assist her out.

She rose gracefully, her eyes on his with a wicked twinkle as the full effect of her gown was revealed: a clinging cream sheath with a slit high on one thigh, cut so low in front that she must have used tape to keep her breasts covered. A lasso style rope of diamonds sparkled with cold fire in her cleavage, one end of the strand brushing her tiny waist.

"No one will be able to look at anyone but you, Delphine," Raveaux said.

"*They* know a good thing when they see it." Delphine tossed her coiffed blonde head and gave a little sniff. Clearly, she was still smarting from his rejection earlier. She passed by a little too close, trailing Shalimar perfume in her wake.

Raveaux was not even marginally tempted. Several women he'd spent time socially with in Hawaii passed before his inner eye; each of them, and particularly Sophie, appealed to him more than this porcelain doll of a woman.

But Gita had loved Delphine, and his wife had been a good judge of character.

Perhaps Gita's death had changed them both, and he was judging the new Delphine Arles too harshly. She had been generous and helpful to him, and she was under no obligation to do so at all.

The driver pulled away to make room for the next arriving vehicle. Raveaux tucked a luxe fur throw around Delphine's bare shoulders against the fall chill and took her arm. They proceeded up wide, shallow marble steps leading into the magnificent Palais du Paris, where tonight's occasion was being held.

The modern building, used for exhibitions and events, had been modeled after a Greek temple and consisted of a main ballroom in a circular shape, surrounded by Corinthian columns that held up a domed roof.

Delphine squeezed his arm against her side as they stepped inside the event space. "Oh!" she exclaimed, tipping back her head.

The enormous arched roof had been darkened and was filled with three-dimensional holographic projections of classic art pieces: Monet's wife with her parasol flirted with Michelangelo's Creation of Adam, Van Gogh's Starry Night segued into Degas's dancers.

Raveaux resisted the spectacle of the stunning display.

Keeping Delphine's arm tucked in his, he maneuvered carefully until their backs were against one of the massive columns. Delphine was still raptly watching the ever-changing sight overhead as Raveaux scanned the room for anyone he recognized.

The lighting had been orchestrated for the event; the ballroom was dark except for recessed dimmers between the columns that allowed staff to circulate with trays of champagne and hors d'oeuvres. An attendant came by and took Delphine's wrap, handing her a ticket to retrieve it later.

Tiny, globular LED lanterns powered by mini drones floated above the guests' heads, their seemingly random patterns adding to the spectacle above while casting a glow over the crowd that didn't interfere with the art show overhead. Even so, the illumination was too dim to see more than a few feet around them in any direction.

Raveaux finally allowed himself to feast his gaze on the riveting reinterpretation of beloved and famous artworks going on above.

The art show repeated for another fifteen or twenty minutes as attendees continued to arrive. A waiter dressed in a suit embedded with tiny lights offered them champagne; Delphine took one of the flutes, but Raveaux waved it away, asking for water. The man soon returned with a large wine goblet of sparkling water.

When it seemed most of the attendees had arrived, the holographic show gently faded, and the dome filled with golden light.

Spontaneous applause broke out. A man with a vigorous mane of white hair in a tux appeared on a dais at one side of the circular expanse.

"Welcome, friends and patrons of the arts!" The master of ceremonies for the evening spoke in French, and an interpreter, a woman in a gold spangled dress, translated into English beside him. "We are so glad you could come support and enjoy our annual fundraiser. As usual, we will offer dancing and refreshment while you have a chance to peruse this year's silent auction."

The interpreter reached behind the MC and pulled a cord; everyone gasped as one side of the room, which had appeared seamlessly as a continuation of the space, dropped to the floor in a puddle of plain white fabric. The illusion projected onto it had been perfect. Beyond that barrier, a semicircle of movable display units had been set up. Each artwork on offer was beautifully lit and mounted on a freestanding structure.

Another cover dropped away on one side to show a fancy buffet spread with an area of raised tables to rest drinks and food upon. No seating was offered—a clever way to keep people moving.

A third drape fell away to reveal a classical musician group consisting of harp, flute, cello, and violin.

Delphine turned to smile at Raveaux. "*C'est magnifique, oui?*"

"*Oui. Vraiment.*"

"I assume each of you have your bid numbers; see me immediately if there is any problem," the Master of Ceremonies said. "Every piece available tonight is labeled with as complete a provenance as we were able to put together, and a minimum bid is clearly displayed on the electronic tablet beside the artwork. Bidding will close at midnight; you may begin now."

The ballroom dimmed once again, but not as much as before. The crowd burst into murmuring conversation as the hologram began playing above them again, but now as a background. The quartet broke into a light jazz piece.

The crowd moved around the space and toward the silent auction; there was now enough illumination to dance, eat, and make bids by.

Delphine prepared to go look at the artworks, but Raveaux tightened his grip on her arm. "I want to find the target first."

"Oh, right. You're working," Delphine said, with a bit of a pout. She sipped her champagne, scanning the room. "I will try to find that odious Mendoza for you."

She didn't have a chance to, though, because a socialite friend swooped in, husband in tow, to buss Delphine on both cheeks and demand an introduction to the "yummy date" she had brought.

Raveaux heaved an inner sigh, curved his lips as best he could into what passed for a smile, and extended a hand. He had all night to spot his prey.

Chapter Twelve

Later in the evening, Raveaux stood beside one of the artworks for sale in the auction area, ostensibly examining it with a loupe and a penlight.

Live music swelled around him, the holographic art show danced above, and he was doing the purported job he'd come for as an "art appraiser." This had not been as easy as he'd hoped because he'd spotted several acquaintances from his past. He'd had to make a quick exit to the restroom or take shelter behind a pillar to avoid these awkward encounters.

It also didn't help that Delphine had been swilling champagne and refusing to eat any of the glorious hors d'oeuvres filling the banquet table.

His blonde nemesis reappeared suddenly, her cheeks flushed and rope of diamonds bouncing fiery sparks of light as she towed a man dressed in a pearl-gray tux toward Raveaux. Delphine had abandoned all pretense of subtlety, and he tightened his back teeth in annoyance as she deposited Mendoza in front of him.

"Pierre. I brought you what you asked for." Delphine gestured to the man theatrically. "This is Enrique Mendoza. Mendoza, my associate, Pierre Raveaux."

Mendoza's handsome, tanned face reflected confusion, but also a subtle gloating. Being grabbed by the hand and dragged across the ballroom by Delphine had obviously increased his social cachet.

Raveaux's attention sharpened on the petite woman trailing in Mendoza's wake, a remora following a shark. The woman's slight height and build were those of the target, Pim Wat, but there any resemblance ended. Her face was reminiscent of the American actress, Halle Berry. Her hair was a sleek platinum cascade sparkling with crystals; her gown, a mermaid style in clinging red, trailed the floor revealing high Lucite heels. Modish black glasses set off dark blue eyes of an unusual shade.

She was exquisite and looked nothing like Sophie.

Mendoza's intelligent brown eyes glittered with speculation. "A pleasure to meet any friend of the lovely Delphine Arles. And I see that you've been captivated by my colleague at Kaleidoscope Tastemakers, Vivian Moran."

Mendoza was shrewd—he had spotted how Raveaux's attention was riveted on the woman who might be Sophie's mother.

Raveaux wrenched his gaze away and focused on her employer. "Pierre Raveaux with Art Assessors." Raveaux shook Mendoza's hand, and then that of his companion.

Their eyes met; hers were assessing behind those glasses, which had to be smart lenses connected to an uplink. She was casing the room. Hopefully, the hastily constructed, back dated business website with resume that he'd had Connor put in place would hold up.

He lifted Moran's hand, clad in a delicate black lace glove, to his lips and pressed a kiss upon her knuckles. "*Enchanté*, madame."

He wouldn't be getting a fingerprint from her tonight, as he'd hoped. The tresses flowing down her bared back were likely a wig, so plucking one of those hairs wasn't going to help either.

Heat flushed under his tux at the challenge ahead—he was going to have to get close enough to get a DNA sample some other way.

"*Merci beaucoup* for your indulgence." Raveaux addressed the two with a slight bow. "I asked Madame Arles for an introduction to you as a favor. I'm building a portfolio of clients for my new business here in Paris. Kaleidoscope Tastemakers provides the kind of services that might interface with mine. I assess art pieces for purchase by collectors."

Mendoza would investigate Raveaux's background; they'd find out he was ex-police. His current cover as an art assessor building a new business was plausible. He'd prepared for this; the skills he'd used for a decade to recover stolen and forged works were the same he'd need now.

Delphine, belatedly remembering her part, burped delicately behind her hand even as she reached for another bubbling flute off a passing tray. "Why don't you wow them with your skills, Pierre? Tell us about this painting I've got my eye on."

"*Oui, madame.*" With a small, theatrical bow, Raveaux stepped back. He removed a small steel pointer from his jacket pocket, extended it, and indicated the eighteen-inch-square canvas before them in its ornate gold frame.

"The description accompanying the piece indicates that this is an early work by Mary Cassatt, signed and dated with its provenance bills of sale included, a nice touch." He pointed to the printed placard beside the painting. "Madame Arles has hired me to verify that information via other means." Raveaux swirled his pointer over the painting. "Art historians know a good deal about Cassatt's work and how it intersected with that of the other Impressionists of her time. The subject matter, that of a child sleeping in her bassinet, is consistent with Cassatt's early subjects." He then pointed to Cassatt's signature. "An artist's name added to a painting is a calling card. It claims ownership and completion of a piece and adds value to it. This lettering is also consistent with Cassatt's known nomenclature and positioning, but of course, could be forged."

A small crowd of attendees had drifted over to watch this spectacle, but Raveaux kept his eye contact confined to Mendoza alone, with the occasional glance at Delphine, his ostensible client. "The work has been mounted for this show so that we can examine the back of the piece, without disturbing it *in situ*. Let us observe the canvas from behind, if you please."

Raveaux walked around to the back of the wall easel; Delphine, Mendoza and Moran trailed after him.

The display mount held the canvas so that the back of the painting was visible for inspection. Raveaux extended his pointer. "Note that the painting was done on a piece of discarded paneling. This was a practice painting for Cassatt; she was honing her craft and didn't spend excess on materials in the beginning of her career. Again, consistent with the stated period of the piece." Raveaux pressed a button on the pointer, and a bright beam turned on, highlighting the area he pointed it at. "I give you a fingerprint in the upper right corner of the panel. Too bad Cassatt didn't leave her prints on file with the Sûreté; I would be out of a job." A polite ripple of laughter. "Note that the material is a thin rosewood panel. Rosewood was a material used for decorative home paneling during that era— popular then, and hard to find today." Raveaux, trailing his audience, returned to face the painting from the front. "Now, I address the color palette and brush style of the artist."

Raveaux opened a slim laptop he produced from his leather satchel, delivered to the area for this purpose by the chauffeur. "Here is an extensive computer file built of Cassatt examples, complete with a swatch sample catalogue of different strokes she used in her body of work." He held up the laptop for Mendoza to see. "I submitted a photo of the painting for comparison with this database. Brushstrokes are within a solid confidence ratio as authentic and consistent with Cassatt's art of the period." He pressed another button, and a color wheel appeared. "I'm going to run a spectrometer over the painting now."

Voices murmured behind him, but Raveaux paid them no heed. He ran a handheld device slowly over the surface of the painting, coming close, but not touching it. "This device measures the distance between light waves bouncing off the pigments. I can then verify if the pigments used are consistent with those available to Cassatt in her time."

The laptop beeped.

Raveaux swiveled the monitor toward Delphine and Mendoza.

"*Voila*. This painting is a Mary Cassatt of the period stated in the provenance literature, to within a plus or minus 90% confidence ratio." He nodded to Delphine. "It appears to be an excellent value at the moment."

"Thank you, Pierre." Delphine stepped forward and wrote her number and bid on the electronic tablet mounted beside the painting. As soon as she stepped back, onlookers clustered in eagerly to submit bids.

"And thank you, Madame Arles, for the opportunity to demonstrate my knowledge publicly," Raveaux said. He then turned to Vivian Moran. "Would you honor me with a dance, Madame Moran?"

"*Mais oui*," the lady said, and took his proffered arm.

Raveaux ignored the murmuring and stares. Head high, he led the woman who might be Sophie's deadly mother out onto the ballroom floor.

Chapter Thirteen

Vivian allowed the art assessor and former policeman Pierre Raveaux to sweep her onto the dance floor.

The man was of a good height for her. She rested a gloved hand on his shoulder, and he held the other in tanned, well-kept fingers—she noticed those details: his nails were clean and buffed. The arm he slid around her waist was steely strong and guided her confidently but did not press too close. She also liked the way the olive-tan column of his throat contrasted with the tux's blazingly white collar and tie. A faint whiff of cinnamon cologne teased her nose.

Vivian gave his shoulder an exploratory squeeze; his eyes met hers. Espresso dark and framed in thick lashes, they hid secrets and a past. "You honor me, madame."

Vivian was intrigued. "Do we know each other, Monsieur Raveaux?"

Raveaux's interest in her had been instant and unfeigned. She sensed tension humming in his whipcord frame as they moved to the music. A smile that didn't reach his eyes curved a mouth clearly unused to that expression; his gaze was intense. "I would have remembered meeting you, *madame*."

"I will take that as a compliment."

"It's meant as one." Raveaux's arm tightened as he moved her into a turn; she was flush against him. Vivian heated beneath her clingy red dress; an attractive man who moved confidently was catnip, and it had been regrettably long since she'd shared her bed.

Raveaux was a good dancer. Vivian let her body go fluid in his arms, following his lead.

All was a delightful whirl until the train of her gown caught on a heel, bringing her up short. Vivian clutched at Raveaux for support and felt something scratch the bare skin of her back as he steadied her. "That dress is a menace," he whispered in her ear. "Perhaps you're better off without it."

She smacked him playfully. "Help me out of it, then?"

"*Bien sûr.*" Raveaux steadied her with one hand, then squatted to undo the fabric twisted around her heel with the other. "I'm afraid I left my client rather abruptly. We should return."

Vivian cocked her head, pouting. "If we must."

Raveaux led her back to where Mendoza and that awful snob Delphine Arles stood talking in front of the Cassatt that he'd evaluated. Mendoza raked the man whose arm she held with an assessing glance, but he addressed Vivian. "Nice to see you enjoying yourself, *ma cherie.*"

"I like a dance with a man who moves well anytime I can get one," Vivian replied.

Delphine rolled her eyes. "And yet I'm the one who's purchased Pierre's time for the evening. Come, Pierre. I require sustenance." The socialite teetered toward the refreshment table. Raveaux rushed to support her—but he gave one glance over his shoulder at Vivian.

That look was dark, unreadable: *I see you*, it said. *You're mine.*

A heavy pulse beat between Vivian's legs; she shifted uncomfortably. She recognized a fellow hunter when she danced with one.

"He is not what he seems." She accepted a glass of champagne from Mendoza. "Raveaux might be one of us."

Mendoza's voice was cold. "My thoughts exactly." Her boss took out his phone and worked it with his thumbs. "I'll have our team do a workup on him. I did enjoy his performance as an art expert, however. Our traditional clients will eat that shit up. If he's clean, we'll interview him more closely."

"Much more closely," Vivian murmured.

Strangely, though she knew she'd never met him before, there was something familiar about Pierre Raveaux as he walked away. She had seen him somewhere; she could swear it.

A

They did not stay long enough to find out who had won the silent auction for the Cassatt, though Vivian was curious enough to download the app that was tracking the auction and input the painting's number so that she could find out what it ultimately sold for, and the number of the winner.

"Our job was to see and be seen," Mendoza said as he helped her into his limo. "And that we did. I am satisfied that those ridiculously expensive tickets were a good investment. I'm glad you approached that society pages photographer; the picture could end up in Harper's Bazaar or Vogue—perhaps the French version of People Magazine."

"The least I could do to thank you for a lovely evening." Vivian cast her eyes down modestly, suppressing a qualm at the exposure she'd attracted by posing with Mendoza for the paparazzi. Hopefully her dangerous situation would soon be remedied with the help of the Chameleon, and she could lean into her new identity—strut it around Paris a bit more.

She'd run into several acquaintances from her days as Pim Wat, and none of them had so much as batted an eye of recognition at her.

Mendoza owned a whole floor of a swanky apartment building and sublet the units to his assets and colleagues, so the limo deposited them together at the front of it. They rode up on the secure elevator in silence.

"Let's meet at the office in the morning and review what the team has discovered on Raveaux," Mendoza said as he escorted her to the door of her apartment, down the hall from his huge suite.

"Perfect," Vivian said. Mendoza waited courteously while Vivian unlocked her door and deactivated the alarm; she blew him a kiss and gave a finger wave from inside. "Thank you, Enrique. I enjoyed myself tonight."

Mendoza smiled with genuine affection. "You are so lovely, my dear. Even more so than before."

"*Merci beaucoup, mon cher*," she replied, and closed the door.

Too bad he had to go; people who genuinely liked her were few in the world.

Mendoza might, in fact, be the only one.

Grief wrapped its familiar talons around her heart.

The Master had liked her.

Loved her to excess, in fact. He'd accepted her as she was, and hadn't judged her innate difference from "normal" people. Instead, her lover had celebrated her uniqueness: her ruthlessness, her cruelty, her murderous impulses.

"My deadly viper. My Beautiful One." The Master's voice still spoke in her mind, and it brought her to tears.

Would she ever be loved again in this life?

Vivian shed her clothing as she walked toward the bathroom to shower; the maid would be by the next morning. But she took time to hang her wig on one of the many stands in her dressing area. She removed the net of crystal dangles and brushed the wig carefully.

In the shower, Raveaux's lean, handsome face appeared in her mind's eye as Vivian washed tension and stress from her body with rich scented soap. She caressed herself, remembering being in his arms as he swept her confidently around the dance floor.

She'd enjoyed every minute of it.

He'd seemed captivated by her, too.

Perhaps she could still make a connection with a man; but worthy partners were so hard to find.

Chapter Fourteen

Sophie settled herself in Kendall Bix's office at the conference table with its video console, ready for the update on the hunt for Pim Wat.

Bix still sat behind his computer finishing something; they'd each carved out time to meet at the Security Solutions headquarters at the request of Pierre Raveaux, who'd reached out from Paris. Connor was going to be looped in from Thailand, too.

Sophie busied herself booting up her laptop and organizing the contents of her briefcase as she waited. She hoped she was projecting the calm and serene mask she'd perfected; inside, she was anything but.

Three months of maternity leave had made the tools of her trade feel unfamiliar; even her laptop had dust collecting in the keys. Her briefcase hadn't been touched since the day Sean had decided to arrive.

Sophie smoothed the easy movement dress pants she wore with a sleeveless knit top and matching loose cardigan. The shirt strained across her full breasts. But given the challenges, she was satisfied with her progress in losing baby weight and tightening up after her second pregnancy.

She wasn't back to where she'd been, but she'd get there; she'd done it before.

Bix looked up. "Five more minutes, okay?"

"You're the boss," Sophie replied.

He grinned and shook his head briefly. "We both know that's a lie. Speaking of, keep an eye out for Connor and Raveaux calling in, will you?"

"Of course." Sophie's palms prickled.

She'd be seeing Connor for the first time in a year; they'd parted on strained terms on Pali Island after he'd tried to kiss her. Sophie'd given him an unequivocal "no" to anything more than friendship. The next thing she knew, a helicopter had arrived to take him back to that stronghold in the Thai jungle that clearly exerted a tremendous pull over him.

Sophie found a small vial of coconut-scented sanitizer and rubbed it into her hands, her eyes on the communication monitor with its video chat program already open for the meeting.

Raveaux appeared in one of the panels. "Pierre!" She admitted him to the meeting, donning her headphones and engaging audio. "How is Paris?"

"*Très bien, merci.* As if I never left. A bit of a time warp that way." Raveaux's eyes were ringed with dark circles she hadn't seen in months. "But it is good to be here. I'm taking myself out to my favorite restaurant tonight. *Coq au vin* to die for."

"Surely there's a pretty lady willing to keep you company," Sophie teased. "Someone from your past, perhaps."

Raveaux tightened his lips. "None I want to spend time with." Clearly the subject was distasteful.

Sophie cleared her throat. "We're waiting a few minutes until Bix finishes something up and Connor calls in from Thailand."

"All right." His expression brightened. "How are the children? The dogs?"

"Momi has asked for 'Uncle Perro' every day since you left." Sophie smiled. "And Sean has slept through the night twice this week. I am beginning to feel sane again. It's great to be back in the office, even if it's just for a meeting."

Just then, Connor appeared.

Sophie stifled a quick intake of breath; her former lover looked so much better!

He'd been thin then, wound too tight, grief and stress etched all over him, his blond hair shorn in the way of the Yām Khûmkạn when last she saw him. Now, his blond locks had grown out, nearly touching his shoulders; his turquoise-blue eyes were clear, his tanned skin glowed even in the grainy video.

"You look well, Connor." Sophie said. "I like the hair."

"Thanks, Sophie—so do you. I'm feeling fantastic. Ready to take on the world."

Was he sending her a message in those words?

"On my way." Bix got up from behind his computer and came to sit beside Sophie, donning a pair of headphones and logging in. "Thanks for waiting, people. Glad we could find a time that worked, given our global distance." Bix tapped an electronic tablet with a stylus. "Monsieur Raveaux, you asked for this meeting to report on the search for Sophie's mother, Pim Wat, in Paris. Why don't you bring us up to speed?"

The three of them listened intently as Raveaux described his contact, Delphine Arles, and how she'd taken him to an event to meet Mendoza and Vivian Moran, the woman who might be Pim Wat. "She is the right height and body type to be Pim Wat but bears no resemblance at all to her previous appearance. Even her eye color has been changed. She was wearing gloves and a wig, so no finger-prints were possible, but I got a DNA sample." He held up a gold watch, encased in a small Ziploc bag. He indicated a small, dark area on one of the links. "I had to think on my feet. I hadn't come prepared to collect more than a fingerprint or a hair. Turns out the antique watch I got out of my safe deposit box for the occasion had a chip in one of the links that gave it a sharp edge. I nicked the skin of her back while we were dancing and procured a blood sample."

Sophie could imagine the scene; Raveaux in a tux, swirling her beautiful mother on the dance floor, "accidentally" scratching her skin with his watch. She'd probably been wearing a backless gown; she liked those. The scenario made her stomach clench with fear for Raveaux. "I hope she didn't realize it."

"She gave no sign that she did."

"Excellent work!" Connor exclaimed. "Did she make you?"

"Not that I could tell. She seemed to enjoy the attention. It's actually Mendoza I'm worried about." Raveaux described the man's wary demeanor. "I'm hoping my semi-truthful cover holds up. Quite sure they've already done a background workup on me."

Sophie leaned forward. "The DNA will take time to process. How will you manage that?"

"I have a contact in the Sûreté; I've already asked him to run it for me. For a fee, which I'm assuming Security Solutions will cover."

"Of course," Sophie replied. She took a deep breath to regulate her pounding heart. "What is your intuition telling you about this woman?"

"Vivian Moran is your mother, Pim Wat," Pierre Raveaux said without hesitation. "And she seems to be thriving in Paris."

Chapter Fifteen

"Vivian Moran is my mother." Sophie's hand covered her mouth; her eyes were enormous. Even in the low-res feed of the video, Connor could see how pale she'd gone.

Connor tugged at the collar of his button-down shirt as he stared into the three video windows of the meeting. Seated in the tower room, he'd barred the door for privacy and had worn the musty-smelling garment for Bix's benefit, but Western clothing no longer felt comfortable. With Raveaux's confirmation that Pim Wat had been found, he wanted to rip the shirt off and go punch something—perhaps a few trainees in lieu of that murderous witch.

"Sophie," he said, low and firm, his words for her alone. "It's a good thing Raveaux has identified Pim Wat. We've got her now. Two of our best ninjas are already en route to meet Raveaux in Paris; they will move against her when the time is right." He raised his voice. "Isn't that right, Raveaux? Or do you need more men?"

"No, two will suit nicely. I need help finding her location and tracking her. If Kaleidoscope is what you say it is, there are quite a few assassins in their stable. We don't want to alert them in any way. Mendoza seems protective of Pim Wat; he was watching me like a hawk when I made my move on her." Raveaux shifted uneasily in the monitor. "I'm concerned that the men don't tip our hand."

"The ninjas I sent you were chosen for their ability to track and observe and remain undetected," Connor said. "Though admittedly, neither have been outside of Thailand and the language will be new to them."

"We'll do the best we can, then," Raveaux said. "When should I expect them?"

Connor gave him the date and time of the ninjas' arrival in Paris.

Connor had also sent the President of Operations all the raw data his programs had mined on Kaleidoscope, and Bix lifted a finger to get everyone's attention. "I'd like to share background on the company and Mendoza. Kaleidoscope is indeed much more than just a lifestyle consulting firm," he said. "I was a bit late for our meeting because I was going through their digital footprint. One of the useful things I pinpointed was Mendoza's dwelling; he owns the top floor of a downtown apartment building and rents out units on that floor to his associates. That address is where Vivian Moran is currently living." Bix punted the address to all three of them via text. "I have a schematic of the building's floor plan that the ninjas might find useful; I'll send that on as well." He did so, with the punch of a few buttons. "What I want to know is this: are we capturing her dead, or alive? Because if the plan is to take her out, I must recuse myself. Plausible deniability."

Connor quirked a brow at the man. "Trust you, Bix, to keep an eye on your personal bottom line. Don't blame you a bit; you've got no skin in this game. But you can stay, for the moment. The plan is to take her alive and hand her over to the CIA. After this meeting, I have a chat scheduled with Agent McDonald, my contact from the international task force. We're going to review the current situation and make sure they have people in place to back us up before anyone makes a move." Connor sipped from his earthenware teacup. "Raveaux, you're in charge of the operation. The men will look to you for orders. Just use them for surveillance of Moran at first; do not engage until you get word from me. We spook her, or Mendoza, and we'll have a shitstorm on our hands that we are ill-equipped to handle—and my guess is that her first stop would be Sophie's place, trying to get her hands on those babies."

Sophie straightened, her arms tightening, her eyes narrowing. "She won't be able to get anywhere near them."

It was good to see Sophie riled—better that than the dismay she'd shown earlier. "Great attitude, Sophie, but your mother is resourceful as hell. She hasn't survived this long and killed so many without considerable skills. Let's not underestimate her, or this new crew she's with. Wait until the CIA is on board and in position. I'll send word, Raveaux," Connor said.

The Frenchman nodded. "*Bien sûr*. I must go." He blipped out of view as he exited the meeting.

Connor addressed Sophie and Bix in their video views. "He's good."

"Very good," Sophie said. "And I trust him."

Was she telling him something deeper? They had a history of broken trust, and Connor didn't know how to repair it.

"Good help is hard to find," he said at last.

"Pierre is more than good help," Sophie snapped. "He's a close friend, and the godfather of my children. Since you were no longer available."

Bix cleared his throat. "I'll let you two carry on." He exited the meeting. In the background, Connor watched him walk around past Sophie to sit at his desk; he put on sound-canceling headphones to give them privacy.

Sophie leaned in. Her riveting face filled the screen. "I need you to know how things stand with Pierre. He is important to me."

"Is he—more than a friend?" Connor's vocal cords felt paralyzed; he had to force his throat to work.

"No. But he wishes he were. He's made that clear." Her eyes were dark, unreadable, hypnotic.

What did she feel for that man?

What did she feel for *him*?

"When this is all over . . ." He couldn't form the words.

Sophie smiled, so warmly it felt like a touch. "We will see where we are. And I will bring the children to Phi Ni. You said the island's being released?"

"Yes. Nam and Kupa are already home."

"Fabulous news," Sophie exclaimed. "I am delighted to hear that. They must be so happy!"

"They are." Connor relaxed at last. "Nam called me earlier. The property is a mess, though. The house got hammered in that latest typhoon after being empty for too long. They have their hands full getting the island livable again. I told them I'd send some trainees over to do the heavy lifting—clear the storm debris and whatnot."

"I wonder how the boathouse held up," Sophie said. "I have a soft spot for your boat." Sophie'd had a harrowing time driving his low-slung pleasure launch all the way across open ocean to the Thai mainland to rescue her infant daughter from Pim Wat's kidnap attempt when Momi was born.

They gazed at each other for a long moment; he thought he might even be able to see her energy signature brighten in the video feed as she remembered happier times on their beautiful private island.

"Nam says the boathouse roof is gone, but the structure held up and protected the Chris-Craft. She got banged up, but it's just cosmetic."

"Maybe it's a good thing we won't be there for a while," Sophie said softly. "Sounds like the island isn't ready for the full invasion of my household, complete with dogs."

Connor smiled. "I'd meet you there in a heartbeat. Just say the word."

"The word is—Pim Wat." Sophie's smile was sad. "My murderous mother."

Connor winced. "I guess I wanted to forget, just for a moment. Remember the good times and hope for them again."

"It appears the new Master is human, after all," Sophie said. "I've got to go. I timed this meeting between Sean's feedings. Let's stay in closer touch."

And with the touch of a button thousands of miles away, she disappeared.

Connor stared at the blank monitor, letting his roiling emotions billow over him.

He shut his eyes to observe them better.

Longing.

Loneliness.

Emptiness. Sorrow. Regret.

An ache in his chest that refused to be named.

But also, hope.

He was still seated before the monitors, eyes closed and legs folded, when Nine appeared.

"You have a meeting with the leaders of the various training squads." Nine dropped his hand to Connor's shoulder. "Are you all right, Master?"

He forced himself to smile. "I will be."

Connor stood, stretched, and went to do more of what must be done until he saw her again.

Chapter Sixteen

The next day, Connor, flanked by armed ninjas with Nine at his back, watched CIA agent Devin McDonald walk toward him at a deserted Thai airstrip once used for military maneuvers.

McDonald hoisted the belt that girdled his gut and lifted off a straw hat to wipe his highly colored face with a forearm. "I don't know how you stand this heat. I've been in the Pacific Rim for close to twenty years, and it never gets easier."

"You're the one who asked for an outdoor meeting in person," Connor said mildly.

"And you're the one who wanted it at high noon," McDonald shot back. "Would you mind stepping into the jet? They've got the AC going. Every comfort."

Connor shook his head. "Sorry. I'm not about to let you fly me off to Gitmo to be tortured, before the ink is dry on my immunity deal."

McDonald huffed. "At least let's sit in the shade. I've got someone you need to meet on video call."

Connor pointed to a table with a battered palm frond umbrella set up in the lee of the abandoned hangar. "That will have to do."

The group walked across the hot tarmac. Connor read McDonald's energy signature out of the side of his eye; the man's aura was a sickly yellow streaked with dark patches. Ill health on several levels plagued him; but was any of it indicative of a double cross?

Too soon to tell.

Connor's guards spread out to surround the area from vantage points they'd already selected; they'd checked the area thoroughly before the meet time. Short of an air strike, he and his retinue would be safe for the duration.

McDonald sat on one of the benches at the splintery wooden table and produced a laptop. He opened it and pushed a few buttons.

Connor's new body servant, a man named Three-Hundred-Forty-Two who went by Two for short, brought Connor's ergonomic stool from the large military helicopter they'd arrived in. McDonald rolled his eyes but said nothing as Connor seated himself, arranging his gi for comfort and air flow. Two then handed them each a cool drink in an insulated cup. McDonald accepted the beverage, and the man retreated with a bow.

Nine barked an order for the men to withdraw out of hearing range, and the ninjas backed away.

He and McDonald were now as alone as Connor was comfortable with.

"You've sure got these Thai fanatics bamboozled," McDonald hissed, his yellow-black energy field pulsing with venom.

Connor blinked at his tone and did not reply. Nothing he said was going to dissuade this man from his opinion.

McDonald hated him.

Hated the Thai brothers who served the Yām Khûmkạn so faithfully.

Was McDonald racist, or just an asshole?

Probably both.

McDonald, having failed to bait Connor, swiveled the screen of the laptop so that he could see it.

Connor's eyes widened involuntarily at the man he saw on the screen: Frank Smithson, Sophie's father. The Ambassador was immaculately barbered, dressed in a suit and tie. He was backlit, and that, along with his dark complexion, concealed his expression, but it was likely irritable. An American flag hung limp in the background; he was probably tuning in from his office in Washington, D.C.

"I wanted to speak with you before this deal went any further," Smithson said.

"It's good to see you, too, Ambassador. Are you enjoying your grandchildren?" Best not to let on that he'd had any contact with Sophie; Frank Smithson had never been a friend.

"This is not a social call," the Ambassador said, his resonant voice sounding like Morgan Freeman in an apocalypse movie. "I wanted you to know that I voted against this immunity deal happening at all. I was overruled."

"Thanks for being honest with me." Connor could respect the man's position; he'd always liked Frank's unstinting support of Sophie, even when the ambassador interfered with his own plans.

"I want you to stay away from my daughter and her children. You're a danger to them."

Connor didn't disagree. "But she has worse threats in her life than me," he said. "Everything I have done and will do is for her—and by extension, her children. The justice the Ghost deals out is so that the world will be a better, safer place. For them."

"If you take this deal, you'll be agreeing to no longer practice that brand of justice," McDonald reminded him.

Connor inclined his head in outward agreement.

"I need a verbal response," McDonald rapped out. "This meeting is being recorded."

"You might have informed me," Connor said. "But I expected nothing less." He opened one panel of his *gi* to reveal a wire, its audio/video recording node near his throat. "I came prepared as well, should I need to correct the CIA's version." He dropped the garment to hide the wire. "Ambassador Smithson. Let's address the elephant in the room, namely your ex-wife, Pim Wat. You'd love to roast me on a spit—I get that. But you want your ex more, and so do I. The enemy of my enemy is my friend, for now. That's the situation we're in."

Smithson folded full lips disturbingly like Sophie's. "Agreed."

"In that case, I'd like to see the written contract, please, for my legal department to review. And so you know, I expect nothing less than a Presidential signature on it."

McDonald's jaw bunched like a prizefighter's fist. "Verbalize aloud what we've agreed to get from you. For the record."

"I've already delivered half of the contract—the leader of the Yām Khûmkạn, a man known only as the Master and believed to cause instability in governments around the world," Connor said. "The second half of my commitment is to apprehend and deliver to the international task force, dead or alive, the assassin formerly known as Pim Wat Smithson. And in return, I get?" He tapped the mic at his neck.

"In return, you will receive a Presidential pardon and restitution of any and all assets seized in connection with your crimes," McDonald said. "Further caveats include an ongoing commitment to no longer operate as the vigilante known as the Ghost, in return for which we will allow you to use your software to track crime and punt those leads to the proper law enforcement agencies for follow-up."

"In other words, I'll be working for you in the future." Connor's smile was humorless.

"I said what I came to say," Smithson growled. "Stay away from my daughter. She has been through hell, and I don't want her hurt again."

Connor's chest tightened with anger. Was it his fault Jake had died? He'd moved heaven and earth to rescue both of them. He'd sacrificed himself by joining the Yām Khûmkạn to make room for Sophie to be with Jake. He'd done all he could to make up for his early failures.

It wasn't enough. Would never be enough. Smithson was another who hated him, whose opinion wouldn't change no matter what he said. He'd have to prove his intentions with time—but in the end, only Sophie's opinion mattered.

"I understand where you're coming from," Connor said. "A father's heart is protective."

Smithson's mouth twisted with anger, and he punched out of the video feed.

McDonald closed the laptop. "Off the record?"

Connor touched the button at the side of the node near his neck. "Off the record."

"I don't like you, Todd Remarkian, Sheldon Hamilton, Connor the Ghost, whoever the hell you really are. You're a dangerous vigilante criminal as far as I'm concerned. But you have your uses, and we at the CIA are smart enough to see them. What are you going to do with all of this . . ." he made a gesture, indicating the men of the Yām Khûmkan, the chopper, the empty airstrip surrounded by steaming Thai jungle . . . "when Pim Wat is in custody?"

"You'll just have to wait and see," Connor said. "I'll be working for you then."

He stood up, picked up the stool, and walked back to the chopper, his men falling in to flank him from behind as he left the fat man sitting in the shade of the umbrella.

Chapter Seventeen

Raveaux opened the door of his hotel room to the ninjas Connor had texted him to look for.

Both were dressed in cheap, off-the-rack suits. Both were slender, of medium height, and shaved nearly bald, with calm, deadly eyes.

Raveaux held the door open. He welcomed them in French and held the door open; they did not reply but entered.

One of them, older judging by the silver bristles at his temples and fans of lines at his eyes, spoke haltingly. "I have been studying English, but Sām Yīsib Sām only speaks Thai."

The younger one bowed at the sound of his name.

"And you are?" Raveaux wasn't going to be able to pronounce their names, let alone remember them.

"I am known as Nk Phirāb."

Raveaux fastened onto the phonetics he could grasp. He pointed to the younger one. "Sam." The man nodded agreement.

Raveaux pointed at the older man. "Rab."

"And you?" Rab's eyebrows rose.

"Pierre Raveaux."

"Pier," both men said at the same time.

"*C'est bien.* Okay. Now that we've got the introductions over, come sit down." Raveaux had swept the room for surveillance devices that morning, but to be sure they didn't have eavesdroppers, he closed the heavy blackout drapes and turned on a tall, standing fan for white noise. "Thirsty, hungry?"

Rab shook his head answering for them both.

Raveaux helped himself to a bottle of Perrier and sat down in an armchair; he gestured for them to sit on the couch.

The two eschewed the furniture in favor of sitting cross-legged on the floor.

"My understanding is that we are only to observe and report at this time," Raveaux said. "I am in the process of getting the target's identity confirmed."

Rab translated this rapidly to Sam.

"I am not sure how long the confirmation of the target's identity will take," Raveaux went on. "A DNA sample is being processed. We can't move on the target until identity is confirmed and law enforcement personnel are in place to take her into custody when we give the signal."

"No kill?" Rab asked, plainly disappointed.

"Not unless we have to, and we might. The target is Pim Wat. I assume you know her?"

Rab's eyes widened. "Pim Wat," he said distinctly to his partner. Sam looked equally dismayed.

"The Master didn't tell you?"

They shook their heads.

"Well, now you know. Do you have all you need? A place to stay, weapons, communication devices?"

"Yes." Once again Rab answered for both. "We will survey Pim Wat. Where is she found?"

"She can't know you're watching her," Raveaux warned.

Rab sniffed contemptuously and said something to Sam. Both glared at him.

"Okay, okay." Raveaux raised his hands in a surrender gesture. "I had to say it. I'll give you what I know. Got cell phones?"

All three carried burners and coordinated phone numbers. Raveaux then sent them the address of Mendoza's building, which housed Kaleidoscope's offices and presumably, several of the company's assets, including Pim Wat.

"She looks nothing like she used to," Raveaux said, and sent them a photo pulled from the gossip magazines that had appeared the day after the ball where he'd met her. Beside her stood Mendoza, looking fashionably lethal. "Watch out for this man. He is keeping a close eye on her. Protecting her."

He told the operatives all he'd been able to find out about Mendoza and Kaleidoscope. "You are ninjas. They are, too."

Rab shook his head definitively. "They are not ninjas. Crude paid killers only. But Pim Wat? She was the Master's woman and his best. *She* is dangerous."

"I'm glad we're on the same page," Raveaux said.

The man looked blank.

"I'm glad we are in agreement. Observe and report only. Do not be seen by anyone at Kaleidoscope."

Rab translated for his partner. Both stood up. "We will report in tomorrow, when we have Pim Wat found."

"Good. I'll look forward to hearing from you."

He closed the door on the pair.

He texted Connor that they'd made contact, and that the ninjas seemed to understand their responsibility. *"They didn't know it was Pim Wat. Seemed to give them pause."*

Connor's reply was slow in coming. *"I didn't want them to have too much information. Better this way."*

Connor was the Master; those were his men. Presumably, he knew best.

Raveaux slid his phone into his pocket.

The night was young, and the Seine beckoned. He owed himself a dinner cruise for one, before this case got too hot for downtime. Should he invite Delphine?

Better not to send any mixed messages. The last thing he needed was for his wife's friend to form an attachment to him. He was already spoken for.

Chapter Eighteen

Vivian sat at her desk, a steaming espresso at her elbow, as she reviewed the specs on the Korean job.

Mendoza wanted the target taken at his yacht, currently docked in a marina off the coast of Thailand. From that position, the Korean arms dealer was easily able to take advantage of loopholes in the legalities of international waters to ply his trade.

Entrance was not a problem for her; the Korean sent for a call girl every Wednesday. She would pose as one. He usually kept the women with him overnight and fed them breakfast, considered a perk, and they left the yacht midmorning of the following day.

Vivian studied the schematic of the boat and timed out her exit using a stopwatch and a drag-and-drop animated software that plotted the positions of everything from furniture to guards.

She frowned. The job itself was simple and straightforward, but the yacht was heavily armed and getting out undetected was going to be tricky, even assuming the Korean died quickly and quietly without raising an alarm.

Any glimpse of her outside his suite prior to morning would raise an alarm.

This job was the perfect chance for her to test out the Chameleon; working together, she could watch the man in action, evaluate his strengths. After they finished the Korean, she'd know better how to move on to hit Connor in his much more difficult fortress.

Vivian depressed the button on her desk phone for her assistant, who now properly minded her manners without excessive friendliness or intrusions. "Find out if Monsieur Mendoza is busy. I need to speak with him."

"Right away, Madame."

Vivian got up and opened the doors of a gigantic, twenty-foot, multilevel armoire that took up the back wall of her office. Ostensibly, it held samples from major designers that she evaluated for recommending to their clientele; in reality, the movable closet held disguises for her characters.

Picking out her costumes and practicing her parts was one of her favorite aspects of planning a job.

Vivian surveyed the racks of every sort of gown and clothing. Jewelry, wigs and shoes lined the bottom cubicles. Hanging on the door behind a rack of scarves was a plastic flipbook filled with laminated photographs of Vivian in her many outfits, costumes, and disguises—a helpful way to find what she needed quickly.

She took out the flipbook and sat back in her chair, opening it.

According to his bio, the Korean liked young, submissive women and enjoyed schoolgirl fantasies and role-play. He also liked blondes, which was convenient since she had the greatest number of wigs in that shade.

The intercom beeped. "Monsieur Mendoza would like to speak with you in person, Madame."

"Perfect."

Vivian shut the wardrobe and password-protected her computer before she left the room.

Every employee in the building was vetted, but precautions were smart regardless. She then locked her office and headed down the hall to her boss's suite without even a glance at her assistant. The young woman was diligently typing on her computer, her eyes lowered now that she'd learned that Vivian disliked interacting.

Mendoza's office commanded a view of the Seine; it was always a treat to enter the suite in the morning when the light beamed over the Pont Neuf and gilded the ancient city with a golden glow. Vivian paused in the doorway to gaze enviously at the view. "You have the best office, Enrique."

Mendoza frowned as he looked up from his electronic tablet. "I'm glad you reached out this morning. I wanted to talk to you anyway."

Vivian heard the warning note in his voice and entered, closing the door behind her. "What's happening?"

"I think you are being tailed."

"How long?"

"At least a day."

Vivian walked across the deep piled antique rug to sit in front of his desk. "I haven't noticed anyone, and since the art ball I've only gone from the apartment to work and back. I've been lying low."

"Even so. Maybe you're rusty, maybe they're good. But two men of Asian extraction have been spotted outside our building; they were picked up by that new AI facial recognition software I installed. It sent our team an alert. They only leave when you do, and they follow you home. They pick you back up in the morning."

Vivian flushed with annoyance. "But why?"

Mendoza sat back and made a pyramid with his fingertips. "You are on the international list of most wanted, with a bounty on your head. It doesn't pay to underestimate how far someone will go to please the new Master in Thailand."

Vivian licked her lips, her pulse speeding. "Shall I go after them?"

He flapped a hand. "Of course not. I just wanted you to be aware, and perhaps you should move up your timetable on the Korean job. A few days out of town would not be amiss right now."

"That's what I wanted to speak with you about. Checking out the specs on the yacht and the intel packet you sent over, I always count six armed guards on board. I could use some backup on exit." Vivian seated herself in the little gold chair in front of Mendoza's desk. "I'd like the Chameleon to help. A chance for us to get to know each other. Build trust. I'm aware how challenging taking the current Master in his stronghold is going to be; I'd like to evaluate the Chameleon's skill level personally."

"Good idea. Contact him. The jet is at your disposal. Your assistant can manage all the travel arrangements for both of you."

Vivian leaned forward and touched Mendoza's hand, giving him genuine eye contact. "I greatly appreciate your protection and help. Once the Master is gone, the price on my head will also be gone."

"And then, you will only have to deal with an international crime task force." Mendoza smiled. "Nothing for a woman of your talents."

Vivian stood. "Want to see me model my choice of outfit for the Korean job? I know you enjoy my little theatrical performances."

Mendoza's eyes gleamed. The man might be gay, but he enjoyed fantasies of a variety of pleasures. "If we can fit that in before you leave, give me a buzz."

Vivian smiled as she left; she had Mendoza where she wanted him, and now she could move up her departure. Maybe being tailed wasn't such a bad thing.

Chapter Nineteen

Two days later . . .

Vivian sashayed down the narrow but luxurious hallway of the yacht, enjoying the stare of the guard escorting her to the Korean arms dealer's suite at the front of the yacht. Her blonde wig was parted in two high pigtails that bounced in long curls to her shoulders. A pleated plaid skirt barely covered her ass, and the long white stockings she wore with high-heeled Mary Janes were held up by ribboned garters. A lace-up bustier with puff sleeves set off circles of red on her cheeks and a Cupid's bow of lipstick.

She was a caricature. The getup was ridiculous. Even Mendoza had thought so, but he'd also given her the nod. "You've still got it, *cherie.*"

There was no such thing as "too much" in this line of work.

Vivian reached a closed panel of dark wood trimmed in gold. She stood respectfully in character, her hands folded and eyes down, as the guard knocked and identified them. "Your weekly visitor, sir."

"Come in." The Korean's voice sounded bored.

Vivian relished that moment before the door opened; it was so much like theater, and she loved her little plays. Adrenaline hummed along her nerves. Her vision was sharp, her hearing sensitive, her skin a-prickle with excitement.

Vivian would not bore this man; not one little bit.

The guard opened the door. As he did so he leaned forward to whisper in her ear. "I'll let you out in the morning for breakfast." He pinched her butt. "We can spend some time together before you leave."

Ha.

Tik Panh, aka The Chameleon, would make sure Vivian was spared that annoyance.

Vivian stepped over the raised jamb, then stumbled "accidentally" forward, tripping in her heels. She clasped her hands together beneath her chin in distress. "Oh! Am I in trouble? I'm so scared, being called to the principal's office!"

The Korean had been staring out at a view of the ocean showcased by one of four enormous portholes of the large triangular room that took up most of the yacht's bow. He turned to catch her as she stumbled. Vivian clutched at him for support, her fake lashes flapping like batwings. "Please, please, sir, don't be too hard on me. I'll do anything!"

Ennui vanished from the arms dealer's broad face; his teeth showed in a wide grin. "Naughty little girl. You need a spanking, at the very least." He drew her against him, eyes gleaming with excitement.

Vivian smiled inwardly even as his hot breath fanned her face and his greedy gaze roamed her body.

"Oh, no, sir. Not a spanking!" She pressed her forehead into the open chest of his silk dressing gown to hide her triumph, her voice wobbling. She wiggled her butt back and forth, flipping her skirt up with a practiced gesture to expose a lacy white thong and the garters. "I can't take it, sir! Spankings make me scream, and I get all red and hot down there."

The Korean only grunted, his hands roaming as he backed up to the edge of the bed and drew her down across his knees. "What service did you come from? You're ten times better than the other girls I've had lately."

"Oh, no, sir—I'm a bad, bad girl. The worst. Please don't punish me too hard," Vivian begged, lowering herself carefully sideways across his bare, hairy thighs.

The target flipped up her skirt and explored her backside with a meaty hand as she checked the big Mickey Mouse watch on her wrist: five more minutes until Chameleon cleared the door.

The Korean smacked her suddenly, and the yelp Vivian let out was genuine. "Ow!"

"Bad, bad girl." The Korean's thick arm lowered heavy and tight across the top of her upper body, pinning her down, and suddenly his fingers were deep inside her, rough and painful.

Vivian writhed. "Stop it!" she cried. "I thought you were giving me a spanking!" This lout was molesting her, damn it. Forget the timetable; she would do him now.

Vivian wriggled the slim, custom-made blade from its taped-on plastic sheath between her breasts. She held it overhand, blade down, and stabbed the four inches of razor-sharp steel deep into the Korean's thigh, hitting his femoral artery with a quick, accurate severing.

As the man opened his mouth to bellow, she reversed direction and shoved the blade straight up through the soft triangle of his palate into his brain.

The Korean fell over backward onto the bed, the blade deep in the underside of his jaw, pinning his mouth shut.

Vivian jumped up and out of the way as blood pumped in jets out of his leg with every beat of his heart.

He spasmed on the bed. His body was already dead, it just didn't know it yet.

She trotted to the door and made sure it was locked; Chameleon would give a coded knock when it was time to exit.

Vivian looked back to the bed; the arterial flow was slowing. His bowels had let go. Shivers racked his frame as he bled out.

The Korean's expression was one of wide-eyed astonishment. He'd never had a chance to make a sound.

Vivian removed her blade. The man's jaw went slack and fell

open, completing the surprise on his face. She wiped the knife on the satin comforter and slid it back into its hiding place.

In the palatial bathroom, Vivian washed her hands and straightened her costume. She checked herself over carefully; only a little spatter had landed on her white tights.

She looked as perfect as when she'd walked in.

But she felt smeared, smirched.

The target had gotten his filthy fingers inside her. Vivian still hurt from it, feeling an unwelcome rasp of pain between her legs.

If she could kill the man all over again, she would, but she'd take her time about it. Pay him back for that stinging spank and those rough, prying digits violating her.

"All part of the job," Vivian told herself sternly. "Don't take it personally."

But she did, and that bothered her. The fact that it bothered her annoyed her even more.

Panh's knock came from the door.

Vivian hurried across the room and opened it.

Panh, dressed in the uniform of one of the arms dealer's guards, held a silenced weapon in one hand and a dripping blade in the other as he stood over the body of the man who'd promised her a date later.

Apparently, the Chameleon also preferred a knife to a gun.

Panh's gaze was on her face. He frowned. "Everything okay?"

"Of course." Vivian opened the door wider to indicate the macabre scene on the bed. "Let's get going."

"Take those shoes off. You can move faster barefoot."

He was considering her. She liked that.

Vivian held his shoulder with a hand for support and unbuckled the shoes, dropping them on top of the dead guard.

Panh led the way back down the hall.

They'd planned the exit from the suite, and Vivian shadowed him as they retraced the Chameleon's gore-strewn route to reaching her.

No one stopped them; no alarm was raised as they descended a spider rope ladder Panh had shot onto the deck of the ship from a small, powerful black jet boat.

Vivian settled herself on the swivel seat of the escape craft. Panh had used a silent electric outboard to approach the yacht, but once the jet motor was turned on, the noise would attract the remaining guards.

They'd be moving too fast for it to matter.

And so it was.

Panh was just a silhouette lit by the glow of the instruments beside her. Vivian clung to the dash just behind the windscreen, loving the way the wind felt flying over her head, the moonlight on the ocean, the powerful engine hurtling them forward into a barely visible vault of stars and sea.

They roared along for a good while.

Vivian had not paid attention to this part; she'd left departure to Panh. This was his chance to show her his planning and execution of an exit strategy. The jet boat circled a few of the atolls that made the area so picturesque; they were just giant lumps of black in the dark ocean to Vivian.

Panh entered a small, sheltered bay at last. No lights showed from the land around them. "This atoll is uninhabited. I thought we could rest here until morning, then return to the mainland when it won't attract attention," Panh said.

"Perfect. I hope you brought something for us to sleep on?"

"I did." He cut the engine and dropped the anchor; the chain rattled and the boat settled into a gentle rocking.

But Vivian didn't feel sleepy, far from it.

She was still jangling with adrenaline, with the thrill of a good performance—and a strange angst brought on by being finger-raped.

Panh turned on a small LED light beneath the dash. By its dim illumination, he pulled two rolled mats out from the bow's storage area. He lay them out side by side, and then followed that with two summer-weight sleeping bags and even small travel pillows.

He extracted a cooler last, and then sat on his bedding cross-legged. He invited her with a gesture toward the impromptu picnic. "I thought you might be hungry."

She was, but for something different than food. "Can you help me get out of this costume, first?"

Panh froze, going still and alert as a hunting dog pointing at game.

"Please," she said softly.

Without a word, he rose and came to where Vivian still sat in the swivel chair.

He moved to kneel between her parted thighs.

Vivian could barely see; his face was just a composite of planes. All was welcome darkness, and he was a silhouette edged by silver.

"Do you want this?" Panh's voice was barely louder than the shush of water against the hull. "Because I want this. You."

Her reply was a hoarse whisper. "Yes."

The Chameleon understood her need for sex after a kill.

She'd thought only the Master knew and accepted that about her.

She wasn't alone, after all.

Vivian opened her thighs. "Make me feel good. I need to feel good."

Panh made her feel good, indeed. He erased the taint of a dead man's hand with overwhelming new sensations.

She was grateful.

In return, she took his violence, held it close, and gave it back in equal measure.

The night was their friend, and in it, Vivian recognized a kindred spirit.

She slept well in his arms, rocked by the gentle lullaby of waves.

Chapter Twenty

Four days after her last visit to the estate, Sophie did a final walk-through with her construction crew and signed off on the immediate work and upgrades. Inside the house, fans were still blowing the paint fumes out through open doors and windows when the movers carried in the family's furniture and personal belongings from the Pendragon Arches apartment.

Armita took Momi to the beach with the dogs for the day to tire her out, while Sophie supervised the movers and the placement of furniture and other items.

She carried Sean, this time in a body wrap over one of her Mary Watson dresses. Still not down to her prepregnancy weight, Sophie didn't want to invest in new clothing for this stage; the breezy dresses she'd worn for that identity were perfect.

Finally, by six p.m., the bulk of the transition was done. The movers, all vetted by Security Solutions, had even unpacked Momi and Sean's room, which they called the nursery. The children had been sharing a room since Sean's birth; Sophie saw no reason to change that even though the house was a lot bigger than the apartment they'd been in.

Sophie stuck her head in to check on how the nursery looked before Armita, Momi and the dogs arrived with takeout dinner.

The room was painted a pale turquoise green on Sean's side of the room, and a soothing lavender on Momi's. Sophie planned to have the muralist who'd worked on Momi's room at her father Alika's house on Kauai come and decorate the walls with fanciful land and sea creatures at some later date. Right now it was important that the babies' beds were set up, the blackout drapes were installed, the white noise machine plugged in, and the smells from painting were entirely gone.

Sophie walked all the way inside the large room and sniffed for any fumes, making a pistol gesture with her hands as she spun around. "Clear," she said aloud.

She thought she heard a chuckle in Jake's voice.

She turned around—*no one was there*.

Of course, no one was there.

But Jake would have appreciated that she was being funny; or, for her, what passed as funny.

"Not exactly the same thing, Soph," she imagined him saying, with an affectionate kiss.

She breathed out on a painful stab of grief. "Walk it off," she said sternly, and exited the room.

The sensor on the front gate gave a *bing* alert that sounded from the wall-mounted monitor and Sophie's phone; it had automatically identified Armita driving the Lexus and admitted her.

Other visitors were faced with a spiked steel gate, the sensor alarm system, and a facial recognition program mounted on a kiosk that only recognized a few, preselected people. Everyone else had to be manually admitted by one of the security team currently living in the guesthouse beside the garage.

Sophie wasn't taking any chances. Once they'd settled in, and the AI video software that watched them day and night had had time to learn their patterns, she would really be able to relax.

Armita parked in the garage; Sophie was able to watch her do so. Armita let the two dogs, tired from the beach, out of the car to explore the enclosed yard of their new home. Her nanny went around to open the SUV's door and lifted Momi out of her car seat.

Her daughter was clearly asleep, ketchup from French fries she'd eaten a dark blur around her mouth.

Sophie smiled and walked to meet Armita at the side door. "Everything's set up in the nursery," she whispered. "Just pop her in bed. It's better this way; she'd be so excited she wouldn't give us a minute's peace until tomorrow."

"Why do you think I took her to the beach for six hours?" Armita smiled over the toddler's curly head resting on her shoulder. "The food's in the back seat. I'll meet you in the kitchen when I've cleaned her and put her down."

Sophie went out to the car and picked up the bags of takeout. Ginger and Anubis, done exploring and peeing on the edges of their new domain, flanked her as she went back into the house, shut the door, and armed the alarm for the night.

"You two don't know what to make of this, do you?" Sophie asked the dogs, whose nails clacked on the terra-cotta floors as they nosed along the hall uncertainly. "This is your new home. You can go outside when we let you out, and that will be often, but here is where your food and water are going to be." She led the animals to the pantry off the kitchen, where she'd set up their bowls. Both dove hungrily into their kibble.

Sophie set the bags of Thai food takeout on the center island. She wasn't a cook herself, but Armita enjoyed whipping up nutritious meals for the household, and she would now have a chef's kitchen to do it in. The stove was under a copper hood that led into the ceiling and was fronted by an eat-in bar done in the gold veined fieldstone that accentuated the creamy walls and tiled floors of the house. The cabinetry in distressed mango wood with hammered aluminum pulls set off stainless steel appliances. Though roomy and top-of-the-line, Sophie liked the homey and unpretentious feel of the kitchen. She opened one of the cabinets, looking for tea makings and mugs. She kept opening doors and drawers until she found the plates and silverware, too.

Armita reappeared, holding up a small laptop with a video feed of

Momi sleeping peacefully in her crib. "Why don't I reheat the food while you put Sean down?"

"Great. He's getting heavy, that's for sure." A knot of tiredness had formed between her shoulder blades from carrying the baby.

Soon, the two of them were seated with their plates of pad Thai noodles and veggies in the breakfast nook, a table with built-in bench seating and a window that looked out at the sea. Momi's high-chair was already in position there.

"I thought this day would never end." Sophie sucked in a big bite of noodles; she was famished.

"Me too." Armita smiled. "Momi was a real rascal today."

"She always acts up when we get off our schedule," Sophie said. "At least we're finally in the house. Now for all the fine tuning. The movers put the dishes away all wrong; I was supervising another area when it happened."

"Easily corrected," Armita said in her serious way.

The dogs had found their beds near the pantry, and Ginger's snores echoed across the terra-cotta.

"Glad someone is settling in well." Sophie pointed with her chop-sticks, and Armita smiled.

Sophie touched the security app on her phone and cycled through the feed, glancing through the property and house views from multiple angles. Thanks to the AI security program, she didn't have to monitor those cameras; the program did and would continue to improve as it learned their normal traffic patterns. Even so, Sophie could look at the feeds at any time, and for now she wanted to be sure everything was working correctly.

The phone, already alight in her hand, buzzed with an incoming call. Sophie answered for Kendall Bix.

"How'd the move go?"

"All right. We're tired, but we're in, and everything seems to be running properly."

"Glad to hear it. Got time to take a video call in your new office?"

Sophie pushed her plate aside. "Give me a moment."

"Will do. Use the usual video channel." Bix ended the call.

"You okay without me for a while?" Sophie waggled her phone. "Work."

"Take all the time you need. This is my rest," Armita said, pointing to the sleeping babies on the monitor. "All I need in the way of TV."

"You're my angel." Sophie kissed Armita's forehead as she stood up. "I couldn't do this without you."

"You are correct," Armita said, and Sophie smiled as she left her half-eaten dinner behind, knowing she'd return to everything cleaned up and put away.

Sophie's new office was at the end of the hall that housed the bedrooms. She'd had the heavy wood paneling and carpets of the previous owner's "den" removed, and a restful gray color scheme replaced it. Sophie'd installed blackout blinds and redone the lighting to use spots with dimmers so she could control how much illumination came in, and the room was temperature-controlled with air conditioning. One of the only door locks inside the house ensured she wouldn't get unexpected visits from wandering toddlers. Her computer corner with her familiar rigs was already set up, along with home gym equipment against one wall. Thick, sound baffling carpet had been laid to keep the chamber quiet.

Stepping into the cool, dim room was a respite for all of Sophie's senses, and sitting down to her computers, even more so.

Sophie video called in to the usual channel used for meetings, sliding on headphones for good sound transmittal.

Raveaux occupied one video panel, while Connor and Bix took up others.

"What's the latest?" Sophie's gaze sharpened on Raveaux's face; his cheekbones looked hollow and there were circles of lost sleep beneath his eyes. "You look tired, Pierre."

"I am tired. The ninjas and I have been searching everywhere for Pim Wat. We had her for a couple of days—but now we've lost her. We think she left Paris."

Chapter Twenty-One

Raveaux clicked the icon that tracked one member of the video conference, and Sophie's face filled the screen in front of him. A wrinkle of worry tightened her brows. "You haven't been sleeping," she said.

She hadn't reacted at all to the bombshell that he'd lost Pim Wat. The woman might even now be on her way to Honolulu to attack Sophie and take her children.

"I've let you down," Raveaux said. "I'm sorry."

Connor cleared his throat and reappeared in the feed. The blond man's sea blue eyes were narrowed. "You must have tipped your hand somehow."

"I stayed out of any direct surveillance, so it must have been one of the ninjas, Rab or Sam, who gave us away. In any case, perhaps she just left for a job for Kaleidoscope and will be back soon," Raveaux said.

"We don't have the luxury of waiting and hoping," Connor said. "I will locate her via tech and find out where she went. No time to lose." His face winked out.

The Master of the Yām Khûmkạn was not happy.

Raveaux glanced over at the hotel couch where the two ninjas, exhausted from combing the streets and the buildings where Vivian

Moran lived and worked, had fallen asleep. Rab and Sam still wore the clothing they'd arrived in, and he hadn't seen them eat or rest since they reported that they'd lost Pim Wat.

"What's the plan if Connor can't trace Pim Wat on tech?" Bix asked.

Raveaux glanced at the two men sleeping on the couch again. "Rab made a suggestion to me before this call, and I can't come up with anything better." He blew out a breath and addressed Sophie. "He thinks only Mendoza will know where Pim Wat went. He suggests we grab the man and get him to tell us where she's gone."

"I'm going to bug out of this conversation. Plausible deniability." Bix's panel winked out, leaving only Sophie and Raveaux.

"I didn't take you for that kind of man, Pierre," Sophie said.

He shrugged. "The ninjas came up with the idea."

"From what I've researched about Mendoza, he is most responsive to money. We could make him an offer for the information, then the ninjas could work him over if he didn't accept," Sophie said.

"I don't like this, quite frankly." Raveaux stroked the swatch of goatee on his chin as he gazed at her. "There are a lot of logistical challenges to grabbing Mendoza. I guess I'll work on those while we wait to hear back from Connor." He frowned. "How did the move to the new house go? It was today, wasn't it?"

"Yes." Sophie pushed her chair away from the desk so he could see the room behind her. "Still full of boxes, as you can see, but we're in and functioning. We are more secure here, with the alarm systems and the safe room."

"Show me that, please." Raveaux had been to see the progress on the new house on numerous occasions, but Sophie had always been short on time or had Momi with her, so hadn't taken him to see the safe room.

"Since we ended early, I've got time. I'll switch you to my personal phone." Sophie blipped out of the meeting. In a moment his phone signaled her call. He enjoyed a sense of anticipation as the device rang.

She had opened her heart and her home to *him*—not Connor.

There was still reason to hope that someday, he'd be the one she chose.

He picked up the video call, uplifted by the sight of her beautiful face. "Thanks for taking the time. I know you've had a long day."

"And so have you." Sophie was on the move, walking down the hall that contained the house's bedrooms toward the house's heart, the kitchen. "But I know you worry about us, and I want you to be at ease. Seeing this will help."

Sophie stopped in front of a tall wooden cabinet with a finger-print lock hidden under the door handle, right beside the large silver refrigerator. The cabinet looked for all the world like a food pantry.

"I didn't have any workmen down here. Minimal exposure for security reasons," she said, opening the cabinet and stepping inside.

The interior was small, just wide enough to admit one good-sized person, or a small one carrying a child. The door shut, a light came on, and Sophie and Raveaux were in a metal lined box. The box began descending. "Weight sensitive, motion activated elevator," Sophie said, smiling at Raveaux's widened eyes.

The lift stopped, and she opened the door. Lights bloomed on, illuminating a large, open room segmented by furniture clusters. "Only downside is that we have to take two trips to get all four of us down here," Sophie said. "I'm planning a couple of drills with Armita and the children tomorrow. We'll both wear sensor alarms that are hooked into the house's AI alarm system. We'll try different approaches from different parts of the house and time it."

"How is the air quality?" Raveaux gazed at the surroundings as she moved the phone slowly around so he could see them.

"Not bad. All systems activate when the elevator does, so it's not an energy drain on the house. It's a little musty down here, but okay." She walked over to a kitchenette area. "I already shopped for nonperishable food and as you can see, there's plenty."

The shelter's pantry shelves were full, and stacks of gallon jugs of fresh water lined one wall. "We have bunk beds and some of the kids' favorite toys down here. My plan is to keep doing drills and bring them down daily for a couple of hours each day. Keep special things down here so they look forward to coming and don't feel scared if we ever have to shelter here."

"I'm impressed."

Sophie reversed the visual, so it was back on her face. "Why do you think I chose this house? Fireproof building materials and this bomb shelter. Just my good luck it also happened to be on the beach in Kailua."

"You did get lucky there." He was smiling, an unfamiliar feeling. "Tell me about the defensibility and communications."

"Of course." Sophie flipped the camera back toward the kitchen. "No entry or egress but the elevator, which is seismically protected and steel lined. I've only got mine and Armita's fingerprints programmed in so far, but I will put yours in when you return."

His heart did a weird flip-flop like a landed fish. "I appreciate your trust."

She went on as if he hadn't spoken. "We've got plenty of weapons." She unlocked a high cabinet to reveal a range of guns, ammo, and explosives. "As far as the systems, we have our own backup generator and satellite enabled communication right here in case power is cut in the house above." She oriented him on the different features. "Additionally, everything that's going on upstairs is still routed to my workstation here, and through my phone." She showed him her work area, separated from the rest of the room by a moveable cubby wall. "I can't expect the kids to stay out entirely—but out of sight, out of mind."

"Genius," Raveaux said. "I am much reassured by what I see."

"Good. Wouldn't want my children's godfather worried unnecessarily." Sophie's smile lit the small screen in his hand.

"*Merci* for taking the time for the virtual tour," Raveaux said, stifling disappointment—she was making it clear that 'godfather' was all he was to her. Still, it was a start. He had to be patient. "Now to wait and see if Connor can find Pim Wat. I don't want to grab Mendoza except as a last resort."

Sophie nodded. "If anyone can find Pim Wat, it's Connor. I don't think you're going to have to resort to that. Get some sleep, Pierre. I don't like those circles under your eyes."

She disappeared, and he was left staring at the phone.

Chapter Twenty-Two

Connor sat back on his ergonomic stool only an hour after he'd left the meeting with Sophie, Bix, and Raveaux, and stared at his monitor with satisfaction.

He'd found Pim Wat.

Doing so had been relatively easy now that he had images of her face to upload to every law enforcement and travel method around the globe—and sure enough, she'd been caught on a traffic cam in the back seat of a limo on the way to the private aircraft section of the Charles de Gaulle International Airport.

Another camera had caught her walking across the windy tarmac, her head down and a hat obscuring her features, but enough of a glimpse to ping on his alert.

She'd been getting into a private jet belonging to a charter company, and she had a male companion with her.

Connor sifted back through CCTV video, looking for more on who she was traveling with, but hadn't found anything.

He *had* found the jet's destination: *Bangkok.*

Pim Wat was coming for him first.

His pulse raced with anticipation, dread—and relief, too.

Stuck here in the compound, there wasn't much he could do to protect Sophie and her family; but if Pim Wat came here, he had a good chance of nailing her first.

He checked his phone.

It was too late to call Sophie in Hawaii; he didn't want to disturb her when she'd already spent a day moving house and dealing with two babies.

But Raveaux and his men? Getting them up was no problem.

He phoned Raveaux directly. "I have a location for Pim Wat," he told the Frenchman without preamble. "She's in Bangkok. I'm likely her next target. Why don't you and my men hop a plane and get to the city, ASAP?"

"Quick work." Raveaux's voice was rough with sleep; he cleared his throat. "Rab and Sam are resting here, so that's easy. How do you propose we travel?"

Connor told him to use the private jet he kept on retainer for Yām Khûmkạn business, and to report to him when they'd reached Bangkok so he could funnel them his latest intel on Pim Wat.

"You got it," Raveaux said, and ended the call.

Connor might have liked the Frenchman in that moment if he hadn't been competition for Sophie's affections.

He got up and rang for Nine.

When his compatriot arrived, he issued a stream of directions: the compound was to be on high alert—the men would be drilling and patrolling. No one was to come in or out that wasn't personally known and recognized by long-term personnel, because Pim Wat was coming for him—and she had an unknown male companion.

Connor shut the door on his worried looking friend, and headed down the stairs, a towel over his shoulder. He'd prepare himself for the coming confrontation from the inside out, in the private thermal bath located in the bowels of the fortress.

Later, refreshed at a cellular level, Connor met with his squad leaders in the enclosed garden that had been the former Master's favorite retreat. The men, seated around the base of the tiger's eye column where Connor sat, gave him their full attention.

He'd been working hard in the time he'd become the new Master to empower the various teachers and leaders within the Yām's existing structure, and he and Nine had been on the hunt for a replacement for his own position as Master. So far, none of the squad leaders had shown the extra spark needed for the position, but in the meantime, the heads of various disciplines had progressed from looking to him and the position of Master for ongoing support, permission, and validation, to producing that from within themselves.

The whole organization was functioning more independently, but still communicating well with him and each other. A new paradigm.

"I want to prepare you in case something befalls me," he told his leaders baldly. "I have not found a Number One yet to be my replacement. This is a concern with Pim Wat, the Master's concubine and his best assassin, coming to the area to kill me."

"We will never let that happen, Master," one of the squad leaders in charge of physical conditioning said. His confidence made his energy field glow with pulses of red and gold.

"You mean well, but the fact remains that Pim Wat is good at what she does. She was able to kill the Master, her lover." The fiction Connor had used to cover his own deed had been believed and become fact. The six men before him fell silent at that reminder. The former Master must have seemed immortal to them, as he had to Connor.

"I want your suggestions for a backup plan should I be gone."

"We rule the compound by consensus," the leader of meditation said. "We vote on what must be done. There are six of us, and Nine can be the tiebreaker and leader of the team."

"I like this proposal," Connor said. "Discussion?"

Nine frowned and shook his head. "I am not worthy to be the team leader."

Connor smiled. "You just confirmed your responsibility. All in favor? Say Aye."

"Aye!" The foreign word rolled awkwardly off the Thai men's tongues, but relief to have the matter of immediate succession settled brightened each of their energy fields.

"Good. Now, let's discuss our defenses. My biggest concern is that we never found the exit Pim Wat used to escape from the Master's chamber. Until she is neutralized, I will be staying in various places throughout the compound, a different room every night. I will just appear where I'm planning to sleep that night, and I will confine my activities to the tower room where I work until Pim Wat is captured."

"An excellent strategy, Master, and it will build your bond with the men," the leader in charge of weapons training said. "They will see you as one of them."

"Which is good, since the color of my skin continues to remind them otherwise," Connor said.

No one made eye contact; the former Master's choice of a white man to be his successor had not been a popular one, and Connor was still working toward the deep rapport he sought with the Yām Khûmkạn as a group.

He dismissed the squad leaders and closed his eyes, enjoying the warmth of the sun on his naked torso as he meditated atop the six-foot-high plinth.

All around him, the life force of the garden glowed: the water lilies in the pond, the orchid tree that shaded the tea table, the borders of tropical flowers and ferns that lined the rough stone walls. Butterflies and birds darted about. The sun was warm, the breeze a caress.

For just a little while the Master could relax and enjoy the peace and protection around him.

Chapter Twenty-Three

Two days later . . .

Vivian lay on her belly along a high limb in one of the massive wild mahogany trees growing in the jungle around the Yām Khûmkạn's compound. She gripped the thermal imaging binoculars as she counted the men on the walls. "They're on alert. Double the usual number of men patrolling."

"They must have got word that you left Paris," Panh said from behind her. "Downside of you coming with me."

Vivian lowered the glasses and reversed direction so that she could rest her back against the bole of the huge tree and sit beside him. "It doesn't matter for our purposes."

"Unless he's found your secret tunnel. And I'm sure he's been searching."

Vivian frowned in annoyance. She gazed around their jungle aerie to distract herself.

They'd gone up the mahogany using climbing gear in the last of the waning light of the day; they'd have to spend the night here with no illumination or comforts, but Panh had been busy while she'd been surveying the fortress. He'd already strung up sleep hammocks and a net suspension platform. She sidled carefully onto the springy surface beside him.

She and Panh wore full camouflage gear, and face paint obscured any contrast of their skin with their surroundings. Vivian's flashy platinum hair was secured under a dark green watch cap.

"We can't go any closer to the compound than this. They've got the jungle mined and seeded with alarms, as I told you," Vivian said as she accepted an energy bar, thoughtfully unwrapped, from her partner. "I just wanted us to get eyes on the fortress. See what we could see. I could familiarize you with the layout from outside. There are many challenges."

"So you said," Panh said imperturbably. "I will be in the supply van tomorrow, going into the compound with the food delivery, as we discussed."

"But if they are on this high of an alert, I can't let you take that chance." Vivian blew out a breath, frightened by the attachment to the Chameleon that she'd developed in such a short time; she didn't want him to die. She didn't want to be alone in trying to take down a tough target like Connor. "They will seize any unknown personnel and ask questions later." She fussed with her leather gloves. "We've lost the element of surprise."

They sat quietly, the sounds of the jungle settling all around them: birds twittered and sang as they came to rest for the night. The rustle of leaves, the creak of branches, the far-off squeal of something dying in the understory was a counterpoint. Ripe smells of moss, mold, and mulch wafted up from the forest floor.

"We don't have to take him now." Panh's tone was gentle. "There's no hurry."

"We need a different plan entirely," Vivian said. She turned to Panh. He was just an outline in the dark, but that was where they were most comfortable. "I think I have an idea."

⚜

Raveaux stepped off the sleek little private jet into a humid, warm evening that smelled of ripe fruit and hot tar. The last of the flaming sunset he'd witnessed coming in was finally fading over the jumble of multi-styled buildings that was Bangkok.

Rab took his bag from him. "Come with me. We are meeting the Master in the Yām Khûmkạn compound."

Raveaux followed the ninja away from the plane and across the asphalt, suffused with a rare sense of excitement. This was an adventure and a truly new experience; he'd never been to Thailand before, let alone to a setting as unusual as the stronghold of the elite and secretive organization.

A small foreign made SUV motored toward them; Rab and Sam greeted the driver in a flood of their indecipherable language, and gestured for Raveaux to get in.

Raveaux got in back with Sam as Rab sat beside the driver, who was another ninja from the compound, guessing by his shaved head, black gi, and general air of lethality.

The drive through Bangkok was a hair-raising experience, though different from other crowded cities Raveaux had experienced. Traffic direction and signage appeared to be mere suggestions rather than any sort of rules, but no one honked their horns. Smiles, waves, and laughter accompanied the weaving in and out of farm animals, pedal vehicles of every variety, and pedestrians.

Raveaux rolled down his window and clung to the strap to get a more in vivo experience; the smells alone were a cacophony for the senses.

He was finally ready to roll the window up and lean on his travel duffel to sleep as they left the city behind and merged onto a well-traveled thoroughfare. Night fell suddenly, as if a black felt curtain had been dropped over the world.

A

Raveaux woke abruptly to being flung against his seat belt and the doorframe; the SUV had hit a chuckhole.

Rab looked back at him from the front seat. "You slept."

"So I did." Raveaux yawned and shifted to stretch his legs. "Where are we?"

"Close to the heart of the Yām Khûmkạn," Rab said.

Hours had passed in a dense darkness, and far from the freeway, the SUV's headlights bucked as the vehicle navigated a rutted, muddy road bordered on either side by enormous trees forming a tunnel draped with dangling vines. Ferns and undergrowth, briefly illuminated by the vehicle's headlights, masked the sides of the road. The jungle appeared too dense to penetrate at all on foot. Now and again, Raveaux glimpsed the gleam of animals' eyes as the headlights hit them.

The vehicle slowed as two ninjas materialized in the road ahead; the men ran forward and yanked open the doors of the vehicle, even as the driver delivered a spate of Thai.

Raveaux instinctively raised his hands; he was pulled from the vehicle, frisked, and his gun and concealed knife removed.

More Thai speech poured over him as the two sentries checked the vehicle over carefully, even shining lights on the undercarriage and examining it with a mirror on a pole.

Eventually, they all got back in and drove forward.

Rab turned to him. "The Master told them to expect us. Even so, no unknowns are allowed in or out of the compound now. You are an unknown."

"But I am not unknown to the Master, or to you," Raveaux said.

"That is why you are still alive."

"Will I get my weapons back?"

"Yes, when you leave."

Raveaux was wide awake now.

The fortress appeared suddenly—a monolithic stone wall crusted with lichen looming out of the night, lit by braziers at the corners. A wooden gate made of logs strapped with metal was inset in it, large enough to admit a tank. The gate creaked open at a snail's pace, and a cadre of ninjas emerged to surround the vehicle.

Once again Raveaux got out, was frisked, and the vehicle was searched, along with his companions, before they drove into a huge courtyard.

"I have notified the Master that you are here," Rab said. "Nine has arrived to take you to him."

Directly ahead a short, compact Thai man approached and opened Raveaux's door. Raveaux nodded to him. "I remember you."

"Welcome to the Yām Khûmkạn," Nine said in halting English. "Come with me."

Raveaux grabbed his bag, nodded a goodbye to his companions, and followed Nine into a nearby stone building.

Raveaux had to trot to keep up, though Nine did not appear to be hurrying as the man walked sure-footedly down a corridor lit by small glass oil lanterns with bronze reflecting shields in niches. "I met you on the Big Island of Hawaii," Raveaux said.

"Yes," Nine said.

Nine had been with Connor when the three of them, flown under duress by a reluctant pilot, had taken a chopper to rescue Sophie and her fiancé Jake from a lava tube, an errand that had ended tragically.

Raveaux pushed the intrusive memories aside and focused on following the Thai man, whose flashlight was a bobbing target.

Soon they were mounting seemingly endless stairs. Raveaux was glad he'd been working on his cardio as they circled higher and higher, eventually facing a heavy wooden door to a tower room. Connor opened the door without Nine knocking.

The leader of the Yām Khûmkạn was even more chiseled than when Raveaux last saw him; his body gleamed like a perfect bronze sculpture between the open lapels of his white *gi*. His hair was longer; eyes the color of the ocean assessed him with unnerving thoroughness. "You're troubled," Connor stated.

"I had occasion to remember when I met Nine last," Raveaux said, seeing no point in prevarication. "Not a happy memory."

"A hard time, indeed." A shadow clouded Connor's aqua eyes. "Do you need refreshment?"

"I haven't eaten," Raveaux said. "And I could use a shower."

"Nine will bring you food now and show you to a place to sleep when we're done talking—but we don't have showers here. You'll have to make do with the geothermal baths—but I promise, the experience is a treat." Connor held the stout wooden door wide. "Welcome to my inner sanctum."

Raveaux entered, and Nine left, presumably to fetch his meal.

The room was circular, with woven native matting covering the harsh stone floor and on top of that, luxurious Persian rugs. The walls were bare but for a violin mounted on pegs. A round table with a couple of chairs and a serious-looking computer workstation with an ergonomic stool were the only furnishings; one window over-looked a lightless black jungle and, perhaps, the ramparts below.

"Spartan work area," Raveaux said.

"My regular chambers are considerably more comfortable, but I've had to vacate them for security reasons. Until we nail Pim Wat." Connor spoke with a bloodthirsty snarl; the man was picturing actual nails piercing his enemy. Raveaux could appreciate that.

"Your security measures on the way into the compound were—considerable and intrusive."

"Can't be too careful right now." Connor brushed past Raveaux and took a seat at the table. "Let's review where we are."

Raveaux shook his head as he sat opposite the blond man. "I hope you've found out something more, because I know as much as I did when I got on the plane—namely, that Pim Wat was last seen headed here with an unidentified male companion."

"And unfortunately, that's where we still are." Connor tightened his robe with a gesture that conveyed frustration. "Pim Wat flew into Bangkok and descended off that private plane with her companion, both wrapped up tighter than mummies to avoid cameras—and then, they disappeared off the grid. I haven't been able to pick them up since. Electronic surveillance is stronger in Western countries, but here in Thailand, we have quite a human spy network. Whatever Pim Wat's done to disguise herself is pretty good because no one has reported seeing her."

"Great," Raveaux muttered.

A coded knock came from the door; Connor got up and lifted the heavy bar that held it closed, and Nine entered, carrying a fragrant bowl of some kind of stew on a tray. Raveaux's belly rumbled loud enough for both men to hear, and Nine flashed brilliant white teeth in a smile. "You're hungry."

"I am." Raveaux picked up the hand-carved wooden spoon that accompanied the bowl and raised it in salute to Nine. "Thank you."

He dug in. Wonderful flavors rolled around his palate: lemongrass, ginger, garlic, onion, and a hint of saffron. Chunks of meat, sliced tuber, and vegetables went down easy. At the bottom of the bowl, a rich slurry of rice rounded out the delicious dish.

Nine sat on the remaining chair as Connor sat quietly, observing Raveaux. "You've driven yourself hard over this," he said at last.

Raveaux pushed the empty bowl aside and patted his full belly. "As have you, no doubt."

"I appreciate you standing in for me. With Sophie and her children." Connor stared at him penetratingly.

"I wasn't aware I was any kind of substitute. She asked me to be godfather to her children; I agreed." Raveaux didn't give an inch.

"I love Sophie. When this is all over, I am going to win her back," Connor said.

"You can try." Raveaux narrowed his eyes. "But are you the best man for her—and for her children?"

He'd scored a hit; Connor's eyes darkened with pain.

"I see how it is." Connor stood abruptly. "We'll get back to the hunt tomorrow. For now, go with Nine and enjoy the baths, and get some rest." He walked to his computers and sat down.

Nine picked up Raveaux's empty bowl and set it on the tray. "Come with me, Monsieur Raveaux."

Raveaux had been dismissed by the Master.

Chapter Twenty-Four

Connor slept poorly, plagued by dream memories of Sophie and their time together.

He woke before dawn had fully bled through the narrow slot windows of the storage room he'd chosen to sleep in that night. He stared at the dim stones of the ceiling overhead, inhaling the musty smell of the bags of rice and beans lining the walls and the faint hint of coffee, spices, and flour.

His new personal attendant slept nearby, a dim silhouette on a pallet like his.

He'd had to accept this staff member because Nine had ignored his directions and quietly inserted him into Connor's life—but he didn't want to remember the man's name, and he ignored his presence.

Pierre Raveaux was a worthy adversary for Sophie's affections, and he was a dirty fighter under that suave manner. He'd hit Connor where it hurt with his question.

Was he the best man for Sophie? And her children?

The barriers to Connor living any kind of normal life with her, and her family, were immense. He shut his eyes, hopelessness rolling over him in a wave.

Connor wasn't going to find an answer to Raveaux's question right now.

But most of those obstacles could all vanish in an instant, if Pim Wat and the danger she posed were gone.

Dealing with Pim Wat was priority.

Connor's phone pinged with a notification that he had a priority e-mail. He drew the device out from under the pillow and opened the message.

He froze, his breath arrested.

A picture of Kupa, her face pale, puffy, and discolored from a beating, filled the phone's screen. Her eyes were closed, but she was being held upright by a fistful of hair. The side of her head where her ear had been was a pulpy mess of blood.

The next photo was of the ear, lying on the upraised paw of one of the bronze dragons that guarded the door of his house on Phi Ni. Blood trickled from the delicate, whorled bit of flesh down the golden paw of the beast—a barbaric image.

Trust Pim Wat to go for the dramatic. Connor would never forget that picture as long as he lived.

Pim Wat's e-mail message was terse. *"Found an unexpected bonus when I came to your island. Come alone, or you'll get them both back in pieces: one body part every hour until you arrive."*

Connor pressed a button on the phone, closed the e-mail, and shut his eyes. His enemy held Kupa and Nam.

He breathed through a wave of nausea.

When he refocused, he was staring at his body servant's back, outlined in the early dawn light.

This was why he'd refused to remember the man's name.

Everyone Connor cared about was a weapon that could be used against him.

A

Raveaux started, awaking, as a hand shook him by the shoulder. "What is it?"

"I've heard from Pim Wat." Connor was backlit by flickering torchlight coming through an open doorway; it was still very early.

Raveaux tossed aside a light cotton blanket and sat up on the wooden platform with a pallet on it that he'd rested on in a dormitory-like room filled with other men. All of them were gone; he must have slept right through their quiet departures.

"What did she say?" Raveaux rubbed the bristle of beard growing on his chin, blinking to clear his eyes. He'd gone down hard.

"Pim Wat has my servants—my friends. Kupa and Nam." Connor's voice was a bleak rasp. "Come with me."

He turned and headed for the door.

Raveaux fumbled for his clothes, pulling a long-sleeved tee on over his head. He'd enjoyed the baths last night; all that hot water had washed away the sweat of tension and travel. He zipped up his pants and slid bare feet into his shoes.

Nine lingered in the hall, but Connor was nowhere in sight by the time Raveaux made it to the door.

"The Master is much troubled," Nine said, gesturing for Raveaux to follow. "He blames himself. His beloved servant Kupa has lost her ear."

"*Merde*." Raveaux broke into a trot behind the man as they moved down the stone hallway to a side door that stood ajar.

Connor stood in front of a large steel locker against one wall, contemplating a variety of guns and weaponry. "She has Nam and Kupa on Phi Ni. My private island." He turned to face Raveaux, and his expressive eyes were the stark blue of an ice floe. "I miscalculated in letting them go home before Pim Wat was captured."

Raveaux's throat closed on any protestations; no response was adequate. "I see."

"Pim Wat demands I come to her alone. I'll take the chopper, and Nine will pilot me. I want you to reach out to Agent McDonald with the CIA. Go to Phi Ni with them by plane. By the time you get there, I will have Pim Wat in hand."

Raveaux frowned. "That will definitely take a bit of time to arrange. You should stall."

Connor held up his phone. "She will cut off a body part every hour that I delay my arrival."

Raveaux approached, took the phone from Connor's hand and looked at the photos Pim Wat had sent. He had never met Kupa, who clearly meant a lot to Connor, but the human misery in the photo turned his stomach. "That's a powerful incentive to move fast, but if you don't give us time to provide backup, she could prevail."

"That's what I told the Master," Nine said. The Thai man's stoic face gleamed with the sweat of stress. "I cannot let the Master endanger himself unnecessarily."

"Then we will watch our friends lose their lives by the hour!" Connor bellowed. "I will not allow it. I am not some child to be coddled. I can take Pim Wat!"

"But Pim Wat has the advantage, and at least one companion we know nothing about," Nine argued, unintimidated by Connor's rage, though clearly glad to have Raveaux there to bolster his position. "She will use Kupa and Nam until the last minute to make you helpless. Neither of them would want that. They have sworn their lives to you." He paused to draw a breath, organizing his thoughts in English. "Pim Wat plans to kill Kupa in revenge anyway; why would she give our friend to you at all? Pim Wat has two hostages; she only needs one."

The man's reasoning was brutal, but sound. Connor turned to face the weapons locker without answering. His hands opened and closed.

"We need a surprise. A distraction. Something to turn the tables and give you an edge," Raveaux said. "Let's call McDonald now and get the task force moving with an aircraft. We need to think outside the box. Do you have a map of the island?"

Raveaux, Connor, and Nine were poring over the satellite map of Phi Ni with McDonald on speakerphone, when Connor's phone dinged with an incoming message.

The clock is ticking," came the message from Pim Wat. A gory photo of Kupa's workworn hand, now missing its smallest digit, filled the screen.

Connor howled in agony. "I cannot wait any longer!"

"We must," Raveaux said. He had some hostage negotiation training; now was the time to use it, while they moved plans into play. "Let me call her."

Chapter Twenty-Five

Vivian set Kupa's finger on the paw of the bronze dragon opposite the one holding the ear. She took a photo of it.

She frowned. The photo wasn't satisfying. Blood had drained quickly from the digit once it was severed, leaving the appendage pale as a slug and quite ordinary-looking. Kupa didn't paint her nails, which would have made for a better shot.

Vivian bent to peer at the finger. There was a bit of white showing . . . She took a photo from a different angle that caught the elusive gleam of bone. "That's better."

Panh was binding Kupa's hand. The woman had fainted, failing to appreciate the first aid the Chameleon had insisted on giving her. "No sense letting a good hostage die of blood loss and shock," he'd said in his practical way.

Vivian wasn't feeling practical; she was riding a powerful, riotous bloodlust. She was enjoying every minute of her long-awaited time with Kupa. She'd been planning to kill her former handmaiden ever since Kupa had stolen poison from her kill stash and given it to the usurper, Connor.

"This one's weak. Leave her alone for the moment. You can cut something off the man next," Panh said.

Vivian curled her lip. She glanced over at the older Thai man, bound and gagged, tied to one of the palm trees that bordered the circular drive.

Nam hung in his ropes, his eyes closed. He appeared as if he'd also fainted, probably at the sight of his wife's blood and the sound of her screams.

Being on this island, a place where she'd last visited with the former Master and played the part of a humble supplicant to her betraying daughter, had put Vivian in touch with a well of rage so deep that no amount of bodies could fill it.

But that was okay; she'd have fun trying. Neither of these people would be left alive by the time she was done with them.

Vivian glanced around the courtyard in front of the cantilevered mansion Connor had designed for its cliff-top view; the place was battered and weather-beaten. Many of the coconut palms had been shredded by the typhoon that had passed over it a few months ago, and the place had been neglected before that when it was seized by the Department of Justice.

The condition of Connor's precious house was a far cry from its former glory, and no more than that usurper deserved.

A touch on Vivian's arm distracted her dark ruminations. "I know you've waited a long time for this and you're enjoying the moment," Panh said. "But we need an exit strategy. Let's go inside and find something to eat and discuss it."

Vivian ground her teeth; clearly, he didn't understand. "I'm not hungry."

Panh's hand tightened on her arm. He pushed his lean face into hers. His eyes were pits of death. "Move, Vivian."

She gave one last glance at her victims: Kupa was bound hand and foot, lying flat on the ground. She'd begun to moan; she was waking up. Nam hung limp and silent from the coconut tree.

The hostages weren't going anywhere.

Vivian allowed Panh to tug her inside the house.

Connor's caretakers hadn't been on the island long, according to Nam; they hadn't yet had time to clean up inside the mansion. Windows had broken even behind the metal shutters that shielded them, and high winds had admitted dirt and leaves that mixed with broken glass and crunched beneath their feet as Vivian and Panh walked down a darkened hallway.

"The power's out," Panh said. "But hopefully there's canned food somewhere. Do you know the layout of this place?"

"No." Vivian had never been inside and had only visited the island that one time when she'd come to lull Sophie into complacency with a false apology.

They passed a glassed-in interior garden; a statue of Kuan Yin had fallen over, and one of the massive sliders was broken. Rain and debris had blown into the room on the other side of the damage.

They reached the kitchen. Panh let go of Vivian and approached one of the windows, pushing the metal shutter up to admit some light. "Look for food," he barked.

Vivian scowled but headed for a likely-looking door in the richly paneled wall of the kitchen and pulled it open.

"Here's the pantry."

Panh joined her in the doorway. They soon located a box of candles and a flashlight. He turned on the beam and shone it around. "Coconut milk. Rice. Canned meat. Curry spice. I will prepare us something on the stove; it's propane, so hopefully it still works."

"Whatever." Vivian could not have been less interested.

Panh grabbed her chin as quick as a snake striking. His fingers bit into her jaw painfully; he forced her to gaze into his calm, deadly eyes. "I am getting out of here alive. I see that you've stopped caring for anything but the torture of your victims; but I assure you, there's more to life than revenge."

He kissed her so hard that she tasted blood.

Vivian clutched at Panh for support. She roared back into her body from that faraway place she'd been as suddenly as if struck by lightning.

Still holding her by the jaw, the Chameleon dropped his flashlight to the floor. His other hand came up to squeeze her throat. He strode forward, shoving Vivian deep into the closet.

She hit the wall at the back of the pantry between a rack of brooms and a shelf containing canned goods. He pinned her there, lightly depressing her windpipe so that spangles and stars filled her vision as she struggled to breathe.

"Feel how alive you are," he whispered. "Even when you're close to death."

Shivers of desire zipped up and down Vivian's spine and pooled between her legs; she panted under his hand, emitting tiny whimpers as she reached for the buckle of his belt.

"I could kill you so easily right now. I choose not to," Panh said harshly. "Feel this. Feel me. Live."

Lust ignited Vivian's spine; she struggled to get his belt undone, his pants loosened. He let go of her jaw and kissed her again; she was dimly aware of his hand fumbling at the leggings she wore, yanking them down. He replaced his hand at her throat with his forearm. The effect was the same: only a whisper of air reached her lungs.

She was dizzy, melting, blind with need.

They came together in a surge of power and heat; their bodies strove, knocking cans over and brooms askew.

Vivian was aware of nothing but Panh's vital, overwhelming force as he invaded and restricted her. Straining against him was pure violent pleasure.

He never decreased that razor edge between life and death; Vivian's scream as she came was strangled into complete oblivion.

A

Vivian came around to the feeling of gentle kisses on her face and neck and a hand brushing through her hair.

She was lying on the floor of the pantry, naked; the tile was cold, gritty against her back.

He'd taken her clothing off. His hands and lips and tongue were everywhere; she rose beneath him as he took her again.

She sat up eventually.

He dressed her tenderly, sliding her arms through her sleeves, maneuvering her as if she were porcelain.

Her throat was sore; she could hardly swallow. She was battered and bruised and replete.

Panh led her out of the pantry's darkness by the hand. Her eyes could hardly stand the light passing through the partially lifted shutter.

"Better?" He tipped her chin again, surveying her.

"Yes." She cast her eyes down; he saw her too clearly. "You mentioned food. I'm hungry, now."

"I will prepare something." Panh busied himself at the stove.

Vivian walked on tottering legs over to a magnificent native wood dining room table, now littered with dust and leaves. She pulled out a chair and sat down, taking out her phone.

She'd missed two calls from Connor.

"He called," she said to Panh's back.

The Chameleon was stirring a pot; delicious smells were already beginning. Her stomach growled. "Give me a minute to get this going and we'll call him back on speaker."

Vivian waited.

She couldn't have moved if she'd wanted to, her body was so satiated. She tried to sift through what had just happened. How had he discerned her secret? She loved to kill, but she also wanted to die. She enjoyed dominating, and she also longed to submit. She loved inflicting pain, and she enjoyed it herself in equal measure.

Vivian fussed with her disarrayed clothing, gathering her dignity. "I should take the hostages some water."

Panh turned from the stove. "Why? You're going to kill them anyway."

Vivian narrowed her eyes even as her body gave a hungry pulse of desire—he knew her intent. "I never said that."

"You don't have to pretend with me." Panh came over and sat beside her. "Call the target."

Vivian took his hand and brought it to her cheek, then kissed the palm. "I like you, whatever your name is."

His expression didn't change, but pleasure gleamed in his eyes. "Make the call."

Chapter Twenty-Six

The phone rang in Raveaux's hand—a call coming in from Pim Wat's number.

Connor and Nine, across the room packing gear, stopped what they were doing and returned to where Raveaux sat on a stool beside a utilitarian shelf.

He held up a finger, then paused to let the phone ring five times. Finally, he picked up and put the call on speaker.

"You took long enough." Pim Wat's voice sounded hoarse, abraded. "Are you on your way?"

"This is Pierre Raveaux, Connor's associate. What are your requests? We want the hostages unharmed."

"I want to speak to the usurper known as Connor," Pim Wat growled. "I only have one demand, and it is for him to come to the island, alone."

"Well, that's not going to happen fast enough to suit you, so I am calling to see what else you want. I assume you're in need of some way to get off the island after the exchange?"

Silence.

"I'll call you back." Pim Wat ended the communication.

Raveaux set the phone down on the nearby shelf. "Dialogue with me as your liaison, established."

"She could just be going to hack off another piece of Kupa," Connor said.

"Doubtful. You said you saw a male figure getting on the plane with her? She is likely conferring with her companion if they are still together. Which, if she's as smart as you say she is, they would be."

"Pim Wat always worked alone in the past." Connor had picked up an empty nine millimeter magazine. He rammed bullets into it. "No reason to believe anything is different now."

"She must know she'd be heavily outnumbered in any attempt on your life," Raveaux argued. "If she had an opportunity for a partner, she would have taken it."

Connor shook his head. "I don't think so."

"Master. She is with Kaleidoscope now, and Mendoza will have his say," Nine said. "She is an asset to him. She owes him for helping her."

"I think we should assume she's not alone. And if I were using that house for a showdown, I'd have been working on an escape route before I even made contact," Raveaux said. "There are a limited number of ways she could have reached the island: by sea, or by air. Do you have any recent satellite footage? Maybe we can spot her transport and guess at her next move."

Connor paused in what he was doing at last. He turned to Raveaux, frowning. "I'm not thinking clearly, or I would have realized this."

Neither man replied.

"Only you can get into the satellites, Master," Nine finally said. "Let me handle packing the gear and fueling the chopper. You and Raveaux go to the tower." He added a rapid spate of Thai, clearly urging Connor to listen.

Connor set down the weapon he was loading at last. "Let's go."

Raveaux followed the blond man through the maze of corridors. Trainees passed them occasionally, bowing respectfully, but no one tried to speak to the Master.

Raveaux was winded by the time they reached the tower; Connor showed no sign of exertion at all as he sat down before his rigs.

"You brought the phone, right?" The man's fingers were already a blur on the computer's keys.

"Of course." Raveaux took Connor's phone out of his pocket and set it on the round table where he'd eaten the night before. "I'll monitor for Pim Wat's call."

The room's starkness had not improved with daylight, but now Raveaux could see out of the single window down into a courtyard below and the jungle beyond. Lines of men dressed in black martial arts clothing, rendered uniform by their shaved heads, practiced maneuvers.

The phone rang again.

Raveaux picked up immediately this time. "Raveaux here."

Connor tilted his head to indicate that he was listening but continued to work his keyboard.

"I want Connor to come, alone and unarmed, with only the pilot for the chopper," Pim Wat said on speaker. "I will trade the hostages for him. He and I will take the chopper to a destination I have in mind."

"Unacceptable," Raveaux said. "You are planning to kill him. He is much more valuable than a couple of servants, and you know it."

"Perhaps he'd like to make that decision," Pim Wat said. "I can always have Kupa scream for you, Connor. I know you're listening."

"I will be on the chopper, alone and unarmed, with just my pilot," Connor declared loudly.

"No!" Raveaux exclaimed.

"I believe the usurper gave me an acceptable answer," Pim Wat replied. "Be here in an hour, Connor, or I start on Nam's extremities next." The line went dead.

Raveaux glared at the blond man. "I thought you wanted me to negotiate. Why did you agree to her request?"

"I never had any other intention." Connor's eyes confirmed his resolve. "But do you think that's the only thing I'm going to do?" He swiveled the monitor for Raveaux to see. "They came in by speedboat."

A sleek, cigar-shaped black jet boat was tied at the dock alongside the boathouse. "That looks fast."

"It does. But we will be faster. I'm going to stall my departure; we will have mysterious helicopter trouble. Long enough for reinforcements to arrive from several directions."

Connor picked up a walkie-talkie and issued a stream of Thai directives.

Raveaux sat back, relieved.

Connor might still be flying straight into danger, but he was not going to be alone, and he'd stopped thinking with his emotions. It was a start.

Chapter Twenty-Seven

Sophie settled herself in the seat of the Security Solutions company jet. The flight to Thailand was thirteen hours long, but the good news about having a private plane at her disposal was that they would be going straight to the isolated island of Phi Ni, with only one stop for refueling.

Ranged around the aircraft, sorting gear and weapons, were eight of the company's best tactical operatives, including Sophie's maternity leave replacement, Lono Jones.

The man had been occupying her office for three months, but she had not heard much about his job performance; she had stayed out of the day-to-day operations and left those to Bix.

The jet had comfortable leather swivel seats and an anchored coffee table; Jones was oiling down a long-distance rifle, sections of which lay disassembled on a rolled-out piece of felt.

Sophie was eager for a distraction after Connor's terse call that Pim Wat had surfaced on his secluded island and had seized Kupa and Nam. She'd put her affairs in order and had assembled the team. They were wheels up within the hour.

"You seem pretty comfortable with that." Sophie indicated the broken-down rifle with her head.

"Did a tour in Afghanistan as a marksman." Jones's shaggy surfer hair seemed at odds with that background, but men living in Hawaii looked and dressed in all sorts of ways. Sophie had given up trying to categorize them as one might elsewhere. "Never know when that background might come in handy."

"As I told you when gathering the team, I really have no idea what we're going into. All I know is that Pim Wat and her partner have hostages, and will not hesitate to use deadly force," Sophie said. "Our function is as backup."

"As soon as we finish organizing the gear, I'd like to get familiar with the terrain we'll be navigating on your island," Jones said. "I hope you brought those topographical maps I asked for."

"I'll get them." Sophie rose from her seat, now that they had reached cruising altitude, and headed to the storage locker behind the cabin's bathroom. The maps she'd brought had been laminated for use in the field and were stored rolled in a zipped case.

She'd had a map of Phi Ni made when the property was seized by the DOJ; a drone had flown over the small island and taken extensive photos she'd then merged with satellite imaging. She'd developed this so that she could track any damage, theft, or wear and tear that happened during the time the property was unoccupied.

Connor also had a copy of this map; hopefully it would help him plan his approach to deal with her mother's abduction of Nam and Kupa.

Sophie could barely tolerate thinking of their dear friends in Pim Wat's hands.

Jones had finished cleaning and checking his rifle; it was now fully assembled. He was attaching a carry strap to the weapon when she returned with the map case.

Jones set the rifle aside and gestured for the rest of the men to gather around the table.

Sophie took the map out of the case and unrolled it.

Jones anchored the corners with a couple of boxes of ammunition so that the plastic didn't recoil, as Sophie located the landing strip and hangar area, pointing it out to the team. "We will be coming in here. I hope we can reach Connor or Raveaux for an update before we land. All I know at this time is that the assassin Pim Wat is at the house and has two valuable hostages—one of whom she has already mutilated." Sophie put her finger on the photo of Connor's cliff-top mansion, roughly at the opposite end of the small island from the airstrip. "As you can see from the map, the house is several miles from the runway. We will have to find transportation."

"There isn't much cover around the house. Or around the landing area for that matter," Jones said. "Looks like mostly coconut palms as far as trees."

"Yes. The most forested area is near the boathouse, here." Sophie pointed to the small bay that protected the boathouse and Connor's pleasure craft. "This makes sense as an entry point from sea."

"In situations like this it's best practice to surround the target area entirely," Jones said. "Doesn't look like we can get around one side of the house at all, though. It's on a cliff."

"Yes, it is. Connor will be arriving by helicopter to this landing pad near the house." Sophie indicated the boldly marked area. "The best cover might be behind the outbuildings, here and here."

"Could you review the chronology for us?" Jones asked. "How long has this crisis been going on? Where in the timeline of events will we be arriving? Most of the action might even be over by the time we get there with a thirteen-hour flight time."

"That's what I'm afraid of. According to Connor, we will be last to the party with our lengthy travel time. He told me he has a plan. We are just—backup, I hope." Technically, she was the team's boss but had never directed military-style operations in the field—nor did she want to start now.

"Backup is good." Jones sat back in his cushioned leather seat. "Glad to hear it. I don't like going in blind at the head of a charge in this kind of situation."

Sophie didn't feel the same. Everything might be over by the time they got there, and it terrified her what that outcome might be. "Why don't you discuss how you'd like to deploy as a team after we arrive?" Sophie said. "Meanwhile, I'll see if I can get a satellite view of what's happening on Phi Ni through a live satellite feed."

"That would be incredible," Jones said.

"It might not be possible in-flight, but it's worth a try." Sophie got up and went into the bedroom.

The cozy room, with its built-in bed, provided a nice respite when traveling long distances. Sophie was far too agitated for that now. She took out her laptop, booted it up, and began searching for a satellite feed that would give her a current visual of the island.

Connor had hacked into a network of spy satellites and had given her his access codes some time ago. She had never connected to them while in-flight, though, and wasn't even sure it was possible.

Half an hour later, the search function icon just continued to spin.

Sophie had to find out what was going on.

She tried Connor's phone.

He didn't pick up at his number, but Raveaux did. Sophie whooshed out a breath of relief. "Pierre."

"Sophie. Are you en route?"

"I, with eight of Security Solutions' best operatives, and a ton of weapons and gear, are currently in the air somewhere over the South Pacific," Sophie said. "I was able to get off Oahu within an hour of getting Connor's message. What's happening right now?"

"Glad you're on your way. Here's the plan."

Sophie covered her mouth with a hand as she listened, her heart pounding in her ears.

Chapter Twenty-Eight

Vivian finished the delicious bowl of rich chicken curry Panh had whipped up on the stove. "A man of many talents." She suppressed a burp and checked her phone. "Time to go cut something off Nam. I'm thinking we should do a toe. Keep up the element of surprise."

"Whatever makes you happy." Panh kissed her. "That was almost too easy, though. The Master agreeing to come alone in the chopper. He's planning something."

Vivian rose, leaving the dishes where they lay on the table. "He is still driven by emotions."

"Still, I think we should prepare for an incursion. He has all those ninjas; he will want to use them. Or at least, his counselors will want him to use them. You go have your fun with the hostages. I'll scout for a vantage point where I can cover the boat area and the airstrip, if possible."

"Seems like a lot to cover, but you are, as I said, a man of many talents." Vivian smiled at her lover. "I'm refreshed in body and mind by this little interlude."

"Just as I was hoping you'd be."

Vivian led the way back through the house and out the front door—and stopped so suddenly that Panh ran into her back.

She cursed ripely.

Nam and Kupa had disappeared; the ropes the couple had been bound with were discarded on the ground.

"This can't be happening." Vivian fisted her hands; her sharp nails bit into her palms. She stomped over to the place where Kupa had lain; Panh had gone to inspect the coconut tree. "Her ropes were untied."

"The husband got loose first, then set her free." Panh held up a frayed, bloodied section of rope that had been severed somehow. "I should have checked his bindings a second time."

Vivian breathed loudly through her nose; rage felt so potent in her veins she was drunk on it. "I will kill them now."

Panh stared at her from beside the palm tree, his gaze speculative. "I know you want to search for them, but those two lived alone on this island for close to ten years. They likely have some hole to hide in that we'll never find. We can't waste time looking."

Vivian spun on her heel, scanning the area. There was little cover, besides the outbuildings. "Give me that ATV and an hour."

"Our time is better spent preparing for a double cross. Besides, they fulfilled their purpose. The target is on his way." Panh approached her. "Capturing them here was an unexpected bonus, and you made the most of it. Time to move on."

Vivian slowed her breathing deliberately, remembering the Master's teachings to rein in her emotions, make them serve her. "What would you have us do?"

"Rearrange one of the dismembered parts you already have and take a new photo of it. That will be enough to keep the pressure on for now."

"I never sent the second photo of the finger that I took." Still trying to regroup, Vivian went back to the entrance of the house and the pair of bronze dragons fronting the door, whose upraised paws each carried a macabre offering.

Panh was right.

She didn't need the hostages anymore; but she'd been planning to kill Kupa ever since the woman spent a season as her very inept personal attendant, failed to appreciate the extensive plastic surgery

Vivian had bought her, and had then stolen poison from Vivian's own stash to try to kill her and the former Master. Kupa couldn't be allowed to live.

Even so, the woman was not a priority. Vivian would wait; she could be patient.

Panh had come up behind her. "You are like a cat denied your mouse," he teased, biting the skin of her neck lightly. "So adorable. I'm going to get our equipment." Panh headed for the ATV they'd stolen from the locked boathouse down at the bay. "We need to get into position for when they arrive."

"I want a moment," Vivian said. "I'll send him the photo of the finger. Let him think it's a second one."

"Take all the time you need, then pick a place to shoot from when the chopper comes in. I'll be back and we can finalize our plan." Panh turned on the ATV. The motorized four-wheeler roared into life and he headed down the long driveway.

Vivian tilted her head, studying the finger. Perhaps a different background?

She picked the thing up, a sad little bit of meat and bone, and placed it back on the dragon paw next to the ear. Those trophies were all she had to show for her time with Kupa—for the moment.

A

The chopper sounded like a far-off hum, rapidly increasing in volume.

Vivian lay on her belly on the roof of Connor's mansion, hidden behind the copper flashed chimney that ventilated hot air in summer. Her rifle, a generalized model useful in many kinds of combat situations, rested on the roof in a tripod, its barrel pointed at the helicopter pad.

Panh had returned with their gear. He'd convinced her that Connor was too wily a target to play games with, especially now that they'd lost the hostages. Once he realized Vivian's leverage was gone, Connor would hold nothing back in taking them both out. Surprise was their best chance: kill the man, overpower the chopper, and get off the island before his ninja reinforcements arrived.

The fact that Connor had taken another hour to arrive told them both that he was marshaling his forces and was willing for his hostages to lose a limb or two to that cause.

Vivian's belly gave a flutter as she listened to the increasing roar of the helicopter's engine closing the distance.

There was more aircraft on the way than just Connor's chopper, most likely.

A glance off the back of the mansion's roof had given her a glimpse of several boats approaching the island, drawing foam-edged furrows in the calm waters. They'd already lost the ability to make it to their jet boat before they were cut off.

She and Panh couldn't afford to stay long.

Vivian calmed her breathing as a black Bell Jet two-passenger helicopter dropped out of the sky toward the landing pad. She ticked over the steps she would take as she drew measured breaths and consciously relaxed her body against the hard ceramic tiles of the roof.

Knowing Panh was providing backup strengthened the steel of her spine.

The chopper slowed its descent, swaying slightly in an updraft.

Two figures were visible in the windows: a dark-skinned pilot, rendered anonymous by his gear, and a blond man, his paler complexion and light hair catching the sun even through the helmet.

Vivian applied her eye to the scope.

The rifle would kick; she'd draped her shoulder with a folded towel to help absorb the recoil. This wasn't a sniper rifle, but the range to target wasn't that far. It would be adequate to the task. She checked the chamber; the armor-piercing round was already loaded but making sure of it was reassuring. She had a couple more, but likely would only get one clean shot.

The chopper settled, beginning to spin down, its blades slowing.

The two men in the cockpit would be looking around for her, for the kidnap victims. They'd see nothing unusual; she had picked up the discarded ropes and Panh had kicked dirt over the blood of the torture site near the front steps.

She had, however, left the evidence of Kupa's sacrifice on the dragon's paws. Hopefully, they'd see that at some point.

Vivian slowed her breathing as she zeroed in on Connor.

The blond man's hair gleamed through his flight helmet, glimpsed through the window of the chopper. The shot was a difficult one with so many layers of tough material to penetrate. She'd have to trust the weapon and the specialized ammo.

Vivian closed her attention to anything but the target circle centered on Connor's head. She exhaled gently and squeezed the trigger.

The recoil slammed Vivian in the shoulder and pushed her a couple of feet down the slippery ceramic tiles of the roof.

By the time she hauled herself back into position using her elbows and knees, the helicopter was attempting to rise, spinning in a crazy arc. The windscreen was blown out on the passenger side, but they were still able to fly.

Connor was slumped in his seat, blood a bright banner staining the broken helmet as the pilot fought to get the bird up in the air again.

They needed that chopper!

Panh was running toward the aircraft from the barn as they'd planned, weapon drawn.

He'd get the chopper and the pilot; all Vivian had to do now was join him.

Vivian grabbed the rope tied around the chimney, clipped it onto the climbing harness she wore, and pushed herself away with her feet to slide down the tiles of the roof toward the ground.

Chapter Twenty-Nine

Nine gripped the collective of the helicopter, lifting it off the ground by main force before the blades were at full rotation. The Bell Jet heeled to-and-fro, spinning in a wobbly circle.

"No!" Connor screamed from the back of the chopper. "We're not taking off until we get Pim Wat!"

He was trapped behind the front seats in the small cargo area of the two-person aircraft by a dummy wearing a flight suit. The dummy's helmet, containing a mannequin's head in a blond wig stuffed with a bag of strawberry syrup, had been blown all over the cockpit.

"Nine!" Connor's precaution had yielded results, but his compatriot in the pilot's seat wasn't following the plan. "Put the chopper back down!"

"Your life is my priority, Master!" Nine yelled over his shoulder. "We're getting out of here!"

His faithful friend was betraying him.

Changing the plan.

Denying Connor his prize.

Rage wasn't red. Rage was white: a white-hot blinding surge of energy that propelled Connor out of the confines of the chopper's tail, through the narrow space between the seats, and out the broken area of the windscreen.

Connor landed in a fighting stance in front of the chopper, weapon drawn, scanning for Pim Wat.

A man was running toward him from the barn, a gun held two-handed.

Something hit him square in the chest, throwing Connor back against the nose of the weaving helicopter whose roar drowned out the sound of the shot.

Connor slid off the aircraft onto the ground. Dimly, he heard the cessation of the chopper's engines.

He struggled to draw a breath.

His lungs were emptied of air; his heart fluttered uselessly.

Connor's gaze was on the sky overhead and the slowing blur of the Bell Jet's whirling blades. He'd been wearing a vest, and the material had caught the round. Still, the impact had thrown his heartbeat off, and knocked the wind right out of him. It hurt like a son of a bitch.

Spots of black filled his vision. His diaphragm spasmed.

Voices were raised in argument over his prone body, speaking a language he didn't know. Pim Wat's beautiful new face filled his visual.

Connor's mouth opened and closed; he'd be able to breathe eventually, but he might pass out first. Passing out right now was a bad idea.

"He's alive!" Pim Wat shrieked. A knife appeared in her hand. She leaned over and stabbed Connor hard in the gut, where the edge of the vest had ridden up. He felt the stab as a blow. No actual pain accompanied it. "This will do for you, usurper." She grinned down at him, a demon from nightmares, her blade dripping. "I'll enjoy knowing it will take a while for you to die."

The scream of the chopper's engine was deafening as it spun up again.

Pim Wat silhouetted above him, her blonde hair whirling, her face dark with anger.

The blades became invisible; the motion was just a vibration roaring all around him.

Pim Wat was the last thing he'd see.

"No." Connor's mouth formed the shape of a name. *"Sophie."*

He pictured her face. His vision narrowed to a black dot and winked out.

Chapter Thirty

Vivian stood over the fallen body of her enemy, blood on her combat knife. She stared in disbelief as the chopper, carrying Panh and the pilot, rose into the sky without her. Panh gazed down at her from the passenger side, his tanned face expressionless.

"So it wasn't mutual," Vivian whispered, surprised.

Surprised by hurt.

By the sour taste of betrayal, then sadness.

Yes, she could still feel all those things. "You bastard. My revenge list just got longer when I thought it was getting shorter."

The chopper rose until Panh's blank dark eyes were rendered invisible by distance.

The aircraft banked, flying out over the ocean.

She looked back down at the living corpse at her feet.

Losing her ride with Panh had been worth it.

Connor wasn't gone yet, but he would be. Nothing could stop that now. He would die the painful, lingering death she'd planned for him. His eyes were closed; he looked dead already.

It would take hours; hours she had to use to find some other way off the island, regrettably.

"Goodbye, usurper. This is for my beloved." Vivian spat on his wound, from which blood welled, soaking the abdomen area of his jumpsuit.

Vivian wiped the poisoned blade on her pants, sheathed it, and trotted to the ATV parked beside the metal barn. She hopped astride, turned the quad on, and roared down the curving driveway, heading for the boathouse.

Of course, she had a plan B.

Being able to take the chopper had not been guaranteed, so she and Panh had discussed other ways to get off this little rock.

They'd left the speedboat they'd arrived in tied up down by dock. She had a decent chance of getting away, if she could make it out of the harbor before the other boats reached it.

She had to try.

Chapter Thirty-One

The Learjet's wheels had barely stopped rolling as the plane landed on Phi Ni, when Raveaux turned the handle on the inside door of the aircraft and pushed it open. Weapon drawn, he took cover behind the doorway as hydraulic stairs automatically began unfolding to reach the sun battered tarmac of the island's airstrip.

Across from him, CIA agent Devin McDonald also scanned the empty area. "No other aircraft here."

"Could be something hidden in the hangar." Raveaux indicated the outbuilding with his pistol.

The huge metal shed was rusted and twisted; several sections of its roof were missing, doubtless from the typhoon they'd heard had hammered the island. Still, the segmented metal main door appeared closed and intact.

"I don't think so. Looks deserted," McDonald said.

"We need to find a way to get up to the house," Raveaux said. "Connor said there should be transport in the hangar left over from before."

Two other agents, all McDonald had been able to round up in Thailand on such short notice, peered out as well.

They'd spent the short flight from Bangkok to the island studying topographical maps of the island's simple geography and discussing their plan to provide support to Connor and Nine, and, hopefully, transport of Pim Wat when she was taken captive.

"If there's anything going down, it's already happening at the house on the top of the hill," Raveaux said. "Let's go check the hangar for the truck and ATV Connor said were there."

The four men, heavily armed, went down the steps to the tarmac, leaving the pilot, who doubled as a medic, guarding the plane.

They'd made it halfway to the hangar when distant gunshots sounded from the area of the mansion. Only a few moments later, a chopper rose, tiny in the distance.

McDonald cursed. "Connor was supposed to beat us to the island by only few minutes. Something's already happened."

The chopper swung out over the sea and turned toward the mainland. "Looks like they're getting away," Raveaux said. "We have to get up there and see what happened." Raveaux broke into a run toward the battered hangar.

Connor had informed them where he'd hidden keys to an extra ATV and a pickup truck used for work inside the hangar; hopefully, they'd still be there. McDonald tried the side door. "It's unlocked."

Suddenly Raveaux heard a high-pitched revving from the direction the helicopter had taken.

He paused, frozen in place, scanning the sky. From where he stood, he had a clear line of sight on the aircraft as it wove back and forth over the ocean, and then abruptly went into a dive—straight into the water.

All four of them stared, open-mouthed, as the aircraft hit the surface with a shriek of metal and began sinking rapidly.

"What the hell?" McDonald exclaimed.

Something was very wrong.

None of the scenarios they'd discussed with Connor had ended with the chopper diving into the ocean! The wreckage was too far away to see, but the thing had plummeted like a stone.

"We have to get out there and see if anyone's left alive," Raveaux said.

"Yeah. If we can get to the boathouse," McDonald finished his thought.

The hangar was empty but for piles of palm fronds and debris from the typhoon.

McDonald swore. "Looks like we're going to have to hike it. Let's split up: two of us go to the boathouse, two to the mansion."

Just then, Raveaux heard the sound of an approaching automobile engine.

He ran back outside to the tarmac, his weapon in low ready position.

The battered white pickup truck Connor had told them to look for was driving toward them, a Thai man with gray hair at the wheel with a woman beside him in the passenger seat.

The agents drew their weapons, tracking the truck as it drew near. The vehicle pulled up beside the group and stopped.

Raveaux lowered his weapon. This had to be Connor's man Nam; the man's face was bruised from a beating. Beside him sat a woman, black hair framing a face that would be pretty when it wasn't pale, streaked with blood, and distorted by swelling.

Nam lowered the window. "We are Pim Wat's hostages. We escaped."

McDonald and the other agents holstered their weapons, and they all approached the truck.

"What's happening up there?" Raveaux asked.

"We don't know. We escaped from Pim Wat and her partner and took the vehicle, which we'd parked near the house," Nam said. "My wife needs medical attention."

"Help her!" McDonald snapped. His agents got moving, rushing around the side of the truck to open the door and support the woman out of the vehicle. "Go with your wife to the jet," McDonald said. "Our pilot is a medic. I will leave a man to guard you."

"I saw the chopper go down," Nam said as he got out of the truck. "That is not good."

"Who was in it?" Raveaux asked.

"I worry that it was the Master, Pim Wat, and her partner. Those two were trying to get the Master to come out to the island by hurting us. They want to kill him," Nam said. "Perhaps the Master or his pilot, Nine, dove the craft into the sea." Nam was tottering on his feet; one of the agents helped him and his wife to the plane.

"We have to get up to the house and figure out who was on the aircraft," Raveaux told McDonald. "Let's go."

"You drive," McDonald said.

Nam had left the keys in the ignition; Raveaux got into the driver's seat. McDonald gave a brief nod and his extra man hopped into the bed of the truck as McDonald climbed in beside Raveaux.

Raveaux threw the stick shift into gear and squashed the gas pedal to the floor. The old truck leaped forward with a roar and charged up the road toward Connor's mansion.

They passed the turnoff to the boathouse and harbor and ascended the long hill toward the house. Raveaux turned his head to look as McDonald pointed out the window. "Check out all those boats."

From the steep ridge they were ascending, a cluster of various types of boats were clearly visible in the waters near the site of the chopper crash.

"Connor said he was sending his men by sea. I'm sure they're investigating the wreck," Raveaux said. "If anyone's alive, his men will find them."

"Probably." But the CIA agent's heavy brow was knit by a frown; clearly, he didn't like not being able to get there first.

Raveaux breathed easier, though; his hope had been that any survivors were reached before the chopper sank entirely.

He refocused on the road. A carefully constructed, curving route designed to make the most of the views on the way to Connor's mansion, the coral stone throughway was littered with fallen palm fronds, pieces of roofing from the boathouse or the hangar, and broken branches, some of which provided a hazard to drive over. Even so, Raveaux was soon pulling the truck around the circular drive and stopping in front of Connor's cliff-top home, scanning for danger. McDonald and his agent exited the vehicle in combat stances, their weapons at the ready, and then spread out to check the area for danger.

Raveaux saw nothing and no one threatening—until he spotted a man's body in a flight suit sprawled on the ground near the helipad.

"There's a victim here!"

Raveaux jumped back into the truck and gunned the vehicle to pull up in a spray of gravel beside the fallen man.

Raveaux recognized Connor as soon as he opened the door.

The Master of the Yām Khûmkạn lay on his back in a pool of blood that had formed beneath the darkly stained flight jumpsuit he wore. His skin was pale as paper, his lips bluish, and his eyes were closed.

Raveaux knelt and felt at Connor's neck for a pulse. Sluggish, thready—but the man's heart was still beating. His chest rose and fell, the movement almost indiscernible—he was breathing.

"Connor, it's me, Pierre Raveaux. I'm with you," he said, scanning for the man's injuries. The main one appeared to be a stab wound to the gut. Blood was still welling slowly from it. Raveaux peeled up an eyelid—no response. Connor was unconscious. "We're getting you help."

True, they had a medic aboard the jet, but the man needed more than that—he needed a hospital, and fast.

Raveaux spoke aloud anyway. "Just hang in there. Help is on the way, and you're safe now. Those two assassins took a long dive into the ocean on the chopper; I have to assume your man Nine gave his life to end theirs."

Connor's body spasmed.

Perhaps Raveaux shouldn't have said that; Nine had been the man's closest friend. "Everything's going to be fine. Just keep breathing."

Raveaux opened the jumpsuit and uncovered a bulletproof vest. A round was lodged in the fabric directly over Connor's heart. "Oh, I see what happened here. They shot you, the bullet knocked you down, and then they stabbed you. Assholes. No honor."

McDonald returned at a huffing, puffing jog, hoisting his belt around his girth. "Area's clear. Looks like two people ate a meal inside the house. We found the ropes the hostages were bound with. No one's here but him. The two perps probably took the chopper and the pilot suicided them all into the ocean."

"Looks like it." This summary fit the facts they had so far. "Connor needs emergency care ASAP. Let's get him into the truck bed and down to the jet. We can fly him to the Thai mainland if he makes it that far alive."

McDonald gave a brief nod. He, his man, and Raveaux gently lifted Connor onto a beach towel Raveaux found in the truck. Then, keeping the towel taut, they carried him atop that and lifted him into the pickup bed.

Raveaux asked them to ride with the injured man in the back, keeping pressure on Connor's wound and stabilizing his body for transport. Raveaux drove as fast as he was able without jouncing too much, back down the long white coral road to the airstrip.

The third CIA man, alerted by McDonald, came running from the jet. The four men each took a corner of the towel and held Connor that way, trotting to the aircraft and maneuvering him carefully up the steps and inside.

The pilot/medic had just administered a shot of something to Nam's wife, who was lying back in one of the reclining seats, her hand and one side of her head heavily bandaged.

"What have we got?" the pilot asked crisply.

"Male, mid-thirties, suffering from gut stab wound and bruising on chest due to bullet impact on a vest," McDonald said. "His blood pressure is lower than it should be, even given the amount of blood he lost. This wound shouldn't be affecting him as much as it appears to be. Perhaps there's another injury we're not aware of."

Raveaux moved over next to Nam and Kupa. The couple watched the pilot insert an IV into Connor's arm, expressions of horror and grief on their faces. "Will the Master live?" Nam asked Raveaux.

"No reason to think he won't," Raveaux said stoutly.

"Pim Wat uses poisons on her weapons," Kupa's soft voice was heavily accented, but clear. "If she was the one to stab him, he will die." With a sudden movement, she buried her face in her husband's chest and let out a sob of utter heartbreak.

Nam embraced her, patted her back.

More sobs followed, escalating in volume. A dam seemed to have broken inside the woman; who knew what she had suffered at Pim Wat's hands besides her obvious wounds?

"Perhaps your wife would be more comfortable in the bedroom where she can rest in privacy?" Raveaux said gently.

Nam nodded. He helped Kupa with an arm around her waist and supported the weeping woman to the jet's stateroom.

Raveaux refocused on the medical attention Connor was getting. "Can you get him stable enough to transport to a hospital?"

"I think so." The pilot had put an oxygen mask on Connor's face and a bag of fluids was now hydrating him. "Fortunately, we have basics on board for emergencies. I need to get a catheter into him and pump in the fluids. If he's been poisoned—which would explain his low blood pressure since the wound is not that severe—getting his system to purge the poison will be key."

"And a transfusion, as soon as we can get him to a hospital, is also key," McDonald added. "Wheels up as soon as you have him ready? We can monitor his vitals once he's hooked up to everything."

"Roger that," the pilot said.

Raveaux turned away to gaze out the door of the jet at the deserted, storm-battered island as the agents worked on Connor.

Sophie was on her way to Phi Ni with a Security Solutions team, but she'd arrive to an empty airstrip and an abandoned island.

He had to call her and let her know what had happened. Leave a message at least. Maybe she could redirect to the Thai mainland and join them at the hospital if she so chose—he had a feeling that she'd want to be by Connor's side.

"We need to find out what happened with the chopper crash." McDonald joined him in the doorway. The portly man mopped his streaming red face with a bandanna. "Would you like to stay here and meet with the ninjas down at the boathouse, or shall I?"

"Leave me one of your men—someone who speaks Thai and can translate—and I'll stay," Raveaux said. Truth was, he didn't want to sit vigil at Connor's bedside to witness Sophie arrive and weep over the man. "I'll call Ms. Smithson now and let her know about Connor. You and your team can get him to where he has a chance at survival."

"Will do," McDonald said. "Agent Baxter will stay with you; he speaks the language."

Raveaux nodded and took out his phone to call Sophie.

Chapter Thirty-Two

❧

Sophie was still trying to connect to the satellite to get a view of the island, when the Security Solutions' jet pilot announced that they were descending to Phi Ni.

She went back out to the seating area. The men were strapped in for landing and slung about with weapons. "Any luck?" Lono Jones asked.

"No." Sophie took her seat. She closed her eyes and focused on taking deep, even breaths.

There was no telling what they'd face when they arrived. She needed to be ready for anything, and she felt far from it. At least she'd been able get a short nap, eat, and dispose of the breast milk that had accumulated during the flight.

She'd have felt better about all of this if she could have contacted Armita to check on the children, but her satellite phone hadn't been able to get a connection either.

Still, a full security detail from the agency was staked out around her house and all the alarms were on. It truly didn't get any safer than that.

Hopefully she'd land and discover that Pim Wat had been neutralized, in whatever form that took.

The jet swooped down and soon pulled to a halt in front of the familiar metal hangar, part of its roof missing due to the typhoon she'd heard about. Sophie frowned as she gazed out the window. There were no other aircraft on the runway—what did that mean?

Sophie thumbed to her phone's satellite connection and pushed the button to try to connect yet again; this time it went through. As the men tossed aside their seat belts and opened the door of the jet, Sophie retrieved a voicemail from Raveaux.

"I hoped your phone was on, Sophie, but since it isn't, I'll be seeing you in person when you land. I'm here on the island with one of McDonald's men who speaks Thai, to assess what happened and coordinate that with the ninjas Connor sent over from the compound by boat." Raveaux's usually pleasant, accented voice was hoarse with stress. "Connor was seriously injured in a confrontation with Pim Wat and an unknown male partner. It appears that the two of them escaped in Connor's chopper with Connor's man Nine piloting. Nine then dove the helicopter into the ocean. His body, and that of Pim Wat's partner, were recovered from the wreck."

Sophie covered her mouth with a hand, her eyes wide. She continued to listen as Raveaux blew out a breath. "We are still looking for Pim Wat's body, but currents are strong where the chopper went down, and she could have washed out of the broken windshield." Raveaux cleared his throat. "On the positive side, Nam and Kupa escaped their captors and are alive and mostly intact. Connor and the two of them were taken on the CIA jet to the Thai mainland to a hospital. Kupa thinks Connor was poisoned, and his symptoms seem consistent with that. Hopefully I will have more information by the time I see you."

He ended the message.

Sophie raised her hand, catching Jones's attention as he and the men prepared to deplane. "Is anyone out there? We have friendlies on island."

"Don't see anyone yet," Jones said.

"I have intel. Gather round and listen." Sophie put the phone on speaker and played Raveaux's voicemail.

"Sounds like we missed all the action." Jones raised a brow. "What do you want to do?"

"I need to find out the location of the hospital where Connor and Kupa were taken. I'd like to leave immediately to see how they are doing over there. Are you okay proceeding on foot without me?"

"No problem. We'll find Raveaux and follow up with him. Take a man with you, just in case you run into anything."

"That's fine—though likely unnecessary." Sophie waved the team off the aircraft and went to the cockpit to speak to the pilot. "Is your radio working? I need to reach the CIA jet that was just here and find out the name of the hospital nearest where they landed."

Sophie walked down the dingy hall of the hospital where the CIA had brought Connor. One of the Security Solutions operatives flanked her; he'd ended up being more of a hindrance than a help, as the two of them presented an intimidating sight that demanded explanation wherever they went.

But she was almost to Connor's bedside.

She'd been able to track down McDonald and his plane, and they'd left the island before she even saw Raveaux. She felt a little bad about that, but McDonald had been blunt about Connor's prognosis. "Looks like he's not going to make it. Get here soon to say your goodbyes. The docs ran a tox screen on him and yeah, the man was poisoned."

Sophie focused on her immediate surroundings: the smell of heavy antiseptic and something musty. Fluorescent bulbs flickering in low electrical current. Stains on the shiny linoleum and acoustic ceiling tiles. The sounds of a hospital anywhere in the world: beeping, amplified calls over an intercom, the distant moans of someone in pain.

She drew in a deep breath and let it out slowly as she arrived at Connor's room. She frowned at several black-clad ninjas and a couple of CIA agents, faced off against each other in the hallway in an unfriendly truce outside the door. Sophie spared them a glance.

"Stay out here," she told her Security Solutions escort. "Looks like you have plenty of company."

The Yām Khûmkạn ninjas on either side of the door eyed her up and down, but clearly recognized her as she was allowed entrance between them. Sophie grasped the door handle, bracing herself for what she'd witness on the other side of it.

She'd seen more than her fair share of men she loved on their backs in a hospital bed with death hovering nearby.

It wasn't fair . . .

"But life isn't fair, is it, Sophie?" her friend and therapist, Dr. Wilson, had asked more than once in the course of their work together. "Thinking it should be fair contributes to depression. Accepting what you cannot change, while working to change what you can? That's what helps you overcome."

She could use a hug from Dr. Wilson right about now.

Sophie pushed the metal handle down on the door and slipped inside.

Chapter Thirty-Three

Raveaux stood on the dock beside the boathouse and watched the Security Solutions jet take off from the airstrip on the other side of the large coconut grove that surrounded the small harbor area. He swallowed, absorbing the body blow of Sophie's departure without even a phone call to him.

The jet had been parked for twenty minutes, max, just long enough for Sophie to tap into Phi Ni's satellite wireless hookup, retrieve his message, and take off again for the Thai mainland, leaving to see Connor in the hospital.

Raveaux pulled his phone out of his pocket and looked down at it.

Would she call him to tell him what she was doing, that she'd see him later, that she was glad he'd left a message for her?

But the phone didn't ring.

She didn't care enough to try to make contact.

Hadn't even sent a text acknowledging his message.

Nothing.

No, not one shred of communication for her good friend, Pierre Raveaux.

Sophie's mind and heart were entirely taken up by Connor and his situation.

But when Connor died, and there was no doubt he was dying, Raveaux would still be there. Faithful friend, loving godfather, shoulder to lean on, confidante, work partner, chef.

Even if Raveaux never had Sophie's whole heart, he'd be happy with whatever she chose to give—and time was on his side.

Raveaux swallowed his feelings and slid the phone back into his pocket.

The radio McDonald had left him with burst into life in a buzz of static. "Raveaux? This is Lono Jones. We're on Phi Ni with five operatives. What's your twenty?"

"Raveaux here. Currently at the boathouse with the translator. I'll let the men know you're en route, and that you're friendlies."

"Roger that. On our way."

Raveaux hung the radio back on his belt and nodded to McDonald's translator. "Let the ninjas know a group of six operatives with Security Solutions are on their way."

"Got it." The CIA operative turned to the squad leader of Connor's men and broke into a spate of Thai language.

He turned to face the two bodies, covered by a tarpaulin, that had been recovered from the helicopter crash area and now lay on the dock. Pools of water had gathered on the deck from the bodies' soaked clothing. One of the men was Connor's closest lieutenant, Nine, according to the Yām Khûmkạn squad leader. The other was the unknown assassin who'd been traveling with Pim Wat.

Of Pim Wat herself, they'd found no trace.

Raveaux walked toward the end of the dock, his gaze passing over the black jet boat Pim Wat and her partner had arrived in, still tied to the dock.

He frowned as he studied the remains of the twisted metal and Plexiglas chopper the ninjas had retrieved. The body of the aircraft was mostly intact; it had been lifted out of the ocean using a net winch and deposited on the broad deck of a large fishing trawler. They'd brought the craft in so the wrecked chopper could be investigated and had tied it off to one of the pilings.

From what the ninjas had ascertained, Nine had dived the helicopter at high speed into the sea; despite that, the aircraft's height and velocity hadn't been enough to tear the chopper apart when it hit the water. Instead, the propeller had crumpled and sheared off, and one door had come away from the metal body. The aircraft had sunk nose first, water flooding in through the broken windshield, a pocket of air in the tail keeping it from sinking entirely.

Nine and the unknown man, strapped into their seats in front, had likely been knocked out by the impact and then drowned as the craft filled with water; but they wouldn't be getting a formal autopsy to find out. This entire operation was going to be handled off-the-books by the CIA—and that was a relief. Trying to explain this complex situation to the Thai police would likely end up with everyone in jail.

Raveaux approached the trawler and stared thoughtfully at the wreckage.

Pim Wat must have been sitting in the small, fold-down jump seat in the tail section, according to the men who'd gone inside to retrieve the bodies.

Could she have escaped? Or her body washed away?

The other men had still been belted into their seats. She would have had to get out of the wreck somehow, or she'd still be there, too.

Currents in the crash area had already carried away the broken door and propeller by the time the flotilla of ninjas had arrived in their varied watercraft; it was possible that if Pim Wat had survived and escaped the wreckage before it filled with water, she'd been swept away.

But she couldn't have survived in the open ocean for long. The ninjas had patrolled the water for hours, looking for her. A few boats were still out there, dragging the area with nets, searching for her body.

Raveaux, trailed by McDonald's translator Agent Baxter, stepped onto the fishing vessel tied at the dock. The smell of seawater, gasoline, and something like burnt hair filled his nostrils, taking him back to other crime and accident scenes he'd worked.

Raveaux approached the tied-down wreck, grateful for the latex gloves in a box he spotted just outside the dripping hull of the chopper. Hopefully the CIA would get their scene techs in here and give it a going-over, looking for trace related to Pim Wat. Much as Raveaux wanted to hope she'd died in the crash, it would be dangerous to assume so without proof.

Pim Wat had more lives than the proverbial American cat.

Inside the chopper, moisture slid down from the roof and walls. The smell of gasoline was almost overwhelming. "Make sure no one has an open flame anywhere near this area," Raveaux barked to the translator.

"Copy that," Agent Baxter agreed.

Raveaux squeezed between the two front seats into the tail area. He navigated around the sodden dummy figure Connor had put in the front seat; its helmet was still in place, but the faceplate was blown out. Red syrup stained the jumpsuit it had been dressed in.

Connor had been smart to use the decoy. Nam and Kupa's escape had probably been discovered by Pim Wat by the time he arrived in the chopper. With no hostages to negotiate with, she and her partner had nothing to lose by taking Connor out right away.

Raveaux squatted in the narrow tail area, lifting the wet, slack belt of the small, fold-down seat to examine it.

Someone had sat here recently; the belt was not retracted. Raveaux held up the restraint. Its flip open clasp was set at a familiar length, maybe a little longer than he used himself.

Raveaux's heart rate sped up.

Connor, who had a similar waist size to Raveaux, had been the last person to sit in this seat—not a petite woman of a hundred pounds or so.

Raveaux's head spun. He hadn't eaten that day, but that wasn't the reason he felt sick.

Pim Wat hadn't been on the chopper when it went down; she'd never been on it at all.

The woman could be anywhere right now—on the island, or off

it. They'd lost valuable time thinking she'd gone down on the chopper.

Raveaux whirled, startling the translator. "Pim Wat was never on board. Shut down the island; no one gets on or off Phi Ni until we check every single boat, plane, vehicle, or other means of transport. She might still be here."

Chapter Thirty-Four

Lono Jones jogged toward Raveaux as he stood on the dock. The blond man wore camouflage fatigues and a distance rifle slung across his chest, with a backpack of outdoor gear, weapons and equipment strapped to his back. Four other Security Solutions private operatives fell in behind him.

"Raveaux." Jones halted, his gaze on the draped bodies. "Ms. Smithson took the jet and one of our men to the Thai mainland to meet with the CIA and check on the health of the Master of the Yām Khûmkạn."

"I guessed that was the case when I saw the plane take off again," Raveaux said. He'd been working with Jones for a couple of months now as he filled in for Sophie's position during her maternity leave; he'd found the man to be tough, quiet, hardworking and a solid investigator. "Pim Wat never got on the aircraft. She's still somewhere on the island."

Raveaux gestured to the ninjas, working with Agent Baxter to separate themselves into parties of two. "We're organizing a search grid. Going to start at one end of the island and go all the way to the other. No stone unturned, no hole in the ground unexplored, no coconut tree unshaken."

"And the boats?" Jones's sun-bleached brows had drawn together over sharp hazel eyes. "That's where she'd have been heading to first."

"Of course." Raveaux inclined his head. "The translator is working with the boat captains. Every single craft that came here from the mainland is being accounted for and searched, as we speak."

"Have you checked the boathouse?"

"Not personally, no." Raveaux's brows lifted. "What are you thinking?"

"I spent the plane ride over looking at topographical maps with Sophie and re-creating, to the best of her memory, the contents of the house and buildings. The boathouse contained not only Connor's luxury motor launch, but a couple of inflatables, including a survival boat on the launch itself. A storage room inside held recreational scuba gear and a cache of survival gear in case of being stranded at sea or on the island."

"The ninjas verified there is no one inside the boathouse, but that's all I know." Raveaux spoke over his shoulder to Jones and his operatives, already moving toward the entrance to the large wooden building. "But they assumed she was on the chopper, as did we all."

The wooden side door of the boathouse creaked open when Raveaux tugged on the handle.

The typhoon had wreaked havoc in here, too. Sunshine beamed down into the cavernous interior where roofing had been torn off the sturdy building. Random beams of light landed on the motor launch, still tied in its berth, though the shiny sides of the Chris-Craft were dinged and scratched. The sectioned door that let out to sea had been torn away by surf that had pounded the normally placid little bay, and the contents of the boathouse, once neatly organized, were tossed hither and yon by the elements.

Lono slipped past Raveaux and headed to a storage room on one side of the building, its door twisted and warped but ajar.

Raveaux, following, noticed an ATV parked on one side of the wall. "Did Sophie say anything about an ATV being down here?"

"Yes. She said there was a pickup truck and an ATV kept at the hangar. A second ATV was stored here for coming to and going from the boathouse."

They passed the ATV, but Raveaux paused to examine it as Lono moved on to open the storage room door with the help of one of the Security Solutions men.

The heavy-duty four-wheeler had coral stone dust embedded in its nubby tires, but that wasn't what gave him pause; it was the lack of any dust on its seat and the smell of fuel and oil around its engine. The keys dangled from the ignition.

"If we took prints off these keys, I believe they'd match those of Pim Wat," he said. "She was here."

"What?" Lono and his companions had finally wrenched the warped, twisted door fully open. "This is where the spare inflatables and survival gear were stored."

The operatives moved aside so that Raveaux could enter behind Jones. They stood in the doorway and surveyed the once tidy storage area. Lined with large, bracket style hooks upon which gear was hung, the room was well-organized. A section of roof had been torn away, exposing the room to the elements, and bringing in storm debris. Wind had knocked things about, but heavier items were still in place.

A clearly labeled survival raft, still in its plastic zip-up duffel, hung on one wall, along with collapsible oars and paddles. Oxygen tanks, spears, fishing equipment and scuba gear including masks, regulators, inflatable vests, fins, and snorkels took up the rest of the wall. Medical equipment, enough to run a small field hospital, took up a second section of the room. A generator and survival style dehydrated food and large containers of water filled floor-to-ceiling shelves on a third wall.

"She had everything she needed right here."

Raveaux didn't realize he'd spoken aloud until Jones gave him a sharp look. "Do you notice anything missing? Because I do."

Raveaux pointed to the wet suits, hanging on a small rack. "If Connor kept scuba gear here for his vacations with Sophie, there would have been a wet suit in her size. I don't see one."

"Exactly. Sophie told me he had two sets of gear for himself, and one for her. They never got to use the equipment before the island was seized; it was brand new." Jones indicated the remaining equipment. "All I see are two sets of men's scuba gear."

"And didn't you say there were two survival rafts?" Raveaux pointed to the single one hanging there.

"I did say that."

"So, here's what I think happened," Raveaux said. "Pim Wat and her partner took a break from torturing their captives to go into the house and raid it for food. They left Nam and Kupa tied up. One of them should have kept an eye on them, because somehow the hostages got loose. They ran off and hid. Pim Wat and her partner came out and discovered they'd lost their leverage."

"They decided to get the drop on the Master when he arrived. No more negotiation," Jones filled in.

"Right. They tried to take him out, but he had the dummy in place and that took the bullet. He should have just pulled out on the chopper once that happened, but instead he got out of the chopper and got shot for his trouble. The round hit him in the vest and took him down; then, Pim Wat came in and tried to finish him off with a poisoned blade to the gut."

"Pretty theatrical." Jones scowled. "Very *Game of Thrones*. Why didn't she get on the chopper with her partner?"

"I don't know." Raveaux stroked the swatch of goatee on his chin, staring at the hook with the missing scuba gear. "Some kind of disagreement?"

"So, she left the Master there, certain he'd die—and then what?"

"The two split up for some reason. Maybe a falling out, maybe wanting to spread the odds of escape. The partner took the chopper, and Pim Wat took the ATV back to the boathouse. She probably wanted to get to the jet boat they brought here, but the other boats had cut her off. She had to improvise. She came in here and helped herself to a set of scuba gear and an inflatable, and whatever else— maybe some food and water. But it couldn't have been much, because she likely evaded the ninjas patrolling the bay here, by staying underneath the water in the scuba gear."

"The ninjas need to know all this. So does the CIA," Jones said. "We need to close the noose around her. She must still be on the island."

"I'll tell the ninjas. I've been communicating through their squad leaders. We can move the search from the land to the water," Agent Baxter said.

"I'd like to be the one to make the call to McDonald," Raveaux told Agent Baxter. "I'd like a sit-rep on what's happening over at the hospital, too."

"You got it." The man took a satellite-enabled phone off his belt and handed it to Raveaux. "Direct line to Agent McDonald, and from him to the international task force."

"Good." Raveaux took the heavy phone. He glanced at Jones. "Why don't you and your men help with the search?"

"On it." Jones and his companions went off at a jog with Agent Baxter.

Raveaux cast one last glance at the rack of wet suits and the empty bracket where the inflatable had hung. Had they covered every possibility of where Pim Wat could have gone? Something was still nagging at him—but he had a phone call to make.

Chapter Thirty-Five

✤

CIA Agent Devin McDonald picked up on the second ring. "Agent Baxter. What's going on over there?"

"Agent McDonald, this is Pierre Raveaux." Raveaux paused to gather his thoughts. "Your man is translating our most recent discoveries to the ninjas of the Yām Khûmkạn. His help has been invaluable."

"Gotcha. Proceed." McDonald was puffing as though he were walking somewhere.

Raveaux gazed around the storage room, breathing its musty odors. "Pim Wat is alive, and she never got on that chopper." He walked out of the oppressive atmosphere of the little room, summarizing the deductive process he and Lono Jones had used to figure out Pim Wat's likeliest escape route. "We think she stole the inflatable and used scuba gear to evade detection in the boathouse area."

McDonald cursed for a bit; Raveaux heartily agreed with his sentiments.

"Don't you have a shit ton of boats staffed with ninjas patrolling around? How far could she have gone, in a survival inflatable that's neither fast nor maneuverable?"

"Valid points," Raveaux said. He'd left the boathouse to stand on the dock, looking out past the wrecked chopper on its fishing trawler platform. The gentle sunshine of the fading day felt good on his skin. Where would he spend the night? He hadn't brought camping gear. Once again, a wave of dizziness struck—he needed food and rest. "My guess is that Pim Wat is hiding out, waiting for darkness to make a run for it—or push off in her raft, more likely." He cleared his throat. "How is Connor doing? Has Sophie Smithson arrived yet?"

"He's in intensive care and not likely to survive," McDonald said. "Yes, Ms. Smithson's here. Just went in to see him, in fact. We've got guards on the room, and so does the Yām Khûmkạn." A pause—McDonald was clearly thinking about something. "With Pim Wat still out there, Connor has not fulfilled the terms of his immunity agreement."

Raveaux clenched the phone, biting his tongue on an angry response.

He was in no position to advocate for the cyber-vigilante currently at death's door due to his efforts to stop Pim Wat, an enemy of the United States as well as countless countries around the world. No, he was not going to say a word about the relentless and unfair way the CIA was using Connor, when he, himself, was vulnerable to deportation as a French citizen.

McDonald seemed to have reached a decision. "If Connor stabilizes enough for transport, we'll take him to where he can get better care."

Meaning—they'd be flying him to Guantánamo Bay and holding him indefinitely for interrogation. That had always been their ultimate goal; Connor, and his computers, held the secrets of criminals around the world.

Raveaux couldn't advocate for the man, but he could call someone who would: *Sophie.*

He needed to get off the phone now and reach out to her before McDonald had time to kidnap Connor out of his hospital bed. "We'll continue to comb the island and its surrounding waters for Pim Wat."

"Thanks for keeping me posted." The CIA man ended the call.

Raveaux speed-dialed Sophie, but her phone went straight to voicemail. His gut clenched.

He left a terse message: Pim Wat was missing but likely alive, and McDonald was going to try to take Connor at the hospital. Raveaux ended the call with a punch of his thumb.

If they could just arrest Pim Wat, all the drama would be over.

Lono Jones came striding back, the translator in tow. Jones had a distinctive, graceful way of moving, while Agent Baxter bobbed like a duckling in his wake. "Nightfall's coming. We organized the boats; they are going to make a ring around the island and keep watch for her. Tomorrow, when there's enough light, we'll do a grid search of the island and check every square yard of it."

"Good plan." Raveaux yawned; his jaw cracked. "I didn't pack for camping. Do your men have any extra gear and rations?"

"Unfortunately, no." Lono cocked his head, gazing uphill in the direction of Connor's mansion in the waning light. "But according to Sophie, there's a whole empty house up there on the hill with top-of-the-line beds and food in the cupboards. Take the ATV; you and the translator can bunk up there."

"Good idea." Now that there was a possibility of rest and food, Raveaux swayed on his feet. He gestured to Agent Baxter. "Let's get the ATV and go up to the house."

Jones frowned. "Pim Wat's still out there. I don't think you should go alone. We'll come and set up our tents. The ninjas can cover the boathouse area and do the stakeout by water."

"Agreed." Raveaux yawned again. "See you up there."

Raveaux and Agent Baxter went back into the boathouse and fetched the ATV.

"We're right behind you." Jones and the Security Solutions men put their packs on and headed for the road at a jog.

Agent Baxter had his weapon out as they pulled into the deserted parking area beside the large metal barn near the house. He hopped off the back of the ATV and headed for the large double doors.

"We should wait for Jones and his men to make sure the house is clear," Raveaux said.

Agent Baxter halted at the dramatic bronze dragons guarding the door. "Aw, crap." He pointed to an ear and a finger decorating the upraised paws of the dragon. "Looks like your friend left something for us to find."

Raveaux approached slowly, his dicey stomach rolling as he regarded the mangled bits of flesh. "Pim Wat is anything but my friend."

"A figure of speech. I meant no offense."

Raveaux regarded the translator. A youngish man of mixed race, Agent Baxter had the kind of pleasant, forgettable face that performed well in espionage work.

The CIA agent had turned to watch the progress of Jones and his men as they tackled the hill on foot. "I feel bad for those guys."

"They got plenty of rest on their flight here," Raveaux said. "We have had none."

"True that." Agent Baxter's gaze swiveled back to Raveaux. "Should we bag this as evidence?"

"Do you have any bags on you?"

"No."

"Hopefully Jones has some in his gear."

"Any chance Pim Wat's in there?" Agent Baxter's eyes gleamed. "Maybe we should go in and see. Nab her ourselves."

"Pim Wat is both competent and deadly, and she's somewhere on this island or in the water around it—so yes, she could be inside. We'd be fools to think we could take her when she's got the advantage," Raveaux said. "Do not underestimate her because she's a woman."

Agent Baxter checked the magazine of his nine-mil pistol, clearly torn between caution and ambition. "I'm going in."

Raveaux opened his mouth to protest, but the agent had already slipped between the massive wooden double doors and disappeared inside.

Chapter Thirty-Six

Lono Jones and his men reached the front doors of Connor's mansion where Raveaux waited. "Where's Agent Baxter?"

Raveaux threw a thumb over his shoulder. "Went inside."

Jones's brows shot up. "She could have circled back around and holed up in there."

"He wanted a chance at her."

Jones jerked his head to the men. "Check if it's clear."

Raveaux watched the cadre of men open the big doors and enter. He felt no compulsion to follow.

Instead, he rummaged in Jones's discarded gear duffel for an evidence bag. He found several, along with latex gloves. He donned the latex and returned to the bronze dragon. He carefully peeled the bloody, sticky ear off the dragon's paw and placed it in one bag, then slid the finger into another. He closed and labeled them.

Agent Baxter and Jones reappeared, holstering their weapons. "All clear. No sign of anyone inside. Leftover food on the stove and table was the same as what the original reports indicated," Agent Baxter said.

Raveaux stowed the grisly reminders of Kupa's suffering in his leather satchel. "Let's go see if there's anything edible in the pantry."

He wasn't hungry any longer, but the needs of his body would resurface again soon.

An hour later, his belly full of a cobbled together meal of rice, canned beans, and vegetables, Raveaux bid adieu to the men, who'd broken into Connor's stash of high-grade liquors. They had lit candles around the dining room table and had settled in with several bottles and a deck of cards.

Raveaux didn't drink and was too tired for socializing. Carrying his precious satchel and an LED lantern from the pantry, he left in search of a place to sleep.

The bedroom wing of the house was on the opposite side from the kitchen/dining area. Raveaux peered into the rooms he passed, curious about them. He located Connor's computer office, a cool musty space with sliding glass doors that faced the fallen goddess Kuan Yin in the center of the house's interior courtyard.

He found a luxurious restroom with a bath big enough to descend into via built-in steps. The bath had a view of the darkened sea dotted with atolls, a-shimmer in moonlight. The master bedroom adjoining it was unabashedly masculine in design and color scheme.

Nearby was the guest suite Sophie had described staying in when she visited here: a series of rooms with comfortable tropical-themed furniture and fans made of woven palm fronds overhead, frozen in stillness now that the power was out.

Raveaux found a queen-sized bed, already made up, in Sophie's suite. The room was intact and only a little dusty. He set his LED lantern on the stand beside the bed and stripped off his clothing. He splashed water from a gallon jug of drinking water into the nearby bathroom's sink. He washed up, eager to cleanse away the filth of the day before resting.

Clean at last, he slid his weary, naked body between the slightly musty sheets, closed his eyes, and was gone.

Raveaux slept heavily, but his dreams were disturbed. All of them rotated around chasing Pim Wat; she was always just ahead of him, a deadly phantom with bone-white hair, carrying a blade that dripped poisoned blood.

Raveaux woke suddenly, reaching for the weapon stowed under his pillow.

Agent Baxter stared down at him. "The ninjas found something. We need to get down to the boathouse."

Raveaux and Agent Baxter roared down the drive on the ATV in a morning so new the sky barely blushed with color. They'd left Jones and his men undisturbed, sleeping off their night of debauch; there was nothing they could add to the current situation.

Agent Baxter hopped off the back of the ATV before it had even stopped rolling, speaking in rapid Thai to the squad leader of the Yām Khûmkạn he'd been liaising with. The squad leader pointed to one of the fishing boats the ninjas had commandeered; the boat was towing a yellow inflatable raft.

Raveaux waited at the end of the dock, shifting impatiently from foot to foot, until the craft squeezed in beside the trawler with the wrecked chopper on it.

"He says the boats were patrolling as we set them to do, and this one found this inflatable at first light, adrift off the south end of the island," Agent Baxter told him.

"Looks like the inflatable Pim Wat stole." Raveaux jumped onto the deck of the fishing boat, pressing through a knot of ninjas to survey the inflatable bobbing off the stern. The small round raft was empty but for a wet suit, buoyancy vest, regulator, and a scuba tank. "She abandoned this equipment. Why? Where did she go?"

"No idea," Agent Baxter said from his shoulder. The men around them were speaking rapidly among themselves with many hand gestures. "The ninjas say they saw a flare go up very early this morning. All the boats went to investigate, and crisscrossing the area, they found the inflatable. They are still off the south point of the island, searching the water for her."

Raveaux's heart gave a sudden lurch. He whirled and pushed his way through the men, jumping out of the boat and onto the dock.

He pounded down the wooden timbers to the boathouse. Powered by adrenaline, he yanked open the heavy side door and ran inside.

Connor's powerful luxury motor launch was gone from its berth, and the broken exit door that opened into the bay was raised just enough for it to escape.

He cursed.

Agent Baxter and the ninja squad leader reached him. "What is it?"

Raveaux pointed to the empty mooring. "The whole thing with the inflatable was a diversion so that she could steal Connor's motor launch and escape in it."

Chapter Thirty-Seven

The guttural rumble of the motor launch's engine as it roared toward the mainland lifted Vivian's flagging energy. She'd hardly slept all night, but she'd done it—she'd escaped that awful little island. Thumbed her nose at the CIA, and at the Yām Khûmkạn, too.

Vivian checked the instrument panel and her heading. Using her phone's GPS, she'd chosen a small fishing village on the Thai coast to head for. It wasn't the closest bit of coastline from Phi Ni, but they'd be looking for her there, and Google Earth had shown her that area was a hellish mangrove swamp.

Once she reached the village, she'd have to change her appearance, contact Mendoza, and figure out where to go next—all before the ninjas and the CIA caught up with her.

Hopefully Mendoza would have some ideas for her—she was counting on it.

Vivian ended up being glad of the two large gas receptacles that had been left full in the stern of the Chris-Craft. She used both to make it all the way to the fishing village.

After tying up at the weather-beaten community dock, Vivian told the fishermen who flocked to examine the exotic motor launch that she'd been out for a drive on the boat and got lost from the island she'd been vacationing on. Where was a hotel where she could eat, rest, and call her husband to figure out a return?

She was practically carried on the shoulders of helpful villagers all the way to a rustic little inn whose rooms were located over the only restaurant in town. Once there, Vivian asked to hire someone to fetch and carry. For a few American dollars, she was able to have a teenage boy run around town and bring her all the supplies she needed.

Meanwhile, she called Enrique Mendoza on a freshly charged, brand new burner phone.

"I thought they got you." Her boss's voice was crisp. "Is this a secure line?"

"The best I could do." The phone had been the first thing Vivian's teenage helper had fetched, purchased in its packaging from someone's uncle who imported such things. "The Chameleon is out of the game." She described the events of the last few days. "I'm getting a new look, and then I need to move. Where should I go?"

"Certainly not back to Paris," Mendoza said. "As you know, I keep a network of operatives around the globe. I want you somewhere with no extradition to the USA, and that limits us."

"Extradition is the least of my worries. Do you think the CIA is going to give me due process? Don't forget, I've already spent two years in Guantánamo." Vivian stroked her jawline as she spoke, remembering her mutilated face and the terrible years she'd mentally escaped by going into catatonia. "I'm not going back."

"Of course you aren't," Mendoza snorted. "You're only good to me somewhere you can blend, where you can't be taken legally, and where you can move about and do jobs for me. I have a couple of countries you can pick from for a new home base."

"Oh, good. Anything but Russia. I've lost my taste for cold." Vivian paced in the small but cozy room; woven matting softened her footsteps on the wooden floor, and colorful linens brightened a bed draped in pretty mosquito netting. "I like the Arab Emirates. Indonesia. Taiwan."

"You can coordinate some of our textile and furniture design when we pick a place as a part of your duties for Kaleidoscope; I know you'll be good at that." She heard Mendoza shuffling some papers. "Where are you hunkered down? Are you safe to stay there a few days while I get you new ID documents?"

"I can't stay here." Vivian walked to the window and gazed down into the dirt street of the village and at the dock beyond. "I'm very noticeable, unfortunately; word will get out to the Yām Khûmkạn that I'm here. They have spies everywhere. I'm just in this village long enough to dye my hair, get new clothes, and find transport. I'll go to your safe house in Bangkok."

"Perfect." Mendoza rattled off an address. "I'll have new ID documents messengered to you there ASAP."

He ended the call.

Vivian slid the phone into the pocket of her filthy pants—everything she wore was the worse for wear after her time on Phi Ni. She couldn't wait to get clean and get rid of these clothes.

A knock rattled the inn's thin door.

The teenager she'd hired stood in the doorway, his arms laden with a woven basket filled with bright fabrics, cosmetics, and a bottle of henna, probably the best he could find as far as hair color. "What you asked for, miss."

Vivian gifted him a genuine smile. "You were quick, young man. And did you keep my purchases confidential?" She winked at him and made him blush. "I'm going to surprise my husband with a new look."

"Of course, miss." He handed her the basket. "Is there anything else you require?"

"Yes. Women's shoes in size six. Preferably black Western style high heels," Vivian said. "If anyone has a pair they're willing to part with, I will pay handsomely. My husband likes them, thinks they're sexy."

The boy blushed, doubtless entertaining a mental movie starring Vivian with nothing on but dyed red hair and high black heels. "I will try to find some, miss."

"I also need transportation to Bangkok. A driver with a reliable car. I'd like to leave as soon as I am ready."

"I know a man who can take you there for a fee. Very good, very fast." The boy nodded emphatically; the driver was probably a relative.

"Good. Come back in an hour with the car and my new shoes." Vivian handed the kid a handful of bills. "For your trouble."

The teenager scurried off, hoisting up a pair of ill-fitting Western jeans.

Vivian watched him go thoughtfully.

Should she silence him permanently when she had all she needed?

She was on a clock; the searchers from Phi Ni would be scouring the coast as soon as they realized her duplicity and could reach the mainland in their watercraft. Both CIA and Yām Khûmkạn spy networks could be actively looking for her even now. They'd want a description of her current appearance, and they'd pay well for it. Killing the boy wouldn't stop the gossip about her. Too many people had seen her arrive, and the boy had to buy her supplies from individuals who would also talk.

She needed to hurry up and get on her way.

Vivian took the clothing out of the basket.

Several different traditional Thai women's outfits in different color schemes had been provided. Vivian picked out a tunic in rich purple and a pair of black pants. She'd wrap a scarf in contrasting shades of yellow around her head and wear the large black sunglasses that the boy had included.

Vivian grabbed the bottle of henna and headed for the bathroom.

A

An hour later, Vivian waved goodbye to her teenaged helper from the back of a Toyota Prius as she and the car's driver exited the village.

The hybrid vehicle had been modified for the environment: the suspension was jacked up and heavy-tread tires dealt with the mud and dirt of the road. A woven bamboo luggage rack crowned the roof.

Vivian gazed ahead through the windshield; the dirt road ahead was empty, and it would likely be that way for a while. "As fast as you can, please," she told the driver.

"Yes, miss." The man pressed down on the accelerator.

The driver was the boy's uncle, and he'd been eager to play chauffeur. Seemed to believe her story of going to Bangkok to surprise her husband for their anniversary and make up for her mishap with their boat.

But it didn't really matter if he believed her tale or not, as long as he got her to Bangkok, and quickly. She'd given him an address a few miles from Mendoza's safe house; the Yām Khûmkạn or the CIA would be questioning him later, no doubt.

Vivian glanced down at the lidded basket on the seat beside her; she'd packed extra outfits and cosmetics in it in case she needed further changes. She leaned her head into the corner of the seat as the driver tuned to a Thai radio music channel and traditional melodies filled the car.

Oh, she was tired. She'd only slept a few hours in the dead of the previous night and hadn't been able to rest at all after Panh had abandoned her.

Thinking about Panh's death brought a smile to her lips.

Her erstwhile partner had done her a favor leaving her behind.

Vivian knew how fanatically devoted to the Master the chopper pilot Nine was, but Panh had not. Nine's suicide dive into the ocean would not have happened if Vivian had been on board; she'd have made sure of it.

Instead, Panh had taken that long dive to death while Vivian had driven off on the ATV and reached the boathouse before the ninjas did—but not far enough ahead of them to get away in the jet boat, her original plan. Improvising, she'd taken the dive gear and the inflatable, planning how she could sneak back for the motor launch later by using the inflatable as a diversion.

Getting into the scuba equipment and submerging in the water inside the boathouse had been a bit harrowing; the harbor had been filling with boats and ninjas by then. Towing the unwieldy inflatable, a weight belt wrapped around it to keep it underwater, she'd managed to pass beneath the boats undetected, exit the harbor, and find a little niche in the rocks around the corner from the bay to hole up in until darkness.

She'd still had to drag the inflatable underwater to the south beach, launch it with the auto inflater, shoot the flare, and then hurry all the way back to the harbor on foot.

By then, Vivian's physical reserves were used up—but as she'd hoped, the harbor had emptied, and no one guarded the boathouse. She'd driven the motor launch out without interference.

Hopefully she'd bought a few hours before they discovered its loss, but they wouldn't be far behind her.

Vivian closed her eyes; she might as well rest while she could.

Chapter Thirty-Eight

Connor was adrift.

He was floating on a black sea, with an equally dark sky pressing down on him.

Or perhaps he was floating deep inside the ocean.

Didn't really matter which it was.

Thoughts flickered past with the movement of tiny silver fish; he could catch them if he cared to.

Some part of him was still awake and aware—that part that knew he wasn't really floating in space, surrounded by thoughts taking the form of silvery fish.

He was deep inside his body, and that body was dying.

The process was neither as painful nor as frightening as he'd anticipated.

Connor had passed the point of fearing death some time ago through his spiritual practices; but he'd had a lingering curiosity about how that passage would occur, and a hope that it wouldn't be excessively painful or lingering.

This?

This was a good death.

He'd died fighting formidable enemies and that was acceptable, though he wished he'd inflicted at least a little damage on those enemies.

Did he have regrets?

Only that he had never been able to make it up to Sophie for the lies he'd told her. For the suffering she'd experienced thinking him dead. For not compromising his passion for justice enough to be with her.

The criminals he'd sent to oblivion in pursuit of that ideal were no comfort to him now.

It would've been great to have died of old age instead, his beloved beside him until the end.

He'd lost his chance for that life, and he regretted that alone.

Connor felt a sense of lift within that spark of consciousness.

Readiness, anticipation even.

He was about to fly away somewhere; he was leaving this dark waiting room behind.

"Connor."

Sophie's voice was far away, a reverberation like an echo in a tunnel.

Though there was no direction in this place, he fastened his attention on that vibration.

"Connor. I'm here with you. It's me, Sophie. Please don't go."

A tremble in her voice.

Something warm and wet splashed on his surface.

He had a surface, an edge that was him, and a black that was not.

This was a new awareness.

"I have loved you since before we met, Connor. Even when I knew I was a fool. Even when I knew I couldn't make a life with you, I loved you anyway." Sophie's voice broke. *"Some part of me always thought we would have more time. Believed we could figure it all out somehow, some year."* A shuddering sigh. *"Even when I was with Jake, some part of me was always yours. Please don't go. I want more time . . ."*

Another of those splashes wet the edge of him.

Her tears were striking his surface, amplified, rippling all the way to his core, clamoring through his being like church bells.

"I know I said we were done, that last time I saw you, but I was scared. Scared of our situation, of who you were becoming as the Master. But for better or worse, I've always loved you."

She stopped speaking.

Where was she?

Why had she stopped talking to him?

Her voice had been drawing him closer and closer to that surface that was him and then not him.

The Master, seated cross-legged on his tiger's-eye plinth, spoke in memory. "Reality is just a set of agreements we've made together," he said. "You can disregard them anytime you believe you can."

He had been willing to disappear to whatever was next—even if that was nothing.

But—Sophie was here, now.

She loved him, and she was calling to him. She wanted more time with him.

He had to return to her.

Connor must push the poison that was slowly paralyzing all his autonomic functions out of his system. He could do it; he'd healed himself many times. This was just a different injury.

His consciousness perceived the workings of his body as a landscape: sluggish rivers of blood, glitching threads of nerves, dark pools of dying cells breaking down as his bodily systems failed.

That tiny spark of awareness that was called Connor began to spin; it spun and spun deep within his body. It spun so fiercely, that the poison was pushed out ahead of the light and heat of his essence. The poison and damage rose like oil to his surface and dissolved away at the edge of him.

Connor woke.

Chapter Thirty-Nine

Sophie had rested her head on Connor's sheet-covered upper thigh, carefully avoiding his catheter, IV line, and the strapping that covered the stab wound in his midsection. "Nothing to be done but wait," the doctor had told her. "The wound itself is not life-threatening; it's what was on the blade that made it so."

She'd been there for hours, and she'd been tired when she arrived.

Sophie hadn't realized how she felt about Connor until it was clear he was dying; one look at his bluish lips and waxy skin had told her he was barely hanging on.

She'd said her truth. No point in holding back.

She'd cried.

Sometime after that, Sophie wasn't sure when, she'd fallen asleep.

Now she woke abruptly, sitting upright so quickly her head swam. The tears she'd shed had dried on her cheeks, and on his arm where they'd fallen.

A strange, unpleasant smell permeated Connor's skin. She frowned, staring down at him. Was his color a little better?

She glanced at the monitors; everything looked good. Much better than it had been, in fact; his heart and respiration rate were increasing, strong and steady.

Connor's fingers beside her twitched, then his hand opened and closed, patting the bedclothes as if seeking something.

Sophie grasped his hand in both of hers. "Connor. I'm here!"

His eyes opened; they were bloodshot with petechial hemorrhaging related to the poison. He looked ghastly, but very awake.

"I want to be with you, too." His lips barely moved; his voice was a thread. "The only thing I want is to be with you."

Sophie released a great, wrenching sob, tightening her grip on his hand. "Please don't die."

"I'm not dying anymore."

Sophie leaned over and hugged him gently and awkwardly. She clung to his shoulders and let go the wall of tears she'd kept inside: tears for the first time she thought she'd lost him and all the time they'd never get back because of that. Tears for Jake, who she still grieved. Tears that carried all the stress and fear of the last few days.

Connor's hand came up to stroke her back, her cheek, her hair. He murmured in her ear. "Sophie. My Sophie. I love you so much."

She closed her eyes, letting herself relax into resting flush against him in a moment of perfection, as if a key turned in a lock, opening an entirely new door—and what lay ahead was hope and joy.

The phone in her pocket, which had been on silent, buzzed with a message and ruptured the sweetness of their union.

Sophie fished her phone out and pressed PLAY on a message from Raveaux, which came out on speaker. "Pim Wat escaped, and the CIA is likely to try to grab Connor if he doesn't die. Please be safe, Sophie." The Frenchman's accented voice was rough with emotion. "Lono, I, and the ninjas Connor sent here to Phi Ni will catch Pim Wat. She can't have gotten far. But get Connor out of there before the CIA tries to take him!"

Sophie, galvanized by a flashback to another time she'd had to defend a man she loved while he lay defenseless in a hospital bed, shot to her feet. She ran to the door to shove a chair beneath the handle. A scuffle and raised voices outside the door reinforced her fear as she pressed the alarm button beside Connor's bed to call for help.

Meanwhile, Connor had elevated the back of his bed and detached his IV. More alarms went off; the room filled with beeping and flashing.

"What are you doing?" Sophie exclaimed.

"We need to go." Life appeared to be flowing back into him by the minute as color returned to his grayish skin. "I can move."

"We're surrounded by your men and we're on Thai soil. The CIA can't make a move against you here," Sophie said. As if to give lie to her words, the unmistakable sounds of a conflict penetrated the door: cries and grunts, the thump of a body against the door, a gunshot.

Sophie unlocked the bed's brake and shoved the heavy contraption against the wall, out of the line of fire from the door. More alarms beeped and screeched. She drew her weapon and faced the door, guarding the bed.

"We have to get back to the Yām Khûmkạn fortress." Connor detached the monitor around his chest and took the oxygen cannula out of his nose.

A loud knock came from the door—three long, two short. "That's a signal from my men," Connor said. "Let them in."

"You are not walking anywhere," Sophie snarled. "Stay right where you are. We'll push that bed wherever we need to go."

Connor smiled with a ghost of his old charm. "Love it when you boss me around."

Sophie snorted. She approached the door cautiously and peeked through the small, wire-threaded window into the hall.

The two CIA men lay flat on their faces, trussed with their hands and feet behind their backs. The four ninjas and her Security Solutions man who'd been guarding the door peered in at her anxiously.

Sophie removed the chair and opened the heavy portal. "We need a chopper back to the Yām Khûmkạn fortress, now," she barked in Thai. "The Master needs transportation home to recover in safety."

"A helicopter is already on its way, Mistress," the head of squad said. The four black-clad, shaved bald men encircled Connor's bed, displaying no surprise at all that Connor was sitting upright and looking very much alive. Apparently, medical miracles were not a new thing to them. "We can push the Master to the roof where the helicopter will meet us."

Medical personnel rushed in behind the ninjas to assess Connor, but he waved them off. "I'll be fine. Not right away, but eventually. Send your bill to the Yām Khûmkạn," he told his doctor.

The ninjas maneuvered the bulky bed through the door and down the hall. Sophie hurried after them, her weapon still drawn. "Wait here," she told the Security Solutions operative. "Someone will return to get you."

The group hurried down the hallway.

The whole situation was surreal.

Only moments before, Sophie'd been saying what she'd thought was a final goodbye, and now they were on the move to the stronghold of the Yām Khûmkạn.

She would finally see that intimidating fortress she'd heard so much about.

Sophie knit her brows as she trotted in the wake of Connor's bed. She'd never wanted to go to that place, but now she was looking forward to it. Anywhere that they would be safe from both Pim Wat and the CIA was a refuge she'd happily hide in.

That reminded her of something. "Stop!"

The ninjas stopped. She liked how they obeyed her, how they called her "mistress" so respectfully. What had Connor told them about her?

"We have to bring Nam and Kupa. They're in danger too," she told Connor.

"Of course!" Connor barked orders in Thai. Two of the ninjas ran off to fetch their friends.

They resumed moving down the hall, then got on a wide elevator designed for gurneys. One of the men touched the button marked *Roof* and they trundled upward slowly.

Sophie took out her phone and tapped Reply to Raveaux's number, but the call went straight to his voicemail; he must have his device off, or the hospital elevator had a weak signal.

"Pierre, it's Sophie," she said into her phone. "Bad news about my mother but thank you for letting us know so we can prepare. Connor is doing remarkably better and seems to have thrown off the poison's effects. We got your warning just in time. We're on our way to the Yām Khûmkạn fortress now; please keep us updated." She ended the call, slid her phone into her pocket, and looked down at Connor.

He smiled up at her; his aqua-colored eyes were already clear of redness. "Poor Raveaux. He's in love with you, you know."

"Nonsense. Pierre's just a good friend." Sophie didn't want to get into that topic. She stroked Connor's forehead, frowning. "How are you better so fast?"

"Being with my beloved is a tonic." Connor tugged her hand. "Kiss me."

Sophie glanced at the ninjas flanking his bed; the men were doing a statue imitation, staring fixedly at the slow passage of numbers over the door.

She leaned down and kissed Connor, a lingering promise that they both sank into for a moment.

She straightened as the doors opened onto the rooftop gardens the hospital was famous for. Her lips tasted funny; she dashed away bitterness with the back of her hand. "No more kissing until you've brushed your teeth and had a shower."

"The poison is coming out through my skin," Connor said. "I'm sorry you had to taste it."

"We will have plenty of time for kisses when we're safe and you're better."

Connor squeezed her hand; he didn't let go even as the men pushed his bed through the curving walkways around potted trees and banks of flowers all the way to the helipad.

A jumbo-sized military cargo chopper emblazoned with the name of the Yām Khûmkạn in Thai lettering awaited them, its blades already whirling and its engine so loud that it rendered conversation impossible.

A new squad of ninjas hopped out and ran to surround them.

Soon Connor was ensconced on board, the hospital bed anchored with straps. Sophie sat in a jump seat beside Connor, and the large side doors shut. The men took seats behind them as two pilots navigated from the cockpit in front. The noise of the chopper drowned all attempt at conversation; eventually the ninjas handed them earmuffs to deaden the sound.

Sophie watched out the window as the hospital receded. The skyscrapers and the buildings of Bangkok rose around them. A chaotic but beautiful scene, the city was especially arresting in that moment as sunset gilded the glass of windows and glinted off metal framework and electrical lines. Lights shone from inside homes and the windows of offices; in that way it was like a city anywhere—but the unique shapes of the architecture made it Bangkok.

Connor found her hand once more.

She held his tightly, needing the comfort and reassurance that he was still here, still alive, still with her for as long as they might have to be together.

Chapter Forty

Raveaux slept for the second night in Sophie's bed at the Phi Ni mansion after a long day keeping up the search for Pim Wat. He woke heavy-eyed and lay in the bed staring at the dusty palm frond fan overhead, its woven blades slowly coming into focus in the low morning light.

The Yām Khûmkạn had picked up her trail in a fishing village on the mainland; the villagers there had been eager to tell Connor's operatives of her purchases and the car she'd hired to take her to Bangkok.

But after that, nothing. Not a whisper of her.

McDonald had told Raveaux he was coming to Phi Ni that morning to strategize. Outside his bedroom, voices carried down the hall from the Security Solutions men who'd taken up residence in the house with him.

Raveaux needed to get up. Get some coffee and food into his belly and prepare to talk to the CIA man.

But Sophie's message kept playing in his mind.

Her voice, all business, except for that telltale "we." Repeated several times.

She'd never been a "we" with Connor before. Now, those two were an "us."

His chest felt heavy, as if a sandbag rested on it. Every breath was an effort.

Raveaux tossed the cover aside in an act of will. He swung his legs to the side of the bed and sat up.

He went to the bathroom, poured water from one of the plastic bottles the Security Solutions men had brought up from the boathouse, and brushed his teeth.

He didn't care enough to try to shave, just pulled on clothing from the day before and headed down the hall to the kitchen.

Someone had made a pot of strong pour-over coffee, and Raveaux helped himself to a cup of the black brew.

Jones looked up from where he was packing his gear. "Sleep okay? You look like hell, man."

Raveaux shrugged. "Did McDonald say when he'd reach the island?"

"Oh nine hundred." Jones resumed packing.

The men had bedded down in the various rooms; they were tidying up, preparing to leave. The Security Solutions jet was already fueled up and parked down at the airstrip, but they wouldn't leave until after the meeting with the CIA.

Raveaux took the mug of coffee back to the room he'd been occupying; he needed to stop thinking of the bed he'd slept in as Sophie's.

He gathered his belongings, packed them in his travel duffel, then rejoined Jones and the others at the front of the house.

The truck Nam had been driving, along with the two ATVs, had been parked by the ninjas for the group's use in reaching the airstrip.

Raveaux approached Agent Baxter, who faced away from him, speaking Thai into a walkie-talkie.

"When's your boss getting here?" he asked.

"He's just landing." Agent Baxter pointed at the flash of metal descending toward the island, then gestured to the ATV. "Just you and me going to meet with McDonald?"

"Jones, too." Raveaux inclined his head to Lono Jones, who was exiting the mansion. The man looked laid-back but deadly in dark blue camo, slung about with weapons and gear. "Let's all move down to the airstrip so we're ready for wheels up as soon as we're done."

"Right on." Jones got into the driver's seat of the pickup. "I'll take the guys down the hill. Why don't you lock up and bring the ATVs?"

"Sounds good."

The Security Solutions men piled into the truck, and Jones drove off.

Raveaux and Agent Baxter did a quick walk-through, making sure all lights and water sources were off in case utilities turned back on at some point. Raveaux pulled the heavy teak front door shut behind him, then tossed one set of ATV keys to Agent Baxter. "What were you telling the ninjas just now?"

"More like what they were telling me. They've had orders from the Master to stay here on the island for as long as it takes to clean up the house and the storm damage to the buildings. They're staying in their camp area down by the boathouse until it's done."

Raveaux felt a twinge in his chest—neither Sophie nor Connor had seen fit to apprise him of that. He didn't merit such personal plans. "Seems smart. I haven't seen the caretaker and his wife since they went to the hospital—are they okay?"

"Apparently the couple went to the Yām Khûmkạn fortress with the Master and Ms. Smithson." A tightness around Agent Baxter's mouth was all that revealed the man's annoyance that Connor, Sophie, and Pim Wat's hostages had been able to evade the long arm of the CIA. "Let's roll. Agent McDonald doesn't like to be kept waiting."

Raveaux stowed his gear bag in the carrier on the back of the ATV and slung his leather satchel across his chest. A slight odor rising from the bag reminded him he still carried evidence that desperately needed refrigeration.

He mounted the ATV, turned it on, and fell in behind Agent Baxter as the man roared down the coral stone road.

Once at the airstrip, Raveaux handed his gear off to one of the Security Solutions men and, after parking the ATVs alongside the truck in the metal hangar building, fell in behind Agent Baxter as he walked to the CIA's Learjet.

Agent McDonald didn't get up from his cushy leather recliner to greet Raveaux, Agent Baxter, and Jones as they joined him in the jet's lounge area. "I'm recording this meeting. You okay with that?"

Raveaux and Jones exchanged glances. This was the CIA's meeting, but they represented Security Solutions and would need to report in later. "I'll document as well," Raveaux said, removing his phone and thumbing to an audio recording app.

He set the phone down on the coffee table and took one of the loungers.

McDonald stated the date, time, location, and names of the people present. "I've asked for this meeting to brainstorm about the current situation."

"And what is that, exactly?" Raveaux cocked an ankle on one knee and straightened the pleat of his rumpled trousers.

"Pim Wat, international fugitive, is still at large. We tracked her as far as Bangkok but have lost sight of her after her driver left her off—at a street corner that's equidistant from a shopping area, a train station, a bus station, and the airport," McDonald said.

"We should have someone representing the Yām Khûmkạn at this meeting," Jones said unexpectedly. "The ninjas have plenty of skin in this game."

"The vigilante known as Connor, aka "the Master," is *persona non grata* with the international task force and the USA in particular," McDonald said. "Now that he has been unable to seize Pim Wat, his immunity deal is on hold. We don't want the Yām Khûmkạn at any table with us."

"Jones makes a good point, though," Raveaux said. "The Yām Khûmkạn has an interest in capturing Pim Wat. We'd be wise to keep them on our side and not work at cross-purposes."

A short silence.

Agent Baxter leaned forward. "I may not represent them, but as the translator who's been collaborating with the squad leaders since we were all thrown into this barrel together, I believe I can speak to what their plan is."

McDonald heaved his corpulent form out of the lounger to go to a refrigerator with a bar area atop it. He poured a mini bottle of Scotch into a cut glass tumbler and returned to his seat. "Enlighten us, Agent Baxter."

"The Master and Mistress—they are calling Ms. Smithson that— have withdrawn to the Yām's stronghold so that he can recover from his wounds in safety. The search for Pim Wat continues, with a bounty on her head and the full scope of their spy network activated. The only reason we know anything about Pim Wat's escape and where she ended up is because they chose to tell us." Agent Baxter furrowed his brows in sincerity. "It behooves us to keep the Master on our side, Agent McDonald. No disrespect intended."

"Of course." McDonald flapped a hand. "That incident at the hospital? Two overenthusiastic agents made an unsanctioned move. They certainly came to regret it, and that's what I told Ms. Smithson when she called for more information."

Raveaux frowned, thinking back to Sophie's message. "What are you referring to?"

Agent Baxter turned to him, a smile lurking around his mouth. "Two of the CIA's finest tried to grab Connor at the hospital and ended up trussed like turkeys."

McDonald scowled, pointing to the recorder. "As I said. Unsanctioned. We've apologized to the Master through channels already."

"Where do we go from here? And how can Security Solutions help?" Lono Jones spoke up. "I'm not sure what our position is in all of this."

Raveaux was glad he'd asked; the CIA was holding out on them but wanted their intel, should they get any.

"You can go back to Hawaii and wait for word from the international task force on how you can support the manhunt from there," McDonald said, dripping condescension. "We'll continue to coordinate efforts to find Pim Wat as an international team."

"Sounds like we're done then." Raveaux turned off his device. So did McDonald.

Raveaux and Jones rose from their seats. "Thanks for the waste of time," Jones said.

Raveaux smiled at Lono's back as he followed the blond man down the steps and out of the oppressive atmosphere of the jet. He was really getting to like their newest operative.

Chapter Forty-One

Sophie followed Connor as he was carried on a wooden pallet by four ninjas. The group moved carefully down a flight of rough-cut stone steps into the depths of the Yām Khûmkạn's forbidding fortress in the jungle.

"I'd love to tease you about how these men treat you like a king, but I'm too grateful that they're carrying you," Sophie said in English, for privacy. "This outing better be worth it."

Connor, lying on the litter, turned his head to smile back at her. "I wouldn't be asking them to haul me all the way down to the basement if there wasn't a real reason for it."

They'd arrived at the compound three days before. Sophie had been at Connor's side ever since as he rested and recuperated, his care overseen by a man called the Healer.

The Healer's treatment process had consisted of bowls of tasty broth, a course of antibiotics to prevent infection, strengthening tinctures and teas, and lengthy body massages with herb-infused oil, "to pull the poison out of his system."

Sophie had consented to one of the oil massages as well and found it to be one of the most relaxing and nourishing experiences of her adult life.

Sophie had called McDonald for more information about Pim

Wat's escape, and she and Connor had heard his protestations of ignorance about the attempt to grab him—and the terrible news about Nine's suicide dive which had also taken out Pim Wat's partner.

Connor had gone silent for an entire day, grieving for the loss of his friend and feeling responsible for it, most likely, though he refused to speak of it. Sophie had no words to comfort him for such a loss.

Even with that setback, the wound to Connor's abdomen was healing without complication. He was still weak, barely able to walk more than a few steps to reach the built-in privy closet in the gorgeous suite of rooms where he lived. She was becoming comfortable with him: sleeping platonically in the king-sized bed, playing chess, and taking long naps together.

The rest of the fortress was spartan in the extreme. Sophie joined the men in the courtyard daily as they worked out in rows, perfecting their martial arts forms. Even now, her body was pleasantly sore and tingly from hours of intense training that morning.

The men called her "Mistress," and she was okay with that. Connor always wore a white *gi;* apparently, here, it denoted rank. Sophie had been given the same white robe to wear. The men treated her deferentially, though many a sideways glance came her way from the shaved headed trainees as she practiced with them.

The culture and emotional tenor of the fortress was more supportive and accepting than she'd anticipated—that had to be due to Connor's democratic-style leadership influence. From what Nam and Kupa said, it hadn't always been that way.

Nam and his wife were staying in a suite of rooms close to Connor's. Kupa spent a good deal of time with the Healer as well; he was doing energy work with her and cleansing the trauma from her body and soul with hot oil treatments.

Connor was carried daily by his men, up to the tower room at the top of the highest building, and he and Sophie went online to follow up with the search for Pim Wat.

The first day they'd gone there and Sophie'd had access to a secure phone line, she'd called Armita.

She replayed the conversation in her mind as she navigated the stairs behind Connor and his bearers.

"I'm finally in a place where I have signal. How is everything? Is the security detail still there? Because we didn't get my mother. She's still out there . . ." Sophie was in a rush to know all she could. In the background, Connor reclined on his litter in front of three monitors, a pair of soundproof headphones guaranteeing her privacy.

"All is well. Slow down. Take a breath," Armita said in her severe way.

Sophie did so, blowing out audibly. "Situation report, please."

"Baby Sean is sleeping well, taking his bottle, and adjusting to 100% formula. I've maintained his daily and nightly schedule. Momi's a rascal, as usual, but her father is here to help, visiting with us at the house since I told Alika we didn't want her to go to Kauai until Pim Wat is in custody. The Security Solutions men, and all the alarm systems, are working just fine; we've tested them daily. Or, I should say, Momi has tested them daily." Armita's voice brightened. "Here's our Little Bean now. Come say hi to your mama."

Sophie switched the call to video and was then able to verify that both of her children were in fine form. They loved their new home, and swims in the pool and at the beach, heavily guarded, were a daily part of their routine that seemed to help keep everyone on a good nap schedule.

Sophie greeted Alika and asked that he continue to spend time with Momi at her secure home until Pim Wat was captured. "I know what my mother wants, and more than anything, it's my children. You'd never forgive yourself if Momi was snatched again while at your place on Kauai," Sophie said.

"I agree. But I don't have to like it," Alika grumbled. "I guess Oahu's Fight Club gym will benefit from monthly attention until you nab that witch."

"Thank you," Sophie said sincerely. "I know it's not ideal. And I have some other news. I want to let you know that . . . Connor and I are together now."

Alika's good-looking face was expressionless in the screen on her phone for a long moment. "As your child's father, I wish you had chosen someone closer to home—who wasn't an internationally wanted criminal."

Sophie bit back an angry response. Alika had every right to say he didn't approve; it wasn't fair to expect more from her ex than honesty when the choices she made affected the child they shared. "Connor would no longer be a wanted criminal if we had been able to apprehend my mother. I'm sure it's just a matter of time until we do."

Alika gave a brief nod. "I hope so. I'll give you back to Armita. Momi has gone quiet, and that's never good." He hurried off to see what the foreboding silence from the nursery was about.

The nanny came on to the screen, holding up plump, smiling baby Sean for Sophie's virtual air kisses. "When will you be home?"

"I'm not sure. Connor and I have a lot to figure out now that we are a couple. I may want you and the children to come here where it's safe."

Armita narrowed her eyes. "I lived in that fortress. It's no place for children."

Sophie couldn't disagree; hard stone steps, a damp environment, and limited living area safe for children were not selling points. "I'll call every day now that I have a place where I can reach you regularly." She'd said goodbye, her throat thick with tears, her breasts aching with milk she'd have to express and throw away.

She could not be away from her babies for much longer.

Sophie slid a hand along the worn wooden safety rail as they navigated another turn in the stairs.

The litter bearers made one more turn and arrived at a large wooden portal flanked by torches set in brass holders in the rock wall. They carried Connor in through the door.

Sophie could not withhold a gasp at the sight of a huge, steaming bath the size of a swimming pool lit by flickering flames in holders along the walls. Tendrils of steam wound up from a natural geothermal spring; a flight of steps led down into clear, bubbling water.

"The spring has healing properties," Connor said in Thai. "The men have their own bath for bathing and rejuvenation."

"This is incredible," Sophie sniffed. "It even smells good."

"Leave us in privacy," Connor told the ninjas.

The bearers set the litter carefully on the paved apron around the hot spring pool and departed; they would assume stations guarding outside the door.

"Are you sure you should go in the water with an open wound?" Sophie helped Connor up off the litter.

"It's the best thing I could do to speed my healing," Connor said. "The men are outside. Please make sure we have total privacy."

"All right." Sophie walked over and dropped a heavy wooden bar into a metal stanchion to lock the door. "What is all this secrecy about?"

"The waters have healing properties, as I told you." Connor winked; his playfulness was returning, but he still bent over with one hand pressed against his abdomen as he rested his weight on the wall. "Maybe I just want to be alone with my beloved."

Sophie approached him. "Let me help you get that robe off and down into the water, then."

"Would you please come in with me?" His eyes and voice beseeched her. "It's a special experience, I promise."

"Of course I'll come in, too."

Connor was naked under his robe, and so was Sophie under hers; but this wasn't sexual. They hadn't even kissed since that time in the elevator that had left her mouth tingling with a dangerous, bitter taste.

Sophie helped Connor disrobe, and she slid out of her *gi* as well. The two robes fell onto the blue-gray stone, white clouds against a dark sky.

Sophie took Connor's arm, scanning down his body. The stab wound had been covered with a heavy-duty plastic bandage that seemed to be sealed around the edges. When she brushed it with her fingertips, the ridged muscles of his abdomen quivered, but it wasn't with pain. She pretended not to notice. They walked slowly to the edge of the pool, and then down the steps into the water to take a seat on a built-in stone bench that ran along one side of the pool.

"Oh," she sighed, as the heat enfolded her. "This feels so good."

Connor rested his head on the rim of the pool; Sophie did as well. The water was just right for comfort, and it must have minerals and salt in it because her muscle-heavy body lifted off the bench to float freely. Her very bones were melting inside of her flesh, and when she closed her eyes all she could see was warm red where the torches flickered.

"There are things about me you don't know yet," Connor said from beside her, his voice drowsy and content. "Through the practices I have learned here, I am able to . . . take certain shortcuts."

Sophie turned toward him, her body rotating weightlessly. Even that gentle movement in the hot water was like floating in a primordial sea. "What kind of shortcuts?"

"One of the things I discovered was that the original Master might have been very old. This bath was part of his secret. He was able to come here and heal himself, restore himself. And now I can do it, too."

Sophie's pulse sped up. She gazed at him; brown eyes met turquoise. "Show me."

Connor closed his eyes. His head remained resting on the lip of the pool, but as he relaxed, his body floated to the surface.

Nothing happened for a few long moments. Perhaps whatever was going on was an invisible, interior process.

And then, he began to vibrate.

There was no other word for it. In the dim of the chamber, lit only by flickering torches, his body trembled, generating tiny waves around it, as if he were moving faster somehow, while staying still. A faint glow began to surround him.

Sophie blinked. Rubbed her eyes. If only she had a camera to record the phenomenon! "What is happening?"

"I'm speeding up time inside my body. The glow is the molecules moving faster. I wondered if anyone else could see what was going on, or if only I could." Connor's voice was completely normal.

"Speeding up time! Can you slow it down, too?" Sophie flashed to Raveaux's description of how Connor had seemed to appear and disappear when he was rescuing her and Jake. That must have been how he got them out of the lava tube!

"I'm only able to affect my immediate self and the space around me. I can move time forward, or back just a bit. It takes concentration, though." The light and vibration had faded slightly as he spoke to her. "In its way, this is a natural process. I would recover soon anyway, but coming here, I'm able to do so much more quickly by increasing the speed of healing."

Sophie reached for Connor's hand, needing reassurance. The digits of his fingers shone like burnished metal; his hand held more heat than the water surrounding them. "How did you learn this?"

"I—don't really know. It just began happening when I was meditating with the Master, then when I was sparring with him. This is the great secret of the masters of the Yām Khûmkạn; and it's not written anywhere in any of the literature. I've come to believe it's only passed on experientially. This chamber—this bath—enhances my ability."

"Your own fountain of eternal youth." Sophie pressed his hand against her cheek, then kissed the palm in wonderment. "You are, indeed, the Master now. I feared it at first. On Pali Island. I saw that you were changing—becoming different somehow."

"I was grieving then. I was fighting what had happened with the Master. I never wanted to be his chosen one, and then he forced me to kill him. I lost it emotionally."

"You did what you had to do. Just like I did with my ex-husband. We are killers, you and I."

"And we are also warriors, in our way. Leaders. Teachers. Mentors. Parents, even." Connor smiled with his eyes still closed; the faint light within him faded. "You are the most wonderful distraction."

Sophie pressed close against his side, taking his body in her arms so that they floated, drifting away from the edge of the pool.

Holding this amazing man and being held by him was the purest magic. Connor was healing her, too, in ways she didn't yet know and couldn't express.

Gradually, his internal heat began to dissipate, and soon it was just the two of them, floating in each other's arms in a warm mineral spring deep within the earth.

"I hope this means we get to kiss now," Sophie said.

"I was hoping for much more than kisses."

That set up a throb deep inside; she lowered her legs and stood up in the chest-deep water. "Let me see you. Make sure you're okay."

Connor rose to his feet beside her. He stretched fully upright, his muscular arms rising high above his head. He seemed taller; but likely it was just that he was no longer hunched over, protecting the stab area.

"I can take this bandage off now." Connor reached to his abdomen and, before Sophie could object, ripped off the waterproof bandage. He tossed it onto the lip of the bath.

"I want to check your wound." Sophie bent to look but couldn't see beneath the water in the dim light.

"Let's get out and cool off a bit. You can check for damage in the torchlight." The underlying vibrato of pain in Connor's voice was gone. He sounded as young and energetic as he'd been when she first met him, each word holding a smile. "I think you might be surprised by what you find."

Sophie kept hold of Connor's hand as they ascended out of the pool, their nakedness dripping water on the stone coping. Connor walked over to stand directly in front of one of the torches.

Sophie bent to examine the site of the wound. She had to feel his skin to locate where the poisonous stab had been. Nothing was left but a thin hairline scar.

Her gaze traveled over him, checking for injury; there was none. Connor stood quietly before her: ageless, perfect, a golden god of a man.

"Like what you see?" One of his brows went up; his turquoise eyes twinkled, teasing.

"Of course, I do." Sophie's throat closed. Her eyes filled. "You're —unbelievable."

"And you're the most beautiful woman I've ever seen—but that's not why I love you." Connor took Sophie's hands, drawing her up against his chest. Everywhere that her skin touched his caught fire. "I love you for how brave you are, how intelligent and persistent. You challenge me. Your integrity teaches me. Inspires me."

"Enough talking. Kiss me already," Sophie whispered.

And so, he did—and much more besides.

Everything felt brand-new, like the first time—and in the steamy darkness that enfolded them after the torches finally flickered out, Sophie found peace.

Chapter Forty-Two

One week later . . .

Raveaux pulled his little silver Peugeot into the turnoff for Sophie's new house. He'd been to see the place early in the process of her buying the Kailua estate, but hadn't visited since she'd finished improvements and upgrades and moved in.

The tall, solid, spiked metal gate decorated with ornamental copperwork was an intimidating barrier, with high lava stone walls flanking it. Native Hawaiian plantings, leaning a bit after a recent rain, appeared to be trying to find purchase in the iron red soil they'd been set in.

Raveaux pulled abreast of a sleek black admittance kiosk adorned with a blank screen. He looked for a call button or keypad; there was none.

Sophie's slightly husky, accented voice spoke suddenly from a speaker in the kiosk, making him jump. "Welcome, Pierre Raveaux."

The gate swung open, slowly but smoothly.

Raveaux drove forward, his brows furrowed. Was Sophie home? He'd been trying to reach her for a week since he got back, with no response.

The driveway ended in a circular turnaround. Raveaux parked in front of the wide front verandah, scanning the area and noting changes: more new plantings and a miniature child's bike, fallen on its side beside a red wagon near the stairs.

Sophie's dogs barked from inside the house, but it was the pair of Security Solutions operatives in trademarked black polo shirts and pants approaching from the nearby guesthouse that captured Raveaux's full attention.

"Welcome, Monsieur Raveaux," one of them said. "We just need to check your car, and you can leave any weapons you're carrying with us."

"Check my car for what?" Raveaux got out of the Peugeot. "And I'm not armed."

"Hope you won't be offended if we verify that," one of the men said. "We understand you're the children's godfather?"

"I am." Raveaux submitted stiffly to a pat down. "Is Sophie here?"

"My name is Bill," the older, white operative said, not answering his question. "Since you'll be a frequent visitor, we might as well get to know each other. We're part of a regular team who will be on hand here at the estate to provide the family's security."

Raveaux shook hands with Bill, and his younger Asian partner Clement. "I'm relieved to see that security is so stringent," he said. "Though the greeting at the kiosk surprised me a bit."

"You're one of only a few people Ms. Smithson pre-admitted to the security system at the gate via facial recognition," Clement said.

Raveaux's chest tightened—she had thought of him, after all. "That's good. I'd like to get familiar with the security measures Sophie has left for the family in her absence. If you don't mind."

"I'm afraid we'll have to get permission for that directly from Ms. Smithson herself," Bill said. "But since we know you also work for Security Solutions, I can assure you that every bell and whistle the company offers, and more besides, make this one of the most secure locations we've ever provided services for."

"Good. I'd like to see the family, then, if you don't mind. I have gifts for the children." He reached back inside the Peugeot. He wasn't surprised when Clement wanded the wrapped presents he'd brought for Momi and Sean from his recent trip abroad. The items had been purchased in the airport, but still—a godfather had certain obligations.

Formalities observed, Clement led Raveaux to the front door of the house and rang the bell for him. It was a long couple of minutes with the dogs barking hysterically on the other side of the door before Raveaux heard the pattering of Momi's footsteps and the little girl pulled down on the handle and opened the door.

"Unco Perro!" She flung herself on Raveaux and hugged his legs. Ginger and Anubis sniffed him over, wagging their tails. Clement waved goodbye and he and Bill made their way back to the guesthouse.

Raveaux picked Momi up and tickled her with his nose, making her giggle.

Armita, dressed in her habitual all-black yoga outfit, appeared carrying Sean. The plump, sturdy baby had filled out even more since Raveaux had seen him last; his toothless grin was a treat to see.

"Good to see you at our new home, Raveaux," Armita said. "Momi has been asking for you. Haven't you, my girl?"

"Unco Perro! Did you bring me a present?" Momi was already tugging at the wrapped gift under his arm.

"Little Bean. Manners!" Armita said. "Offer Uncle Pierre some refreshment, first."

Momi wriggled to get down. Clearly this was a new routine, but her brown eyes were bright as she took a couple of steps back to look up at Raveaux. "Unco Perro, would you like something to eat or drink?"

"Why yes. Thank you, *ma petite*," Raveaux said, interested to see where this went.

"Follow me!" Momi turned and ran off down the tiled hall. "I get you something!"

Raveaux followed at a more sedate pace beside Armita. "May I hold Sean?"

"Of course." The nanny handed the baby over.

Raveaux hugged Sean close, inhaling the warm scent of his skin. Sean emitted a chuckle as Raveaux tickled him gently with his whiskers and blew on his neck, reveling in the sweet, solid weight in his arms. "Where's Sophie? She hasn't returned my calls."

"She's still in Thailand." The nanny seemed to be avoiding his gaze as they entered the great room that looked out over the infinity pool and yard with the ocean in the distance. "She has limited connectivity. I'm sure she'll be in touch soon."

Momi was in the kitchen; the tot was filling a plastic drinking glass with water from the door of the big steel refrigerator. She walked toward Raveaux with it held in both hands and presented it proudly. "Here you go, Unco."

"Thank you so much, Little Bean." He bent to kiss both of her cheeks European style; Sean still clasped close to his chest. "And you offered me something to eat?"

Momi popped a finger in her mouth, suddenly unsure, and her gaze swiveled to Armita.

"Ask Uncle what he feels like having. Then I will help you make it."

"Unco Perro, what you like?" The little girl's combination of Hawaiian pidgin and baby talk was adorable.

"Well, I don't know. I haven't had lunch . . ."

"A sandwich!" Momi shouted. "I know how to make peanut butter and jelly!"

"That would be delightful. I'll wait with Sean out here," Raveaux said.

Armita followed Momi into the kitchen and their murmuring voices were a gentle music in the background as he sat on the low couch in the great room. He joggled baby Sean on his knees, offering a rattle he found on the nearby bouncer seat.

Soon Momi reappeared, carrying a sandwich on a plastic plate. She navigated over to Raveaux and offered it. "Now can I get my present?"

Armita rolled her eyes heavenward, but Raveaux laughed. "Thanks for the refreshment, Little Bean. Yes, you may have your present." He gave the gift to Momi, then picked up the sandwich and took a bite. "Mmm. Delicious."

Momi uncovered a hand-carved wooden puppet with strings, a traditional Thai toy. "I like it, Unco Perro!"

Raveaux handed the baby to Armita and undertook to demonstrate the puppet. It was a bit beyond Momi's current motor skills to operate, but she loved watching Raveaux make the jointed arms and legs move as if walking and dancing.

Sean began fussing—it appeared to be time for his nap. "Want to take Momi to the pool for a swim while I put him down?" Armita asked.

"I would love it, but I didn't bring a bathing suit," Raveaux said.

Armita smiled. "Sophie already ordered you one—and a robe. They're in the cabana outside."

Raveaux must have revealed how that touched him, because Armita's face sobered into its usual severe lines. She took a breath, then blew it out and said, "Sophie is not for you, Pierre. She is with Connor now in Thailand. As a couple."

"Ah. I see." The sandwich Raveaux had eaten turned to a ball of lead in his stomach.

"I'm sorry to tell you, but I would not want you to imagine something that wasn't true," Armita said in her dignified way. "I hope that does not change your feelings for the children."

"Of course it doesn't. I love them." Raveaux kept his gaze on Momi as she played with the jointed legs of the puppet. "Thank you for letting me know."

Sean wriggled and let out a howl, clearly ready for nap time.

"I have to put him down," Armita said. "You will be all right. Go out with one of the other women who like you. I hear there are several." And with that pithy bit of advice, she carried the wailing baby away.

Momi jumped up and grabbed his hand. "Let's go swimming, Unco Perro!"

Raveaux followed the little girl out through the sliders to the pool.

He *would* be all right, eventually. He'd been through much harder things than having his hopes dashed.

And in the meantime, Sophie had shared her children with him. He had a chance to be a father figure again, and for that, he'd always be grateful.

Chapter Forty-Three

Sophie pulled her SUV into the garage at the house in Kailua a little more than ten days after rushing out of it in pursuit of her mother.

She and Armita, seated beside her, turned to look back at the children in their car seats. Both had fallen asleep during the drive home from picking Sophie up from the airport.

Twilight, lit by motion-activated sensor lights, wrapped around the buildings. The security team had waved to the arriving car from the guesthouse but, per their usual protocol, didn't come to speak unless she requested it. Sophie would meet with them the following morning for a check-in.

"It's too early for bed, but too late for naps," Armita said. "But the children got plenty of exercise at the fast-food play place on the way home. Let's try to carry them inside and put them to bed without waking them up."

"Sounds good. Stay put and I'll let the dogs out and open up the house."

Armita inclined her head.

Sophie got out of the car, stepping into a velvety tropical night scented with the blooms on the mature plumeria tree that grew beside the garage. She walked around the vehicle and opened the hatch; Anubis and Ginger hopped out and ran out to sniff around the yard, checking the security in their own way.

Sophie unlocked the side door into the kitchen with her key fob. "Welcome home, Sophie," the alarm console spoke, in her own voice.

"Good to be home." Sophie gave her stock greeting. She had another phrase to say if she ever returned to her home under duress.

Sophie walked quickly through the house, glancing around at the immaculate space as motion-activated lights bloomed on. It still didn't feel like "home" yet, but it certainly was beautiful, especially after the spartan furnishings of the Yām Khûmkạn fortress. The house's smart computer made sure it was a cool 70 degrees, and more illumination lit the way as she walked down the hall and entered the nursery.

Sophie paused in the doorway; a maid came to clean even when they weren't in residence, so the room was neat: a toddler bed draped in a colorful quilt where Momi slept, and Sean's crib, empty but for a bright sheet and a couple of pacifiers—he wore a sleep sack outfit at night instead of using blankets.

Along the walls, colorful storage bins on shelves held toys and clothing. A small trampoline and basket of balls were pushed to the side. Everything seemed in order—but still, Sophie felt a tingling at the back of her neck.

Something wasn't quite right, here in this precious sanctuary at the heart of her home.

Frowning, she walked deeper into the room, scanning around— and then she saw it: an unfamiliar vintage teddy bear sat on the bookshelf surrounded by stuffed toys she recognized.

Sophie advanced to the bear and lifted it off the shelf.

An expensive, classic vintage teddy made by Steiff, the toy had jointed arms and legs and the trademark wiry golden fur that had made the bears a household staple for generations. Its stiff body felt heavy, as if stuffed with sawdust or even sand. Someone had probably given this expensive toy to Momi or Sean while she was gone, but she hadn't heard about it.

Sophie tucked the bear under her arm and hurried down the hall just as Armita, with the sleeping baby in her arms, opened the side door with the dogs alongside of her.

Sophie held up the bear. "Who gave this to the children? Did it come into the house while I was gone?"

Armita frowned, clearly annoyed as she adjusted the sleeping infant in her arms. "I don't pay attention to every single toy they have."

"Then I need you to go back to the car and stay there with Sean and Momi, until I have this bear checked out by the security team," Sophie said, steel in her tone.

Armita's eyes widened. She spun on a heel and exited back to the garage without a word.

The dogs scrambled to follow Sophie as she left the main dwelling and headed for the guesthouse. The two men on duty saw her approach because both met her at their door with wide grins. "Welcome home, Sophie. Was awfully quiet around here without you," Bill said.

"Good to be home," Sophie repeated automatically, but she was frowning.

"Everything okay?" Clement asked.

"I hope so." Sophie produced the bear. "I've never seen this toy before, and it was on the nursery shelf. I want to know who gave it to the children and how it got there."

"I don't know offhand, but we'll have video of anyone entering and exiting the nursery, which won't be many people since you left," Bill said. He took the bear. "Come in. Let's check it out before we do anything else."

Sophie closed the dogs outside after giving Anubis the command to patrol the grounds. Ginger wasn't trained for that, so the yellow Labrador trotted purposefully back to the garage to wait with Armita and the children.

Clement turned on the lights over the house's kitchen island as Bill slipped some gloves on. "I hope we're all overreacting," he said with an avuncular chuckle.

"We can't be too careful right now," Sophie said. "My mother is still free. You've read her file."

"We have," Clement said soberly. "I'm sorry you didn't catch her. We were all hoping for that when you left."

Sophie shrugged one shoulder with fake nonchalance. "Pim Wat's good at what she does."

Bill put the bear on the cutting board and began a thorough investigation, turning the toy to-and-fro, inspecting it with a magnifying glass.

"One of the eyes," he said in a moment. "It could be a camera."

"Foul offspring of a two-headed goat!"

Both men swiveled to look at Sophie.

"I curse in Thai when I'm upset. Better around the children." She grabbed a knife out of a nearby butcher block and advanced. "Let me see." She elbowed Bill out of the way and bent over the right eye of the stuffed animal.

Sure enough, the round black bead had a certain dimensionality to it the other eye did not.

Sophie plunged the knife into the bear's head, immediately encountering resistance. She dug her fingers savagely into the hole she'd made. Sawdust seemed to explode all over the cutting board, but along with it came a slender wire connected to the eyeball of the bear, and a little black box with a stub of antenna attached to a wire. Sophie continued to rip at the bear, and pulled out the antenna wire, which traveled all the way down the stuffed animal's back. "This is a remote transmitter."

"Crap," Clement said.

"Crap, indeed." Sophie glared at the two men. "Find video of whoever put this in the nursery. Call in an emergency support team from the company. I want the whole house searched from floor to ceiling for any further devices. Meanwhile, I have two very tired babies to put to bed somewhere secure. You can reach me on my cell when you have a full report. I'll be at my father Frank Smithson's apartment in Nu'uanu."

"Sorry, Sophie," Bill said. "We don't know how this happened . . ."

Sophie whirled and headed for the door. She had no time for apologies. She needed to get her family somewhere safe—and the new house she'd spent a fortune on making secure no longer was.

Sophie accepted a homemade Blue Hawaiian, her favorite drink, from her father. She sat on a stool at the island where he'd often fixed her pancakes when she lived with him.

"Any idea who planted the surveillance device?" Frank asked.

"My security team is reviewing the footage from the last few weeks. We should know soon." Sophie took a morose pull of the sweet, frothy drink through the festive striped straw he'd added to the glass. "I looked up the camera device; it's expensive, but not government issue. Could have been purchased on the darknet. Whoever put the bear together did a very good job with it. If I hadn't been looking for anything out of place . . ." Words failed. She took another swig of the drink.

Armita appeared in the doorway of what had been Sophie's room when she lived here years ago. "They're sleeping. So are the dogs."

"Care for a nightcap?" Frank gestured to the blender, still half full of the blue blended drink.

Armita shuddered. "No thank you. I'll have a bath instead." She went into the nearby restroom, carrying her small overnight bag and a robe.

"Sorry to drop in on you like this," Sophie told her father. "I was so excited to be home in my very own fancy new house." Tears filled her eyes, surprising her. "I put so much into making that place safe. It was supposed to be a fortress."

"Ah, Sophie." Her father, dressed in long satin pajamas and a matching robe, came around the island to give her a hug. "You of all people know that nowhere is impenetrable. Not even this apartment, in the most exclusive building in Honolulu, is entirely secure. As you have reason to know."

Yes, she did know that. Sophie let her head rest on Frank's shoulder. "I worked so hard to make sure nothing could get in undetected."

"But when it was, you detected it. Right away, too."

"Someone planted it while I was gone. And for the whole time I was away, they watched my children in their beds. It makes me want to vomit."

Frank patted her shoulder, comforting. "Maybe you should go away for a while. Maybe back to Phi Ni. I heard it was released from the DOJ and is getting cleaned up after the typhoon."

"Yes, Connor's men are working on it even now." Sophie raised her head to look at her father. "I'd love to take a longer leave—but how would that solve anything? Mother could evade us for years. No. I have a company to run." She frowned. "In fact, I have a few phone calls I need to make. Can I get some privacy in your office?"

His office was an open area off the living room with its floor-to-ceiling view windows facing the ocean and Diamond Head.

"Sure. In a minute." Her father firmed his mouth, lowering his brows. "I hear you're with the Ghost now."

Sophie's temper, already frayed by the evening's events, flared. "Yes, I am, though Connor no longer goes by that. He's called the Master now."

Frank narrowed his eyes. "And he's still an internationally wanted fugitive."

"As long as it suits the CIA to leverage him that way." Sophie sucked down the last of her drink and set the glass aside with emphasis. "As you well know, Dad, retired agent that you are. Thanks for giving me and my family a safe place to stay for the night. We'll be out of here tomorrow."

"Don't get snippy with me, young lady," Frank Smithson's deep, resonant voice boomed. "I just want you and my grandchildren to be safe. Connor's not an appropriate father figure, and you know it."

"You don't get to tell me anything about picking partners! You married Pim Wat, the ultimate deadly assassin, while you were a covert CIA operative—and then, you let me be married to an abusive gangster when I was just a teenager," Sophie stood up. The revelation that her father was with the CIA had come out not long ago, and still rankled. "Let this go before you dig a metaphorical hole that causes us a relationship problem."

They faced each other, breathing heavily.

Sophie noticed, for the first time, the many silver hairs at her father's temples. He no longer stood inches taller than she did—his strong shoulders curved inward, and he'd lost weight.

Her strong, invincible father was getting older, and he didn't look well.

Frank dropped his gaze first. "I just worry, that's all."

Sophie softened her voice. "Connor would do anything for me and the children. It's Mother that you and I both need to worry about."

"On that we agree. I'll give you the room for privacy." His shoulders were slumped as he headed for his bedchamber.

Sophie hurried after him. "Dad."

He turned.

Sophie embraced Frank, feeling a new fragility in his frame; her arms reached all the way around his formerly muscular back. "You're my rock, Dad. Are you okay? You seem so thin."

He straightened forcefully. "I'm fine. Now go make those calls so we can both get to bed. It's been a long day." He slipped out of her arms and into his room, closing the door, leaving Sophie staring at the closed portal, troubled.

Chapter Forty-Four

Sophie sat down at Frank's sleek onyx desk and picked up the handset of a phone that looked more like a shiny black sculpture than a communication device. Because her father did ambassadorial business from this location, the phone was a secure line, and for the first call she wanted to make, Frank's number was one that would get attention.

She used her cell phone to look up CIA Agent McDonald's personal number and punched in the digits on her father's device. McDonald's voicemail came on, terse and immediate: "Leave a message."

Sophie told McDonald about the discovery of the surveillance device in the nursery. "I can't think of anyone who'd want to watch the children but my mother. A security team is searching the house for any more devices. Meanwhile, I want to know what's happening with the hunt for Pim Wat. You were supposed to be keeping me updated, and I haven't heard a thing since your men made that ridiculous attempt to kidnap Connor. The CIA has to do better!" She hung up the receiver with a satisfying bang.

For the second communication, she switched her phone to video mode. She dragged over a square padded footstool that matched her father's sumptuous leather armchair and settled in to make her call.

Connor's face, eyes heavy with sleep, appeared in the screen on her phone when he answered. A smile curved his lips. "I've missed you. I thought I'd have to wait a few days to hear from you."

"I miss you too. The fortress as well, surprisingly. Especially that bath in the basement." Sophie sighed and felt an unwelcome prickle of tears. "Maybe I should come back to Thailand. Somewhere safe."

"What's wrong?" Connor was instantly alert, radiating a calm readiness to deal with whatever needed doing that heartened Sophie.

"Someone put a surveillance device in the new house. I suspect there is more than one; I have an extra team doing a thorough search." Sophie drew a shaky breath, blew it out. "The worst thing is that the camera was concealed in a stuffed bear in the children's room." Tears overflowed her eyes, but Sophie ignored them. "I tried so hard with every innovation available to make the house secure. And someone, probably my mother, was watching my children in their beds!" She was yelling by the end.

Connor's expression didn't change, but a muscle ticked in his jaw. "I totally get why you're so upset. What kind of device was it? How did you find it?"

Sophie calmed down as she described entering the house and discovering the bear. "It's a high-end commercial transmitter. Not military."

"If it was CIA who planted it, and I don't know why they would put something in the children's room—it wouldn't necessarily be military. They'd be prepared for you to find it and would make it as generic as possible." Connor angled his chin down to engage her gaze intently. "And if it was your mother, that makes total sense that she'd put it in the kids' room. Why don't you take a little more time off from work? Come meet me on Phi Ni. It's isolated there. No one can approach without us detecting them. My men can keep you safe, and Nam and Kupa can look after us."

"I shouldn't," Sophie's voice wavered. "But I don't like this long-distance thing, Connor. I need you in stressful times like these."

"And you can have me. The island's ours again. The CIA has granted me amnesty in Thailand; they've agreed not to make any more attempts to take me in until the situation with Pim Wat is resolved. Please come to Phi Ni. Bring the children, the dogs, Armita—hell, bring your father if you want to!"

Sophie gave a wet chuckle. "He doesn't love you; you know that —but Dad suggested the same thing."

"He's a smart man. I get why he doesn't approve of me. I respect him for it. I know he just wants to protect you." Connor smiled. "And hey, Security Solutions has done without you for three whole months. What's three more? We can see where we are at the end of that. A lot could change. We might have Pim Wat by then, and then you'll have to find room for me in your mansion in Kailua."

Sophie gazed into Connor's aqua eyes, feeling his magnetism, longing to be back in his arms where she'd felt safe and supported. "All right."

He let out a boyish whoop that made her cover her face with her hands, embarrassed at the flush of feeling that suffused her.

"I'll see you in a day or so, okay? Let your team do their thing at the house and come play on the beach with me. My men will keep us safe, and the babies and dogs will love it."

"You don't need to convince me. I only got a glimpse of Phi Ni out the window of the jet when we landed before I took off to meet you at the hospital. I miss it so much—I can't wait to be back."

"Good. I'll send another team over to work and we'll have it cleaned up quickly. Send me your arrival time, and I'll meet you at the airstrip." He waited a beat for Sophie to meet his gaze again. "I love you, Sophie. I'll keep you and yours safe, or die trying."

A shard of grief pierced Sophie's heart. "Don't even say that," she whispered. "I'll make the arrangements and see you soon."

She ended the call.

A new sense of hope and excitement suffused her. She looked over at her father's door, but it remained closed. She couldn't see any light beneath the portal. Perhaps he'd gone to bed.

That was good; he needed his rest. She'd tell him her change of plans in the morning.

Armita came out of the bathroom, wrapped in her robe with her hair in a towel. "I'll sleep out here on the couch. You can be in bed with the children."

Sophie stood up. "How do you feel about going to Phi Ni for a few months, starting tomorrow?"

A slow smile wreathed Armita's somber face. "A very good idea. The children and the dogs will much enjoy the beach, and we can let this investigation proceed without us."

"Just what Connor said." Sophie approached the other woman and embraced her. "I couldn't do this without you."

"Of course you couldn't," the nanny said, and Sophie laughed with a new lightness of heart.

Chapter Forty-Five

Two weeks later...

Pim Wat swung her legs out of bed and parted the delicate mosquito netting that shrouded the bamboo four-poster. She glanced over at her companion; the much younger man slept on, his back turned. She enjoyed how beautiful he was, every muscle well-defined even in sleep, the way his coffee-toned skin contrasted with the white sheets.

She usually didn't let lovers stay the night, but she'd been in the mood for a cuddle, and he'd obliged. She deserved a little indulgence after all the changes she'd undergone, including shedding the identity of Vivian Moran, a woman she'd just been getting to know and like.

She slipped into a silk robe draped over a nearby chair and padded into the kitchen for a cup of coffee. Her housekeeper was already bustling around and jumped fearfully at the sight of her. "Oh, mistress, you startled me."

"Coffee. And it better be hot and strong." Pim Wat's new voice was a harsh rasp. The doctor who'd altered it had said it would get better; so far it hadn't. Soon, she'd be going under the knife for new alterations to her face, small adjustments to recognition points that would fool those infernal cameras yet again.

The housekeeper handed her a full cup, and Pim Wat took it. She sipped; it was potent. "Thank you. This is perfect."

The woman smiled and nodded. "You're welcome. Have a blessed day."

The people on this island were so infernally cheerful all the time. It was maddening.

Pim Wat padded to the living area, where glass sliders framed a view of a peaceful sea. It wasn't her favorite place, Pali Island in the Philippines, but this wasn't a bad substitute. Mendoza had listened to her request that she be stationed somewhere warm.

She settled on a lounger on the deck to watch the comings and goings from the harbor. There was always something to see here; it helped with the period of isolation she must deal with until the hunt for her died down.

Sipping her coffee, Pim Wat watched the water and reflected.

She'd changed through all of this.

Coming so close to death, facing difficult odds in being able to get away from Phi Ni, losing a man she'd connected with—all of that had combined to help her relish being alive in a new way.

Her fire for vengeance had cooled; she was in no hurry to endanger herself with another overt attempt on Connor. Her failure to kill the new Master of the Yām Khûmkạn had revealed how powerful the usurper was becoming.

"You may achieve awakening yet, my Beautiful One." Her former lover's mellifluous voice resonated in memory. "There are deeper things in life than your basic drives. I hope you live long enough to realize that."

She'd bit him, offended by the comment, and he'd laughed. "My deadly viper. You'll never change."

That conversation had taken place the night the Master had been killed—by Connor. She'd been so blinded by rage at her loss that she hadn't remembered it until now.

What had the Master meant by 'awakening'?

Was it considering whether Pim Wat even wanted to resume the quest to kill those who'd hurt her? Evaluating what she might want for herself, for what remained of her days?

The glass door slid open, and the young man who'd served her needs last night came to stand beside her, his hips wrapped in a pareu. "This is paradise, mistress."

"Yes, it is." She smiled and patted the edge of the lounger. "Sit with me."

He sat, with the grace of the young and very fit—not a whisper of the pain that haunted her joints, especially when she got cold.

His gaze was openly admiring; he was like a child, so unguarded and warm. "May I hold you?"

"Why not?"

He lifted Pim Wat into his lap and settled them back into the cushions. She sipped her coffee, enthroned in his strong arms.

This was a good place to be while she bided time. Mulled over what the Master had meant by "awakening." Maybe she'd even continue to be polite to those who took care of her—being pleasant seemed to get better results.

Pim Wat patted her lover's arm. He was no kindred spirit, as Panh the Chameleon had been, but he was eager to please, and that was something. "You may kiss me, if you like."

He did, and Pim Wat enjoyed it. There was much to relish while she waited.

Chapter Forty-Six

Two weeks later . . .

Connor leaned back on his elbows and stretched out his body on the sparkling white sand, as he relaxed on the beach at Phi Ni. The calm ocean sparkled before him, peppered with stunning rock atolls topped by tropical plants. Sophie and Momi dug in the sand nearby, their murmurs and giggles sweet song to his ears. Beside Connor, in the shade of an umbrella, baby Sean wiggled and cooed in his bouncy seat.

What a change a month could make! The team of ninjas he'd left on the island had done a phenomenal job cleaning up and repairing the storm debris. A regular influx of building materials, ferried over from the mainland, had replaced lost roofing, ruined flooring, and broken windows. Nam and Kupa were back in their cozy home. A temporary agreement he'd signed with the international task force had ensured that Connor would not be grabbed in a raid and whisked off to Guantánamo.

Life was good here.

But he could not return to the United States. He couldn't make a permanent home with Sophie and her family until Pim Wat was detained and his immunity deal finalized.

Sean waved a fat fist clutching his rattle, and gave a loud yell. A good-natured, energetic baby, he promised to keep them as busy as Momi did once he was mobile.

Resting in the shade on each side of the bouncy seat were Ginger and Anubis, tired out from a morning of running, playing, and swimming in the crystal-clear water.

Sophie, digging a hole in the sand with Momi, glanced up and met Connor's eyes. She smiled, a secret promise of time they would spend together later, when the kids were napping.

"How long can you stay?" Connor asked. He hadn't wanted to raise that question and push her too much, but it had to be asked.

Sophie shrugged, her back to him in a bikini that revealed that she'd almost returned to her pre-pregnancy form. "I was thinking of submitting paperwork for another two months, and staying here with you, if you're agreeable. We have to make sure you're entirely recovered, after all." The glance she slanted him over her shoulder was full of mischief and flirtation; he had been back to full strength after that night spent in the underground hot spring at the Yām Khûmkạn compound.

"Sure. I'm fine with that." Connor's grin was huge, but he managed to sound cool.

He still worried about coming on too strong with her. Giving Sophie plenty of space as they found their way forward seemed to be working. Still, his entire being lit up; he joyful energy radiated off him in waves. He would treasure every precious second with her and her children.

And now, he would have more of that time. He could make two more months feel like a year.

Connor flashed back to their reunion on Phi Ni. Sophie had been ashy with stress when she arrived. Several surveillance devices had been found in her Kailua home. The devices had been planted by a painter who'd ostensibly returned to the house to touch up some areas. The AI software in the house had not been triggered by his appearance, because he'd been one of the workmen vetted to be inside. He hadn't been found since, and there were no leads yet on who was behind it—but of course, they suspected Pim Wat.

"Look, Mama! It's getting so big." Momi scooped some wet sand with her little shovel and dribbled it onto the drip castle they were making.

"And so are you, Little Bean." Sophie tousled Momi's glossy black curls. "Looks like Armita's on her way down with lunch. Why don't you go help her?"

Momi hopped up and ran to the long, switchback flight of wooden stairs that led to the cliff-top mansion. They'd been teaching her to take the steps independently, but Sophie got up and followed Momi to keep an eye on the toddler. Momi climbed carefully, holding onto the railing with two hands as she'd been shown.

Armita met Momi halfway and made a fuss of draping a water bottle on a strap over the little girl's back so she could help carry the picnic.

Soon, they were clustered in the shade of the umbrella, digging into delicious food Kupa had made and packed for them.

Connor chewed meditatively, his gaze roaming to the cliffs where hidden sentries with distance rifles watched over them. The motor launch, anchored offshore, contained a couple of ninjas fishing from it and keeping watch.

They were as secure as they could be, outside of the fortress.

Sophie reached over and touched his arm. "You can relax—we're safe here. And now, we don't have to say goodbye so soon."

Connor loved the way her long, strong, golden-brown fingers looked against his skin. He covered her hand with his. "I'm still having a hard time believing we've made it this far, when she's still out there."

She. Pim Wat, casting a shadow from wherever she was in the world.

"I know." Sophie's gaze was a little sad as she met his eyes. "I dreamed of this day a while ago, but Jake was in the dream."

"He's still here," Connor said, indicating Sean, seated on Armita's lap. "He'll always be with us."

The sadness retreated; Sophie smiled. "Yes, he is. Thank you for understanding that I'll always love Jake, too."

"As I will always love and miss my friend Nine. They gave their lives for us, and we honor them when we remember it." He was glad he'd shared that sobering thought when Sophie leaned over to kiss him.

Connor closed his eyes to slow down time, just a bit, and savor the moment.

Thanks for reading Wired Revenge. I hope you enjoyed Sophie's adventure, and it continues in WIRED TARGET!

Check out WIRED TARGET HERE!

If you enjoyed this book, you'll love another mystery series set in the same world of Hawaii with dog-loving policewoman Lei Texeira. BLOOD ORCHIDS is free to download HERE.

If you like my writing voice, you might be interested in my personal story of growing up as a homeless hippie kid on the island of Kauai! Check outFRECKLED: a Memoir of Growing up Wild in Hawaii.

I'd love to see you in my Facebook group, where I do lots of exclusive giveaways and fun community-building! Visit me here: Friends who Like Toby Neal Books

Sign up for my newsletter and get TWO BOOKS FREE!
http://tobyneal.net/TNNews

Want to see a COMPLETE LIST of my books
in all genres? Click HERE!

Sneak Preview

WIRED TARGET, Paradise Crime Thrillers #14, AVAILABLE NOW!

On her first day back to work after six months of maternity leave, Sophie tightened her grip on the sissy strap of a heavy-duty Ford truck as it bumped through a red dirt pothole on the way to Oahu's scenic bird sanctuary at Ka'ena Point.

Marcus Kamuela, a detective with Honolulu Police Department, gripped the wheel tightly as they hit a bump. "Good thing I was able to get this permit for us to drive out to the sanctuary, or we would have had to walk all this way."

Sophie glanced at Kamuela. The detective's jaw was tight, his brown eyes intent behind mirrored sunglasses as he navigated the rough dirt road through the Ka'ena Point State Park toward the windswept, southernmost point on the island of Oahu. "This was one of my favorite run-hike routes before the baby."

"Ka'ena Point's popular, even though it's a two and a half-mile hike each way, with no water or facilities."

"I enjoy this trail," Sophie said. "I've been hoping to do it again now that I'm back on Oahu. But given that we're on the clock, driving is more efficient."

Wedged in behind Sophie sat Pierre Raveaux, his knees folded high in the truck's narrow passenger seat. "Going out to the scene in person is always a good starting point," he said. "Thanks for making the time to show us where this case began."

"The case waited for me to come back to work before moving ahead," Sophie said. "We appreciate you being willing to work with Security Solutions on behalf of our client."

Kamuela nodded. "We're glad for the help at this point because we haven't had time to give this case the man-hours it needs, even though public outrage has created pressure on the HPD. As you know, I work in the Homicide Division, and this was a crime involving animals. Or birds, I should say." Beads of sweat had formed on Kamuela's brow despite the truck's air conditioning, and he swiped a beefy forearm across his forehead. "Nobody can understand why someone would sneak into a nature preserve and kill twelve adult Laysan albatrosses and smash fifteen of their eggs."

"I understand the press are calling it the Moli Massacre," Raveaux said. "*Moli* being the Hawaiian name for albatross."

"Yes, and that's why HPD put me on the case rather than letting the Department of Land and Natural Resources be the only agency to investigate. According to the experts I interviewed, damage to future generations of this endangered species is hard to calculate," Kamuela said.

Sophie shut her eyes, trying not to imagine the scene that had met the sight of park attendants the morning after a savage attack on the peaceful birds at their nesting grounds. "This is cowardly of me, but I'm glad there won't be anything much to see three months later."

"The park rangers cleaned up the mess." Kamuela's jaw was tight. "The photos will be grisly enough for you to review. I've seen some dark shit in my time, but this was—some of the worst."

Sophie gazed out the window at the passing scene.

Ka'ena Point was dry; no large trees broke up the rolling sand dunes, sparkling turquoise ocean and scrubby bushes that dotted the arid landscape to her right.

On the left, towering cliffs in bold red volcanic soil studded with boulders and a few wind-battered *hale koa* and *kiawe* trees contrasted with the ocean's fringe of yellow-white coral beach and aquamarine surf over reefs.

Sophie was happy to be back in the field as a distraction after the last three months spent exclusively in the company of Connor, Armita, Momi, and Sean. Momi was now spending her custody month on Kauai with her father, Alika, with a team from Security Solutions to ensure her safety. Armita and Sean awaited her at home in Kailua, but she'd had to say a wrenching goodbye to Connor when she left Phi Ni.

Even now, the ocean she gazed at reminded her of his eyes . . .

"I'm assuming you will let us review the surveillance video, too," Raveaux said from behind her. "I did a quick scan of your case file, which mentions that two male perpetrators were visible in the footage."

"You're welcome to review it, but the perps knew the park's cameras were recording. They wore bandannas over their faces as well as ball caps on their heads. Other than being able to ascertain that there were two males, both less than six feet tall, one skinny, one heavy, there isn't much to go on. We couldn't even make out skin tone in the low-quality feed."

"Those details show premeditation, though," Sophie said. "The Moli Massacre was not an impulse crime."

Kamuela glanced at her; Sophie was struck as she'd been in the past by the man's handsome Hawaiian features and how fierce he looked when he frowned. "I can't promise that I'd be able to follow due process if I got my hands on those guys. In our culture, the Moli are some of our most revered `*aumakua*, guardian spirits of the ancestors. We treat these birds with utmost respect." He blew out a breath. "The Moli have little fear of humans, and from everything we could tell from the scene, they did not defend themselves."

Sophie looked out the window again. Even grisly murders she'd worked didn't get to her like the slaughter of these rare birds; apparently Kamuela felt the same.

The three investigators reached a dirt parking area at the end of the road. A tall chain-link fence with a turnstile gate and an information kiosk marked the entrance to the sanctuary. Kamuela parked the truck, pointing to the high barrier. "Private citizens raised funds to fence this entire section of the park to protect the Moli's nesting grounds. That fence keeps out mongooses, pigs, and feral cats, which would disturb the birds and feed on their eggs. Unfortunately for the birds in this case, it's designed to allow humans to pass through."

Sophie got out of the cab of the truck, flipping the seat lever so that Raveaux could climb out as well. Raveaux dusted down his trousers as he straightened up from the cramped quarters. He wore a battered but quality straw fedora and a pair of Ray-Ban aviators with a white linen shirt; he was always a notch more stylish than anyone else. Their mutual friend, forensic auditor Hermoine Leede, called Raveaux's elegance "the Paris factor."

The three donned backpacks containing water and their crime kits. Kamuela held aloft a large plastic bag. "Might as well pick up some trash while we're at it."

They proceeded through the turnstile and walked along a well-worn red dirt path between sturdy native bushes and clumps of grass. A boulder-strewn beach they navigated past was empty and stunning; gentle waves lapped golden sand studded with white coral.

Brisk wind tugged at Sophie's curly hair, still thick and long from pregnancy. She swung her arms as she walked, enjoying the strength she was rebuilding; the physical effects of carrying, birthing, and feeding a baby were no small feat for any woman, even the fittest.

Kamuela interrupted Sophie's ruminations with a touch on her shoulder. "Look."

The three of them paused, gazing at a meter-high albatross standing majestically on its nest, a speckled white egg balanced between sturdy yellow webbed feet.

The Moli stood tall, its snowy feathers reflecting the sunshine. The bird's farseeing eyes, framed by sooty black feathers like Egyptian eyeliner, gazed at the three humans with neither fear nor aggression. The nest was a simple construction of twigs and feathers; the egg itself was quite large, at least the size of a mango.

Marcus spoke softly as they walked on. "Volunteers from the local Audubon Society as well as our park service personnel cleaned up the remains after the attack. I just want to check and see if we missed anything."

He described the scene as he and the other staffers had approached it right after the massacre. "You can view the photos back at the station when you look at our case file in more detail, but the perps came armed with weapons. As you said, Sophie, the attack was premeditated."

They passed a few more of the albatrosses, grooming each other and sunning themselves. At no time did any of the massive birds show fear or aggression toward the humans passing through their environs.

Sophie had already been predisposed to not only taking the case but taking it seriously; now that she had been out to Ka'ena Point and seen the regal birds in their native habitat, the deep burn of outrage under her sternum would provide fuel for the investigation in the days to come.

They did a thorough walk-through of the birds' nesting area. Sophie took reference photos of the cameras positioned near the entrance and exit of the fenced protective zone. "Did you ascertain if the perps came in by vehicle?" Sophie asked. "That might provide a source of clues."

"They did not come in by car that we can tell," Marcus said. "No permits for vehicle usage were issued the day of the attack and the gate to the road was locked."

"That's a long hike at night, and a long way back in the dark after the deed was accomplished," Raveaux said as they exited the nesting area. "Maybe they camped somewhere nearby."

"Camping isn't permitted anywhere in the park, but you're right. That's a possibility. We searched extensively inside the protected zone, but not much along the trail," Kamuela said as they approached his truck.

Raveaux raised his brows at Sophie. "What do you think? Should we walk back and look for a campsite?"

"Sounds good to me, as long as we can get some water from you, Marcus," Sophie said.

Kamuela popped open the side door of the vehicle to expose a flat of water bottles. "I'll do you one better and loan you a hat," he said, and clapped an HPD ball cap on Sophie's head. "Unfortunately, I can't come with you; got a fresh homicide back at the office to follow up on. Call me if you find anything of interest."

"Will do."

The detective got in and pulled away with a wave. Once the truck was gone, Sophie and Raveaux scanned the heavy undergrowth and the beach beyond.

"Well, now we have two and a half miles of coastal beach to search. How should we go about it?" Sophie said.

"Put yourself in the mind of the perps," Raveaux said. "They were carrying weapons. They would want to be somewhere concealed, but with easy entrance and exit in case they were confronted." He pointed to a narrow trail leading to the beach. "If I were camping, I'd pitch my tent on the beach and conceal it in the bushes. Maybe they were drinking to get in the mood. Perhaps lit a fire on the sand."

Sophie shivered despite the bright sunlight overhead. She tugged down the brim of the HPD cap. "Let's get started."

The two of them made their way along the beach. They found several possible campsites, with disturbed sand patterns and buried fire rings, but nothing that told them anything pertinent about the bird killers.

Eventually, about a mile from the beginning of the park, Sophie slid on a pair of latex gloves: she'd spotted a rusty tire iron protruding from an old fire ring.

"What do you think? Seems like an odd place to discard this." She held up the tire iron for inspection.

Raveaux frowned. "You're right. Let's give this area a closer look."

They poked around in and among the *naupaka* bushes, *ipomeia* vines, and beneath the umbrellalike branches of a beach heliotrope tree.

"I don't see anything more. What weapons did Kamuela say the killers used on the birds?" Sophie pulled her hair off her neck and twisted it up under the hat.

"A blade of some kind was used—a machete they think, and some kind of club," Raveaux said. "Your tire iron could be the club." Hands on his hips, he stared at the fire ring thoughtfully. "Wouldn't you try to destroy a weapon that could tie you to the crime?"

"We're operating on the theory that it was kids from Kama'aina Schools because the headmaster is our client," Sophie said, fanning herself with a bit of cardboard she'd found. She gazed longingly at the sea—if only she'd put her swimsuit on under her clothes that morning! "Since Dr. Ka`ula hired us. I wasn't at the intake meeting. Was there anything specific he shared that tied their students to the killing?"

"The headmaster was not forthcoming with why he thought it might have been their students. Said he didn't want to open that can of worms until we found out if HPD would share the case with us. Now that Kamuela has allowed us to join, we need to meet with our client again and get whatever he knows." Raveaux stroked the small goatee he'd been growing. "If it was a couple of teens, they probably didn't realize how outraged the community—even the world, when the news got ahold of the story—was going to be."

"Let's dig deeper into this fire ring since there's nothing else nearby," Sophie said. "Maybe another weapon is buried deeper, and they were hoping fires built in this spot would eventually get rid of it."

"Sounds good." Raveaux unbuttoned his linen shirt and draped it over a nearby bush. "No sense getting charcoal all over a perfectly good shirt."

Sophie averted her eyes from his leanly muscled, olive-skinned body. "I wish I could take my shirt off." She dug carefully inside the fire ring with her latex-covered gloves.

"Go ahead. I won't mind," Raveaux said, dropping to his knees beside her.

She narrowed her eyes at him over the rims of her sunglasses in a chastening squint. Raveaux hadn't asked one question, nor made any comment, about her relationship with Connor since she'd returned from her extended leave on Phi Ni. She'd been waiting for it to come up.

One corner of Raveaux's stern mouth tucked in. "Don't worry. I've moved on. Heri Leede and I are dating."

"That's good. She's a fine match for you." Sophie released a breath of relief, glad to put this awkward moment behind them.

They dug carefully, removing pieces of semi-burned garbage and driftwood out of the hole. Sophie felt something larger, flat, and long, and brushed the sand away.

"Look at this, Pierre." She had located a molded plastic handle, halfway melted. She drew a short, lethal-looking, rust-covered machete out of the hole. "I think we found our murder weapon."

Sophie bagged the two items in a couple of paper evidence bags she'd had the foresight to pack.

Raveaux got his phone out to call Kamuela. "No signal, but I picked up a voicemail from a blocked number." He frowned. "Can't retrieve it. We'll have to call at the parking lot."

"Let's go." Galvanized by the discovery, Sophie swung her pack on and broke into a jog, the enervating heat and tiredness dropping away. Raveaux caught up, and they soon reached the parking lot where they'd met Kamuela and left the white Security Solutions SUV.

When Sophie took her phone out, she also had a blocked number. She listened to a short message from Connor asking her to call back immediately. She held the phone up for Raveaux to see. "Your call is probably Connor trying to reach us, too. It's likely about Pim Wat."

Raveaux's expression was carefully blank. "Should we call him back first, or Kamuela?"

"Let's get on the road to somewhere with a better signal. You call Kamuela while we drive, then let's return Connor's call together and see what he's concerned about."

"*Bien.*"

They got into the car, taking a moment to refresh with bottles of water. Sophie turned on the SUV while Raveaux called Kamuela to report their discovery. Hot air poured over them as the air conditioning labored.

"Can you bring the possible evidence in to the station? I'll meet you in the entrance area. I'd like to log them into evidence right away," Kamuela's voice was rough with urgency after he listened to Raveaux. "I'll reach out to the District Attorney and schedule a meeting so we can clarify a legal process. Since this is an animal-related crime committed by humans, we need more direction on what to prioritize as far as building a prosecutable case. In the meantime, can you meet with your anonymous client and get more information? By then, we'll have plenty to discuss about the Moli Massacre."

"Will do," Raveaux said. He ended the call.

Sophie pulled into a nearby gas station and parked. "Let's reach out to Connor here, then take the evidence in to HPD." Sophie plugged the address of the downtown Honolulu Police Department station into the car's navigation system, barely taking a moment to notice the pretty tropical plantings around the gas station and the comings and goings all around them.

Her heart rate had spiked ever since the terse message from Connor.

It had to be about her mother.

After all these months without a trace of Pim Wat, Sophie'd almost begun to relax and hope that the threat was over.

Raveaux had listened to his message as well. "Connor asks me to call back, too. Says it's important."

"Has to be Pim Wat. No other reason he'd reach out to both of us like this." Sophie put her phone into a holder that held the display screen upright on the dash. "Let's use video. Ready?"

"Always." Raveaux's dark brown eyes twinkled; he almost smiled. Someday he'd smile more, and she hoped she'd be there to see it.

She pressed the auto-programmed button to reach her lover, the Master of the Yām Khûmkạn in Thailand, and listened to the pulse of signal for him to pick up.

A

Raveaux didn't look at the screen of the phone as it pulsed, ringing somewhere in a faraway jungle fortress; he gazed at Sophie's face.

She drew the eye, always, with something more than mere beauty. The scar earned on one of her cases bisected a cheekbone and disappeared into her hairline, serving as an arrow to point to her eyes, her mouth.

Right now, those eyes were bright, her full lips pursed in a half-smile of anticipation—she was eager to see the man in Thailand.

Not him.

Raveaux had lied. He hadn't moved on. But if Sophie knew how he felt, she'd distance herself, and that he couldn't stand.

"Sophie! I didn't dare hope to hear back from you so soon." Wreathed in a smile, joy radiated from Connor's handsome face like sunlight.

Connor was different since Raveaux had seen him last, no doubt about it.

"Hello, darling." Sophie was smiling as big as he was. "Pierre is here, too. We were out investigating a new case together when we got your messages." She tilted the phone politely so that Raveaux was included in the frame.

Raveaux made a little half wave. "*Bonjour.*"

"Ah, our French connection." The light that seemed to emanate from Connor dimmed. "Glad you're there to keep an eye on Sophie and the kids. I appreciate it."

Raveaux bristled at the man's patronizing tone. He didn't respond.

Sophie glanced at Raveaux. She frowned back at the phone. "What's so urgent that you reached out to both of us in the middle of a workday?"

"It's your mother, of course." Connor was all business now. His eyes flicked down and to the left; Raveaux heard the rattle of a keyboard. "I've had surveillance attached to Kaleidoscope ever since we found out about Pim Wat's relationship with Mendoza. We haven't discovered so much as a glimpse of her since she escaped Phi Ni, but I think I might have found a job she did for Mendoza—in Bali, of all places."

Grab your copy of WIRED TARGET at your favorite book retailer, NOW!

Acknowledgments

Aloha dear readers!

Thanks so much for coming along on another adventure in Sophie's international thriller world! This series continues to take new directions and surprise me as much as it does you—and one of the ways this story surprised me was in what was revealed about Pim Wat's complexity. I fully intended to have her in a body bag by the end of the book—but the wily b*tch refused to be captured! Argh!

Thanks so much to Angie Lail, the keeper of my Series Bible and copyeditor! Thanks also to Mike Neal, who's helping me with formatting and book design (as well as the brainstorming talks in the hot tub and endless cups of coffee it takes to keep an author writing!)

Until next time, I'll be hard at work on the next book, when I'm not enjoying being a new grandma (one who does not plan to steal her grandbabies, BTW!)

If you enjoyed WIRED REVENGE, please leave a review! Reviews mean so much to me and help the book(s) get discovered in ways you don't even know. They are the encouragement I feed on when the going gets hard, and I thank you in advance!

Much aloha,

Toby Neal

P.S. Grab your copy of WIRED TARGET now and find out what

Free Books

Join my mystery and romance lists and receive free, full-length, award-winning ebooks of *Torch Ginger & Somewhere on St. Thomas* as welcome gifts: tobyneal.net/TNNews

About the Author

Kirkus Reviews calls Neal's writing, *"persistently riveting. Masterly."*

Award-winning, USA Today bestselling social worker turned author Toby Neal grew up on the island of Kaua`i in Hawaii. Neal is a mental health therapist, a career that has informed the depth and complexity of the characters in her stories. Neal's mysteries and thrillers explore the crimes and issues of Hawaii from the bottom of the ocean to the top of volcanoes. Fans call her stories, *"Immersive, addicting, and the next best thing to being there."*

Neal also pens romance and romantic thrillers as Toby Jane and writes memoir/nonfiction under TW Neal.

Visit tobyneal.net for more ways to stay in touch!
or
Join my Facebook readers group, *Friends Who Like Toby Neal Books,* for special giveaways and perks.

www.ingramcontent.com/pod-product-compliance
Lightning Source LLC
Chambersburg PA
CBHW021223250626
47155CB00008B/2907